DE ⸻

A completely unputdownable gritty
and gripping gangland thriller

CASEY KING

The Dublin Thrillers Book 1

Joffe Books, London
www.joffebooks.com

First published in Great Britain in 2023

Cover art by Nebojša Zorić

ISBN: 978-1-83526-105-7

CHAPTER 1

No words spoken, pressure around her elbow. Someone had it gripped tight. Someone was shoving her into a car. That car had cut in front of the cab next in line, and Danielle glanced back at the cabbie, locked eyes with him, hoping the panic showed on her face. Maybe he would leap to the rescue: a lone woman bundled into a motor outside the arrivals lounge of Dublin Airport. Doesn't happen every day. But why should he get involved?

The car sped to the exit. Drops of rain on the windscreen. Wipers going. Every traffic light on green. She felt weak and helpless.

The dark leather interior closed in on her, her head spun. Her throat was tight. She opened her mouth to speak, but nothing came out. The driver circled the roundabout, throwing her to the side. Twice. Maybe they were being followed; maybe someone would stop them and she could get help.

The old Danielle would have swanned out of Dublin Airport all high heels and attitude, but not this new version. At least in the runners and athleisure wear, she'd be able to leg it when the opportunity arose.

The driver had polished skin and gelled hair. She glanced at the hand resting on the gearstick. The nails were flawless. Danielle slid closer to the door and tried the handle. He glanced at her in the rear-view mirror, shook his head and tutted. It was some sort of communication, at least.

'Do you know who I am?' she demanded.

Silence.

'I belong to the Lewis family. Do you know what that means?'

* * *

The bullet struck Dean Lewis in the shoulder. His arm went limp. Blood splattered across the path. He ran. The second shot pierced the back of his thigh, sending him to the ground. In his head, he was still running. Like a snail, he slid forward using his uninjured arm, leaving a trail of red slime. He rolled on to his back. He hadn't expected the pain to be this excruciating. Jesus, he hadn't shat himself, had he? He looked up at a couple of birds that had taken off, startled by the noise. Even the clouds seemed to scatter. Nature running for cover while he lay there, exposed.

In the silence, time seemed to slow. Then he began to hear a repetitive dull thud, like a heartbeat, coming from somewhere nearby. A football against a wall? Cheers for a goal scored between posts made from spare jumpers and jackets. Like he used to do as a kid.

Two scrawny young fellas riding a dirt bike loomed into his line of sight. The one driving had dyed blond hair; the other clung to him, feet loose. They had been in Dean's shadow while he made his collections. What were they up to? There was no trusting little fuckers like them.

He opened his mouth to call them over, but nothing came out. Probably just as well. Those young thugs seeing him in this state. Talk about a reputation in shreds. A player like him, owing them favours for coming to his aid. No way was that going to happen. He eyed them and they took off.

Then the balaclava-clad gunman stood over him. His hand shaking, he took aim at Dean's forehead. Every person he had killed flashed through Dean's head. This was due . . . but why here, in this grotty Dublin estate?

His mind raced. He tried to remember what day it was. What date would be recorded on his death cert, on his grave? He listened for the sound of his crew rushing to his aid. Typical. No sign of them when he needed them most. Probably busy jerking off on to some street whores. They'd regret it. Useless bastards. *Shit*. Ged had called them away. He was on his own, facing this gunman.

Dean looked into the shooter's eyes. Fixed him with a stare. Defiant. Concealing the confusion, his fear. Any minute, the pain would stop.

A loud crack rent the air. The gunman's weapon bounced on the ground beside him. He lunged for it, pointed it and fired. The kickback nearly cost him the other shoulder. *Fuck*. He'd missed.

The asshole ran, his trainers barely touching the tarmac, leaving Dean holding the gun. The next loud bang nearly split his eardrums. He saw the front grill of a car bearing down upon him. He rolled to the side. Rubber missing him by millimetres. He landed beside a gully, the sound of water rushing past his head. He tried to see where the other shots had come from but was unable to lift his head. Fighting the pain, he readied himself to fire again. It took him a while to realize there were no bullets coming at him — the kids on the dirt bike were setting off black cat fireworks. While his buddy steered, Blondie, now at the back, was lighting the bangers and hopping them to the ground. This was the gunshots. The little squirts had saved him. Clever bastards.

The sound of sirens drew near. He dropped the weapon down the gully. The two lads looked around, then sped away. He lay in the rain, amid the piss-stink of wet firecrackers. His leg and shoulder throbbed. The pain grew intense. Agonizing, as if someone held him in a chokehold. His mouth was dry, his lips beginning to crack. He tried to move them, say something, but they remained closed, stiff and painful as if they'd been stitched.

Voices above him. Fuss. Noise. Then everything went quiet.

CHAPTER 2

They didn't even flinch at the mention of the name Lewis. The driver didn't utter a word, not to Danielle nor to his buddy beside him in the passenger seat, just kept driving. The muttonhead who'd bundled her into the car stared straight ahead, chewing on his bottom lip. Every so often he glanced over his shoulder, scanning the passing traffic. Once in a while, his hand went to the left side of his jacket. A nine millimetre? Possibly.

He had pushed back his seat to accommodate his long legs. His window was wide open. Alert as he was, she'd be away before he knew what had happened. She was fit enough. Besides, he'd never take a shot at her out here, in front of potential witnesses or CCTV.

The car slowed at a junction by Penny's on the Swords Road. This was it, her chance to go. Fuck her hand luggage. Muttonhead had probably left it on the footpath anyway. Her passport and wallet were in her pocket. The rest she could manage without. But what if she didn't make it? What if he grabbed her and she ended up hanging out of the car only to be wiped out by some passing motor?

Still, she had to do something.

The car sped up again and Danielle went for it. She squeezed between the front seats and tried to get across him. She ended up half in the front, her legs still in the back.

'Jesus.'

The driver, that man of few words, finally found one.

The car swerved. Danielle, jammed as she was between the front seats, remained rigid. Something sharp dug into her ribs. She lashed out wildly, intending to inflict as much damage as possible on anything within her range. The car came to a halt. The brakes squealed. She heard a click — the door locks. She wriggled backwards and sat down, pulled at the door handle. The door opened. She jumped out, her shoulder hitting the tarmac. She rolled, careering sideways until she hit a kerb wet with rain. She broke into a sprint, but was felled by a rugby tackle, her face in the grassy verge and her arm yanked up behind her back.

'Mad bitch.' Muttonhead tried to haul her to her feet.

Still on her knees, she contemplated ripping his face open with her nails.

'Are you all right, love?'

The kind stranger was accompanied by a German shepherd on a lead.

Before she could answer, Muttonhead intervened. 'The situation is under control. Move along.'

His grip on her tightened until her wrist felt like it might snap. The dog whimpered.

'I'll do serious harm if you don't cooperate,' Muttonhead hissed in her ear.

Danielle stopped struggling. She looked up at the stranger. Maybe he would call the guards. But what use had they been ten years ago when she'd needed them? All they had done then was advise her to leave the country. It'd be the safest option, they said, until they found who had shot her. Meanwhile, their investigation went cold. She had taken a risk in returning, but she hadn't expected to be subjected to something like this so soon after setting foot on home soil.

The man hesitated, pulling the dog closer to him.

'What will it be? Dead hero or continuing your pleasant stroll?'

The man walked on, the dog straining at the lead.

Shit.

If Danielle could just turn herself around, she could reach his gun. But twist as she might, his grip remained firm. He finally managed to drag her to her feet, sopping wet, and jostled her back into the car. Back into her cell.

Now in the back with her, he blocked the gap between the front seats, his knees nearly touching the headrests.

'Someone better tell me what's going on,' Danielle said.

'Button it and don't try that again,' the driver said.

He took the slip road on to the bustling M50, passing Whitehall, then on to the N1. The rain had stopped.

'If you're going to kill me, why not do it now?'

The driver caught her eye in the rear-view mirror. 'No.' He really was a man of few words.

Two young lads on a white dirt bike shot across the road like their tails were on fire. The car braked, sending Muttonhead shooting forward. The driver sat on the horn. Neither of the fellas on the bike looked back. They were away on to Millmount Avenue and out of sight almost as instantly as they'd appeared.

Muttonhead grunted. 'Bastards.'

They turned into Richmond Road and came to a stop outside a block of apartments. A plaque on the wall gave the name as Clonliffe View. The driver pressed a fob hanging from the sun visor, the iron gates parted and the car eased in. None of the windows had blinds or curtains and the apartments Danielle could see into were empty. The car park was empty too, save for a white Volkswagen Passat parked in front of a *Do Not Obstruct* sign.

Her heartbeat thundered in her ears. She barely heard the order to get out of the car. She looked at her hands. They were scratched, her nails in bits. She could just imagine the state of her face. She glanced behind her. The gates were closing again and she couldn't see any other exit. Would they dump her body where it could be found? She hadn't made contact with anyone on this side of the Irish Sea. Her return was meant to be a surprise. This was an unexpected curveball. But would her family care? After all, they'd packed her off to London a decade ago, with plenty of money but little support.

Muttonhead went to the boot and took something out. Her case. He rolled it towards her and led her to a door, where he punched in a code. The man of few words sparked up a fag. Offered her one. She took it. He held the lighter towards her, but didn't let it go. She held his gaze. Defiant.

She yanked it from his grip, but her hands were shaking and she couldn't get a flame. He took the lighter back and gave her his cigarette instead. Was this a last cigarette before her execution? They gave no hint of their intentions. She drew on the cigarette. It tasted good. When she'd finished, she stubbed it out on the wall, a dot of charcoal. She left the butt on the windowsill — a small trace of her presence.

The three of them took the lift up to a penthouse apartment. It had a clear view over Drumcondra, Clonliffe and beyond. Who could afford a place like this? The Flynn family? *Shit.*

'There are outfits in the closet, make-up. You can make yourself more . . . presentable. Get into the shower and spruce yourself up.'

The driver could speak, then.

'Who are you?' She didn't recognize either of them. Should she? 'Presentable for what?'

The driver looked at his watch.

'You had an hour. Now you have fifty minutes.'

'For what?'

No reply. He pointed to a room behind her. 'There's the main bedroom. Go and get on with it. And if you come out looking anything less than how he'd remember you, I'll throw you off that balcony face first, so no one will recognize you.'

'Who's *he*? Who will remember me?'

Again, no reply.

Fuck. It was Jason. Had to be. He must have heard she was coming back, but who the hell from? Saoirse? Hardly. No, this was his revenge for dumping him and leaving the country. The rest of the Flynn family would give him all the backing he needed to . . . What? He was the one who had dipped his wick elsewhere. The final injustice. As if their future wasn't damaged enough. He'd let her down just like her family had, left her alone, abandoned. How could she stay with him after that?

She slammed shut the bedroom door, locked it and ran to the bathroom, making it to the toilet bowl just in time to puke her guts up.

Maybe she'd be better off jumping from the balcony. At least she'd be taking back control. What had she returned to? Did the Lewis name no longer invoke the terror it used to? She rested her head on the cool tiles of the wall. She should have told her family she was coming back; should have got Uncle Ged or Dean to collect her. Too late now. She was on her own. Time was moving on. She had less than thirty minutes to clean herself up.

She heard a low thud coming from the bedroom. She peered through the bathroom door. No one. Maybe someone had tried to get in. Kill her in the shower. That would make sense — easier to clean up the mess.

She went in and opened the wardrobe. A leather jacket slipped off its hanger. Jesus. She hadn't worn stuff like this for a decade. The clothes were all her size, still were. That hadn't altered much at least. She selected a pair of leather trousers and a V-neck satin bodysuit and laid them out on the bed. She stood back, assessing her choices. In the past, this had been her favourite means of distraction — breasts front and centre. Over the years, as she gradually adopted a safer, low-profile, fight-or-flight stance, her style had changed. If this was what was needed now, so be it. Jason wanted her to look like she used to. Maybe it would prevent him from

8

harming her. If she had to talk her way out of danger, she'd have to be ready, wash away the events of the morning. If she were quick, she'd manage to take a shower.

The cubicle was big enough for ten people, with jets everywhere. Hopefully, the warm water would wash away some of the fear. But her strength disappeared down the plughole along with the suds. Her loss. The shooting. She fell to the floor, pain clutching at her heart, the rush of water drowning the sound of her sobs.

Come on now. Not this. She was still alive, wasn't she? So while she had breath in her, she'd fight. She wanted answers. Who was behind the hit? Who had caused the death of two unborn babies, and killed the man who had saved her life?

CHAPTER 3

Useless bastard. Bruce 'Bird' Flynn looked down on him, cowering on his knees, whimpering like a simpleton.

'Brenno fucking Ahearne. Look at you. The hard bastard who was going to wipe Dean Lewis out. Who begged us to trust him to do it.'

'I got him, Bird. I did. I swear.'

Brenno looked up at him, his face all dried blood and snot. He must have put up a fight when the lads dragged him to the yard.

'But is he for the grave? Anything less is no good to me, you thick fuck. The job's not done until there's brains on the concrete.'

'Dunno for sure.' Brenno stared down at the gravel.

'You dunno. The fucking media will be all over this, you useless prick. You told me the arsehole was dead. Fucking dead and gone. And now what do I hear? He's in some hospital.'

'I put a couple of shots in him.'

Bird snorted. 'A couple? You should have emptied the magazine. And then kicked him in the head to make sure.'

'There was no time. I'd have been caught.'

Bird sighed. 'What about the car?'

'Burnt out. Did it myself.'

'That's something at least.'

Sal Fogarty returned from closing the yard gate. Bosco Ryan was crunching his bruised knuckles. Bird had only to give him the nod and he'd bruise them again. Bird was tempted to let Bosco loose on Brenno. Not only had he not made sure that Lewis was dead, but he'd also gone and lost the fucking handgun.

Though if Bosco got started, he'd pulp him to a vegetable. No good. He'd got too much invested for that to happen. Brenno would be more use alive and owing him, for now anyway.

'Why did you try to take him out there of all places? A busy fucking estate.'

'It was his regular money collection run. Predictable.'

'Predictable? You're predictable. A predictable fucking failure.'

'No way, Bird. I've never let you down. You know I haven't.'

'Yeah, but you've never carried out a hit on a major player before. You should have known better. That place was way too open. Too many witnesses.'

'No one would talk against you, Bird.' Brenno spat blood on his hands and rubbed them on his jeans.

'How would they know I had anything to do with it? Eh?' Bird stared hard at him.

'Let me shut him up for good, boss,' Bosco said, and took hold of the back of Brenno's T-shirt.

Bird shook his head. Bosco released him.

Brenno coughed and put a hand to his throat. 'They wouldn't. Of course they wouldn't.'

'Even if no one opens their mouths,' Bird said, 'there's always some self-righteous fuckhead mad to get their mug on TV. Talking bollocks about how that stuff never happens in their estate.'

'If it hadn't been for the lads on the scrambler—'

'What? Two young fellas on a glorified hairdryer? That all it took to put you off, was it? For fuck's sake.' Bird took a deep breath. 'Who are these two heroes anyway? Anyone know them?'

Bird looked at Bosco, then Sal. Both men shook their heads.

'I can find out, Bird. Just let me. Please, give me that chance. I swear I'd know them again if I saw them.'

'And what would you do with them?' Bird said.

'Make sure they don't talk.'

'Even I'm not that bad. You think I'd give you the nod to take out a couple of kids?' Bird said.

'Yeah, true. Bring them on board with us, so.' He looked at Sal and Bosco, then back to Bird. 'I dunno. Something. Whatever you tell me to do with them.'

'I'll have to have a think about that one. But what I want to know now is whether Dean Lewis is dead. That prick has been losing me money with those jobs. Ones he's meant to be getting good info on. Funny, they don't go to plan, yet he, Dean Lewis, never loses a cent. It only ever costs me. It's all a load of bullshit. And now he's stealing my equipment. Nah, the fucker will end up taking me down, so better he's gone. It's the only way.'

'I left him in the gutter, Bird. Blood spouting out of him. He could be dead.'

'"Could be" is not fucking good enough, Brenno, not by a mile.' Bird dragged his hands through his hair. He needed to think.

He paced back and forth for a few moments. Brenno half rose from his knees.

Bird turned. 'What the fuck are you doing?' He picked up a length of pipe and raised it.

Brenno fell back on to his haunches and covered his head with his arms. 'No, Bird. Sorry, man. Don't.'

Bird used the length of pipe to send him toppling sideways against the bucket of a digger. A trickle of fresh blood glinted, vivid on his dust-caked face.

Brenno fell back against the huge rear tyre of the machine and put his hands together.

'I'm begging you, Bird, please, no more. Give me another chance.'

He put one arm over his face to shield it.

'Drop your fucking arm.'

The arm stayed where it was.

Bird whacked his ribs with the pipe.

It must have stung, because Brenno scrambled up and crouched, arms over his head.

'Turn to face me, you cowardly bastard, and put your fucking arms down, or I'll break one off and wave you good-bye with it as you bleed to death.'

Brenno dropped one arm but kept the other up, protecting his head. 'No,' he whimpered.

He looked like he was going to pass out on him. He'd already pissed himself. Bird said, 'I won't tell you again.'

Slowly, Brenno lowered his hand. He was shaking all over, his face wet with tears and snot. Bird swung the pipe high, smashed it down, just brushing the side of Brenno's head and hitting the tyre instead. Brenno's eyes were squeezed tight shut. Bird handed the length of pipe to Bosco, who raised an eyebrow.

'No. Into the skip with that.'

Bird bent and put his face close to Brenno's. 'You fucking owe me, you useless bastard.'

Brenno opened his eyes and nodded. 'Anything, Bird. Whatever you say.'

'Get him up.'

Sal Fogarty stepped forward and hauled Brenno to his feet.

'Ah, quit your whining,' Sal said, dusting him off. 'You'd be dead by now if he wanted it. Come on, tidy yourself up. To survive in this game you've to learn to front the bravery, even if you're shitting it.'

'Listen to Sal,' Bird said. 'He knows the craic. You wanted in, didn't you? Wanted to be the big man. If I didn't take you on, your mammy'd still be putting milk on your Frosties and wiping your arse for you. She thinks you're doing my paperwork and odd jobs. You'd better not let her know any different.'

Bird started to walk away, then stopped. 'This is your own fault, Brenno.' He turned to Sal. 'Get him cleaned up in the Portakabin — the one Dwyane uses is unlocked. There's a sink and toilet in there. Then bring him to the office. I want every detail about those little fuckers on the scrambler — interfering pair of pricks. And find out if Dean Lewis is dead or alive.'

Bird went into the bathroom beside his office, scrubbed his hands and changed his shirt. He checked the internet for news of the hit. Reports had already started to come in of shots fired and a man taken to hospital. Medical status unknown.

Bosco hauled a cleaned-up Brenno into the office, where he stood shuffling from one foot to the other.

Bird shot him a look. 'What's going on in that vacant head of yours?'

'It's not about the hit.'

'What the hell is it about, so?'

'Yeah. Look. I know where your equipment is. I, I mean, I think I know. That is, I know a guy who has an idea where Dean has it stashed.'

'And you're only telling me this now?'

'Sorry, yeah. I didn't get the chance before . . . in the yard.'

'This'd better be true, or you'll be owing me the full value of it.'

'But I'm trying to help,' Brenno whined.

'You could have helped by doing your job and taking the fucker out.'

'But wouldn't it be better to get your stuff back?'

Bird thought about this for a minute. A seven-tonne Hitachi excavator, tractor and trailer worth over ninety grand. Of course it would be better to get it back. It didn't matter that the insurance company was willing to pay out. The insurance company didn't need to know. Theft of machinery was rampant at the moment; construction sites up and down the country were being hit. He knew because he'd organized half of them. And if he hadn't himself, then he was the go-to person to sell them on to gangs in other countries. Dean thought he could join in with that game and get away with it. But he didn't even have the balls to sit on the subs' bench, never mind enter the field of play. He was a disgrace to the Lewis name.

'Knowing a guy and guessing where it might be isn't what I want to hear. If I do claim the insurance, that machinery needs to disappear and never be found. So, if you don't have it back to me in forty-eight hours, then leave it where it is. Now, let me make sure you heard me right, Brenno. How soon do you need to get it back to me?'

'Within forty-eight hours, Bird.'

'Good. And no later. Now, find where I can recover the machinery, or make it so that I can make a legitimate claim for it. If you don't, you'll be working the cost off.'

'Huh?'

'Yep. A hundred and forty-five grand.'

Brenno muttered something.

'Yeah, you heard me. One hundred for the machinery and forty-five for my cut of the ATM robbery that was fucked up two weeks ago, including interest and losses incurred.'

'But the ATM robbery fuck-up was beyond our control. The PSNI were meant to be busy with the twelfth of July parades that day, nowhere near the Monaghan and Armagh currency exchange. We were lucky we didn't get arrested. I thought they were going to cross into the South, they were so close. How there weren't guards waiting for us on the other side, I'll never know.'

'Ye must be fierce lucky altogether.'

'Nothing to do with luck. I'm a shit-hot driver. I fucking floored it and took as many back roads as I could. I got us away that night and back to Dublin.'

For the first time, Brenno looked Bird right in the eye. 'See, Bird, I'm not a fucking failure.'

'Well, Brenno, the jury is still out on that one.'

'You're not out of pocket either. The ATM job just got delayed, not cancelled.'

'Then why do my pockets feel so empty? I don't believe you, because Dean is running those jobs and he has been losing me money. Which is why he had to go.'

Brenno stared at the floor for a beat. 'Would I still owe the money if I told you I knew who the rat was?'

Bird tapped his lip, thinking fast. He had no idea who'd shopped the info on his €200,000 heroin delivery last month. The guards had been all over it. Sources had gone quiet. He'd presumed Dean was in some way behind the info getting to the cops. But on second thoughts, that was unlikely, since it had cost Dean his investment as well. No one could tell him for sure if Dean had fucked him over on that job. Would Dean lower himself enough to rat on him? Probably, if it meant no longer having to share the profits. So he was still justified in organizing the hit on Dean.

'Who?' Bird asked.

'I'm working on a fella who knows,' Brenno said.

'Not exactly first-hand proof, now, is it?' Bird sighed.

'This fella is solid. I swear.'

'Your word's not worth much right now.'

'I'll come through on this, Bird, I swear. On Ma's life.'

Oh, Brenno did love his mammy.

'All right. Go on, get cracking on it, Columbo. And don't come back without good info. This is your last chance to prove your worth, so I want nothing less than gold standard.'

'Of course.'

Bird looked at Bosco and Sal. 'One of you better get him the fuck out of my sight before I change my mind.'

He watched from the window until all three were out of view.

Brenno had no idea how close he'd come to ending up in some landfill or house foundation. Not much brain there, that was for sure, his skull good only for keeping his ears

16

apart. He'd be no use to anyone dead, though, especially if he knew anything about Dean — like, was he dead or alive? — or about any of the rest of the Lewis crowd. But who did Brenno Ahearne know with that kind of information? Someone in the Lewis crew must be flapping the lips — or else the fucker was a good bluffer. He'd find out soon enough.

Alone in his office, he picked up his phone. Marion answered after two rings.

'Did them bandages come off yet, love?'

'Yep, all done and dusted. Clear to go.'

'How are they looking?'

'The right job altogether. You'll love them.'

'Well, in that case, how's about my dog meeting your cat later?'

'Sound, Bruce, hun. I'll be here and waiting.'

She was the only one he let call him by his real name — so long as she called him 'Daddy' in bed. He checked the time. 'I'll be round in an hour.'

'Right, hun. Is Brendan in the office today?'

'Er, yes, he was here earlier, left a little while ago. Why?'

'I asked him to pick me up a bottle of gin. Gave him a fifty.'

'Don't worry, I'll bring you some. Tell him to keep the money and go and do something for the evening.'

'Will you stay tonight, like you promised? I'll make it worth your while.'

'Great. Can't wait.'

'Me neither.'

Lucky for Brenno that his mother gave head like a pro. He'd invested in a new set of knockers for her, and it would be a shame not to get at them 'cause she was looking for her son's body. He'd rather it be Dean's dead body, the thieving fucker. If he wasn't the cop-rat, it had to be someone close to him.

The Lewis family had wasted their advantage. Their so-called equal partnership with the Flynns no longer felt equal, not with Ged losing his grip and Dean itching to take over from his father. Bird now had a chance to wipe them out and find someone else to work with. He hoped Brenno hadn't fucked it up.

'There's news, Bird.' Sal had arrived back, a little out of breath.

'Dean Lewis is dead?'

'Not sure. Still no word there.'

'What is it then?'

'She's back.'

'Who's back?'

'Danielle. Danielle Lewis is back in Dublin.'

'Since when?'

'Flew into Dublin this morning.'

Bird stared beyond Sal and into the yard. This changed things.

'Where is she?' He had already picked up his phone to cancel his visit to Marion.

'Holed up somewhere.'

'Safe?'

'Not sure.'

'Find out.'

'Will do, Bird.'

Sal left. Bird hesitated. He didn't make the call. He'd leave the arrangement as it was, unless Sal gave him an update on Danielle.

CHAPTER 4

A fit of coughing served to clear Danielle's throat. She scrubbed herself all over and dried herself with the soft, comforting towel that had been provided for her. Then she sat in front of the mirror and began to slather her face with the fancy creams and make-up she'd found.

Reminding herself of her strength and determination, she blow-dried her hair, twisting it into a mass of soft curls. By now, she was looking as much like her former self as she could get. An older and wiser version of the Danielle she had left behind when she fled to London.

If she was to be murdered, at least she'd die looking her best.

She listened to the sounds coming from the living room. One voice in particular, though not the one she'd expected. It contained more grit than she remembered. Then again, it had been so long. He'd found her. But how? He'd tear those two idiots apart if he knew how they'd treated her. On the other hand, why should he punish them for roughing her up? Worse had happened to her in the past, and he'd done nothing to avenge it. Not even the attempted murder, the death of her unborn child.

Her relief at hearing his voice was replaced by confusion. Maybe he knew all along. Maybe they worked for him. Maybe her own flesh and blood had in fact orchestrated her terrifying ride from the airport. Well, she'd find no answers in here. They lay out there, beyond the bedroom door.

Taking a deep breath, she unlocked it and stood gripping the handle, fearing to go. Now that she was back, maybe she was afraid of getting the answers to the bigger questions she herself had been asking. Suppose the truth turned out to be too hard to bear? But there was no going back now.

Parting her lips in what might pass for a smile, she walked into the living room.

As soon as she appeared, Man-of-few-words and Muttonhead slipped out of the room, closing the door behind them. She hesitated, watching him warily. His forehead had grown larger as his hairline receded. His light jacket failed to conceal his bulk. He had a yellowish hue to his skin and bags under his eyes, which seemed unfocused, clouded, milky. He opened his arms wide and she moved into his embrace, willing her body not to stiffen. He pushed her out to arm's length, gripping her shoulders, blinking rapidly. He looked much older than his sixty-four years.

'Danielle. Dani, my darling niece. Did you really think you'd get away with it?' He tilted his head to the side.

Her throat gripped in an invisible chokehold. Parched mouth, legs of jelly. Time slowed. Part of her body separated and floated over her. What the hell had she been thinking?

The plan had been well worked out, all probabilities covered. Yet here she stood, alone, in the jaws of the lion. He could see through her, understand her motive. He had to, the way he'd reacted. They were several floors up, and there was no way to make a run for it this time.

His rigid smile softened. 'Relax, my dear. I know we ruined your surprise and turned it back on you. We just couldn't resist when the whisper of your return reached our ears. And it must be as strange for you as it is for me. Tell me I'm not hallucinating.' His face was close, breath sour. 'Did you miss us?'

'Of course I did.' The answer came out as a croak.

'And it's really you?'

'It is, Uncle Ged. It's good to be back.'

'Ah, here, you're exhausted. Let's sit you down.' He pushed her gently on to the couch and plodded over to one of the cupboards, his jacket swinging. He rooted around, found a bottle of Dingle whiskey and two tumblers and fired a good shot into each of them.

'A lovely batch,' he said, bringing one over to her. I bought the cask.' He clinked his glass with hers. 'Cheers.'

He'd served it straight, with no ice or mixer. It gave off an aroma of apricot and honey. She finished it in a single swallow. It burned its way down her throat and warmed her gut.

'Another?' He had already brought the bottle over. It stood on a coffee table by the sofa.

'Uh-uh.' She shook her head. She had to keep her mind as clear as possible. Who had whispered of her return? That wasn't in the plan. What else had her family been told?

Well, fuck the plan. After today, nothing could be assumed. She needed information, whispers of her own, then proof. Until then, she had to stay quiet and deal with whatever was thrown her way. The result would be worth it.

She changed her mind about the drink, poured another measure and gulped that down too.

CHAPTER 5

Bird banged Marion hard, trying to get thoughts of Danielle out of his head. Downstairs, a door slammed and Bird went at it faster, trying to make as much noise as he could. The headboard hit the wall repeatedly, the bedsprings squeaked. Marion didn't seem to mind the lack of foreplay. Her screams rang out across the estate.

It worked, though: she hadn't had time to notice his distracted state. When he was done, he left her lying on the bed, damp and delirious.

Still fixing his pants, he strolled downstairs to the kitchen, where he found Brenno making himself a sandwich, the radio blaring.

'Built up quite an appetite there, so I did.' He passed deliberately close to Brenno, knowing Marion's scent lingered on his body. He switched the radio off, swiped the sandwich from the plate and bit into it, staring Brenno down. 'Christ. What the fuck is that?' He spat it out into the sink and dumped the remainder in the bin.

Without a word, Brenno dumped plate and cutlery into the sink and opened the tap, splashing Bird.

'What the fu—'

A creak on the stairs brought him up short. Marion appeared, in the silk kimono Bird had told her he'd bought for her in Turkey. They were two for a tenner in the Milk Market in Limerick. She wore it like it was the most expensive thing she owned. She was smoking a fag, which she offered to Bird.

'No thanks, love,' he said, dabbing his trousers with a tea towel.

'Any more bread in the house, Ma?' Brenno said.

'Sorry, son, didn't get to the shops. I was busy.' She smiled at Bird.

'It's all right. I'm not that hungry.'

'I hope you're keeping my son busy, Bruce?'

'I sure am, darling.'

'He's a hard worker, but he needs a shove every now and then. I'm so pleased you took him on.'

'Anything for you, my darling. I have plenty for him to do, all right.'

'Good, good.' She turned to her son. 'I hope you're doing as you're told, and doing it the best you can.'

'I am, Ma.'

'Hey, what happened to you?' She turned Brenno around, frowning at the cut under his eye, the swelling and the bruise on his cheek. He flinched. Smoke from her cigarette wafted into his face.

'I fell.' He freed himself from her grasp and turned away.

'Really?'

'Ah, Marion, don't interrogate the boy. He's old enough to take a tumble without his mammy kissing it better. How else will he learn to toughen up?'

'You're still my baby boy, aren't you?' She stood on her toes and kissed the damage on his face, ruffled his hair. She took a last drag on the cigarette and stubbed it out on the plate in the sink.

'Any tea going, then?' Bird plonked himself down on the sofa, arms across the back, legs spread wide.

'Yeah, sure. Brendan, make your boss a nice cuppa while I get dressed.'

'Two sugars, Brenno, that's the good lad.'

'He was christened Brendan.'

'Can't call him that in front of the lads at work, can I?'

'Of course you can — for me.'

'Anything for you, darling.'

The stairs creaked under Marion's retreating footsteps.

Bird watched Brenno's every move. The boiling water poured on the tea bag, the sugar added, the stirring. The boy's hand trembling. He stood over Bird, tall for a moment, as he handed it down to him.

'You not joining us?'

'No.'

'Should you not be out looking for my machinery, then? More importantly, finding out who the rat is?' Bird reached for a coaster and put it under the mug.

'I'm working on it.'

'Do it faster.'

Bird sighed and checked his watch. Singing quietly to herself, Marion clattered about upstairs. She'd been up there ages. Eventually Brenno left via the back door. The tea remained on the coaster, untouched. Marion finally returned, all warpaint and puffy hair.

He smiled and went to meet her, but his phone buzzed with a message.

'Fuck.'

'What is it, hun?'

'Work. I gotta go.'

'I thought we were going for a Chinese? You promised.'

She tried to put her arms around him. He shrugged her away. She lost her footing and stumbled backwards, on to the couch.

'I hate it when you get all clingy.'

'I didn't—'

'The new knockers are the business.'

She glanced down at them and smiled up at him, her teeth smudged with lipstick. 'Um. Good. Glad you like them. I'll have to get a few new dresses; they're straining in the old ones.'

He reached into his trouser pocket, pulled out a roll of cash. Peeled off a wad of €50 notes. 'Here.'

He dropped them in her lap.

'Aw, thanks, Bird. You sure know how to treat a girl.' She snatched up the notes and began counting.

Bird watched her, smiling. He kissed her on the forehead. She reached out to him, but he pulled away.

Outside, Sal was parked round the back, engine running. Bird slid into the back seat.

'You've found Danielle? Where is she?'

'Yes, Bird. She's staying at Clonliffe View. The penthouse on the top floor.'

'Any idea why she came back after all this time?'

'No. I'm working on finding that out.'

'I have to see her, Sal. I have to talk to her.'

'Oh?'

'Yes. Jason hasn't been to see her yet, has he?'

'Nope, he's away trying to sort out something to substitute for the stuff the cops took last month. People on the streets are crying out for it.'

Bird shifted in the seat, cracked his knuckles. 'Fucking guards. At least I'll get to her before he does.'

'Jesus, hang on a minute, Bird. One thing at a time here. What about Dean? The shooting?'

'Is he dead?'

'No word yet.'

Bird nodded. 'Right. How could they know it was us?'

'They shouldn't.'

'Well then, we're okay, so. Take me to see Danielle. There's stuff been left unsaid for too long. My brother did her wrong. It wasn't good enough. She deserved better.'

'No, Bird. No. Don't.'

'Why not?'

'You and Jason are back on track. Don't let a Lewis come between you again.'

'She was once nearly part of our family,' Bird said. 'It's one reason to keep to the arrangement with the Lewis crew.'

'We'd be throwing everything away, all those plans—'

'Things can be rearranged.'

Sal shook his head. 'Not in the way you think, or hope.'

'I don't know what to think, or hope, until I speak to her. Do I?' Bird sighed. 'Just drive, Sal, just drive.'

'Where to?'

'Head towards Clonliffe View. I'll decide what to do when we get there.'

CHAPTER 6

Accident and emergency at St Vincent's Hospital was less than twenty minutes by car from Clonliffe View. They made it in five.

Ged couldn't get a straight answer from anyone about his son's condition. All he could do was pace.

The guys who'd collected Danielle from the airport turned out to be the family's hired goons. The one she'd called Muttonhead was Mark. Pat, the man of few words. Having dropped them at the hospital entrance, Pat was nowhere to be seen, but Danielle doubted he was far away. Muttonhead Mark had positioned himself in a discreet spot opposite the door to the accident and emergency department. He was still there whenever she went to check. It was good to know someone was on the lookout in case whoever shot Dean returned to have another try.

Entry to the waiting room was restricted to the patient and one other person, usually family. The Lewis name seemed to mean something to the security guy, because he allowed Danielle to enter with Ged.

The waiting room was crowded, but there were two vacant seats not far from the reception desk. Danielle led Ged across. He sat down while she went in search of a toilet.

A sign read that both toilets were closed for cleaning, with just the disabled one available. When she returned, Pat was sitting where she had left Ged.

'Where's my uncle?'

'Gone for a smoke,' Pat said.

'Any news?'

'No.'

'How did you get in? I thought it was just family.'

'The lad on security works for us.'

'Really?' Danielle asked. 'Doing security?'

'You don't want to know.'

'Maybe I do.'

'Ask your uncle, or Dean. It's not my place to tell you things,' Pat said.

'Any sign of Ann?'

'Your aunt has been contacted. I'm not sure if she's coming. She's been down in Limerick. Look, Danielle. Don't ask me anything else.'

'Well, you're a fucking mighty help, aren't you? I thought you worked for the Lewis family.'

'I do.'

'I am a Lewis. Therefore, gimme a bit of respect, if you please, and don't be an arsehole, or at least pretend you're not one.'

He pursed his lips. 'What do you want from me?'

'Well, I have another burning question, but not about my relatives, if you don't mind answering.'

'Depends.'

'Arsehole alert it is.'

'Go on.'

'Why weren't you the least bit decent to me in the car earlier? I wouldn't have made a run for it if I didn't think my life was in danger.'

His lips tightened further. 'Maybe it was. Maybe you were right to run. Maybe you should run back to wherever you've been for the last decade.'

'Well, fuck you very much.' She lapsed into silence, chewing on the inside of her cheek.

Pat's gaze followed Ged as he came back inside and went up to the reception desk. 'I'm not paid to answer questions. Direct anything that's burning a hole in your brain to your uncle, your aunt or to Dean. To family, not to me. Keep me out of it.'

'Out of what?'

Ignoring her question, he stood up and went over to Ged, who was now leaning against the wall.

'Fine. Arsehole,' she muttered.

Over the next hour or so, ambulances pulled in and out of the bay. Doctors and nurses bustled about, but none of them stopped to speak to Ged. He stayed by the wall with Pat.

People were called into a triage room. Some were sent back out, others weren't. A woman seated in one corner held her elbow across her body. There was blood on her forehead. She stared at the floor, a man close to her, his arm across the back of her chair. They didn't speak. A baby, dressed in pink, set up a wail, and a woman bounced her in her arms, murmuring to her in a foreign language — possibly Polish. After a while, she took the baby outside. A man with hair that looked like rats had been sucking on it and smelling of shit, shuffled over with his hand out. Before he got to Ged, Pat blocked his way. His voice loud enough for the whole waiting room to hear, he told the man to fuck off.

Hours went by. Eventually, a doctor emerged from the cubicle and asked for Dean's next of kin. Ged pushed himself off the wall and went over. It was difficult to read the doctor's face or guess what he was about to relay. Ged stared, eyes wide, waiting for the news.

The doctor led him into the cubicle. After a moment or two, Ged returned and beckoned to Danielle.

No way was she going in there. Less than twenty-four hours in the country, she did not need to see a dead body, least of all her cousin's dead body.

Fuck. How to get out of this?

But Ged ushered Danielle along, saying he needed her support. Where the hell was Ann? She was Dean's mother, not her. It should be her supporting Ged. This was not why she'd come back.

She had never been that close to Dean. He'd always been a nasty bollocks towards her, though she wouldn't wish him dead. But he was much younger than her. Ten years ago he was still a teenager, thinking he had balls bigger than he did. Then again, his death would distract them from her and her return, leaving her free to pursue answers to her questions. It was hard to feel sorry for Ged's loss when her own had been that much greater. He hadn't been there for her in the aftermath of her loss, yet he wanted her with him now. They both had lost a son.

CHAPTER 7

Out in the corridor, the smell of disinfectant came as a relief from the stench in the waiting room. Nurses rushed in and out of rooms. They passed an elderly person in a wheelchair, drip bag on his lap, eyes dead, staring at nothing. His hands full of papers, the doctor backed in through the door.

About to follow him in, Danielle was jostled by an older woman, who was wailing like a banshee. A nurse in scrubs flattened herself against the wall to avoid being hit by the handbag swinging from the woman's arm. It narrowly missed the orderly in charge of the wheelchair, who was forced to duck.

'Sorry, love. I'm upset.' She caressed his arm, bracelets rattling. The orderly hurriedly pushed the wheelchair forward, while the woman began to shout, 'Where's my boy? Let me see him. I want to see him.' She staggered, slid down the wall and retrieved a wad of tissues from the handbag. 'They better not have shot him in his beautiful face. I want an open coffin.'

'Get up, Ann, please.' Ged hauled her to her feet. 'He's not fucking dead.'

Danielle's stomach lurched. *Not dead.* Having braced herself for the worst, now she didn't know what to feel. She went to help Ged with Ann.

'I told you he was in surgery, didn't I?' Ged continued. 'Didn't Pat ring you to say he was back in the ward and coming round?'

Ann held the bunch of tissues against her chest. 'I thought you were afraid to tell me the truth.'

'I wouldn't do that to you.'

'Take me to him. Take me to my baby boy.'

Ged steered her into the room. Dean's shoulder was wrapped in bandages, so it was hard to see the extent of the damage. Still groggy, he tried to raise himself on to his pillows.

Ann held Dean's good hand pressed against her cheek for a moment. 'Oh, my nerves. I can't take it.' The doctor dropped his folder and caught her as she fell. He guided her to the empty bed next to Dean's. 'Are you okay? Let's take those sunglasses off so we can examine you.' He called to a nurse, who slipped a blood pressure cuff on her arm.

'Can you put the bag down, Mrs Lewis?'

She tightened her grip on the handbag and turned her head towards Dean. 'Look at this now, baby, the two of us side by side. I'm not leaving you.'

Danielle rolled her eyes. 'Stop making this all about you, Ann. It's Dean who's been shot.'

Ann finally took off her sunglasses. 'It can't be. Surely not. Danielle, is that really you?'

'Yes, Auntie Ann. It's me.'

'Come closer, so I can take a look at you.' Ann extended a limp hand towards her.

Danielle smiled, thinking, *I bet if I held out a bottle of vodka towards her, she'd perk up all right.*

In the next bed, Dean blinked. 'Cuz? Is that you?'

'Sure is.'

'That's the job, family reunion. Pity I had to take a few bullets to get you all together in the one room.'

Ged grinned. 'It's great to have her back. Isn't it, Ann?'

'Sure, it is.' She turned to the nurse. 'I'm grand now.'

'I'll get the doctor to take a look at you.'

'No need. I'm fine.'

'Take it easy for now, and I'll be back soon to check up on you.' The nurse left the room.

Ged took a step towards Dean's bed. 'What were you doing when you got shot?'

'Making a few collections,' Dean said.

'I told you to wait till Mark and Pat were free to go with you. Christ.'

'I didn't want to wait. Where the fuck were they, anyway?'

'Picking me up at the airport,' Danielle said.

'So, it's your fault I'm here,' Dean said.

Danielle raised an eyebrow. Some things never changed. 'Hardly.'

'Now, now, you two,' Ann said.

Dean groaned. 'Fucking painkillers are wearing off. Useless as fuck.'

He pressed a bell. The nurse appeared at once. 'The pain! It's excruciating.'

The nurse sighed. 'Let me have a look.' She checked his records. 'Dean, you've been given strong painkillers.'

'They're not fucking working.'

'I'll get the doctor to examine you when he's free. You can't have any more until he says so.'

'Why can't he come now?' Ann piped up. 'Can't you see the pain my son is in?'

'I'll see what I can do.' She approached Ann, who was now sitting on the edge of her bed. 'How are you feeling now, Mrs Lewis?'

'I said I was fine, didn't I? It's my son needs the attention. Why are you wasting your time with me when it's him needs sorting?'

'If you'll excuse me, Mrs Lewis, I'll be back soon.' And the nurse hurried out.

'Fuck's sake,' Ann muttered and laid back down.

'Right. We can reorganize the collections, that's no problem. Just tell me what you remember about the shooting. Did you recognize him?' Ged asked.

'He'd a bally on, Da, but the eyes, they were a weird blue colour. Tall, strong fella. He was shitting it, though, trembling all over he was.'

'Why didn't he go for the kill?'

'Two boys landed on — young fellas on a scrambler. Scared him off.'

'Who were they?'

'No clue, Da. I was busy trying to survive.'

'We need to find them,' Ged said.

'Why?' Dean asked.

'They had to have known who they were helping. Could be useful to us.' Ged stared at the floor, thinking. He looked up again. 'Wait. Tall, strong, weird eyes . . . that sounds like Marion Ahearne's boy.'

'Now you say it—'

'That little shit. What's his problem?'

'That's what I said. I dunno, these drugs are fucking with my memory. Where the fuck is that doctor?'

'No wonder they're not rushing back. The way you spoke to that nurse. Christ,' Ged said. 'A few manners go a long way in places like this, Ann.'

'Oh, you're lecturing me on manners, Ged Lewis, while our son is in pain.' Ann peeled herself off the bed and went to the bathroom.

Ged watched the door close behind her. 'And don't be smoking in there. You'll set off the fire alarms.'

Ged went out into the corridor. Minutes later he was back, dragging a bewildered-looking medic. 'He looks qualified enough to write up some drugs.'

The harassed nurse bustled in to the rescue. 'I told you the doctor will be along soon.'

'Better be. My son nearly died,' Ged said.

The nurse left, pushing the medic in front of her.

Ann came out of the toilet, complaining that it was filthy.

With a glance at her, Ged continued to question Dean.

'Why the fuck would he have a go at you?' Ged asked. 'What's going on, Dean? What have you done? You had to have been targeted for a reason.'

'Nothing, Da. I swear. Maybe it was mistaken identity. No way could it be him.'

'Whoever it is, I'll get the bastards.' Ged paced back and forth. 'But if it wasn't him, who else could it be?'

'Could they be connected to the crew who tried to shoot me all those years ago?' Danielle said.

Ged opened his mouth and closed it again.

'Should she be here?' Dean said. 'We haven't seen sight of her in years, and now she's listening in to everything.'

Ged took hold of Danielle's hand and patted it. 'She's family, Dean.' He squeezed her hand before letting it go. 'What were we saying? Oh, yes. Where else would the danger be coming from?'

'It's nothing, Da. Nothing I can't handle. I'm still here, aren't I?'

'Don't sound like nothing to me. You've two bullets in you. And it's a very fucked-up mistaken identity, if that's the case.'

'Close the door,' Dean said.

Ged gave it a kick. 'Why are you suddenly so convinced it's not him?'

Dean sighed. 'There's too much cash involved for any of them to off me.'

'Go on . . .'

'Brenno came in on the ATM jobs with me. Bird supplied the machinery. I needed a seven-tonne excavator, tractor and loader to do the job. His were just sitting around in the yard—' He winced and touched his bandaged shoulder.

'Go on.'

'Well, word got back that the cops had some operation going and no job around the border was safe. The cops here teamed up with them bunch of pricks across the border. We'd already paid a visit to the place we were going to hit that night when we heard this, but I figured they'd be too busy with them July parades to bother with us.'

'Wait. But if you were only casing the place, what was the problem?'

'Brenno was in one car, I was in the other. He was the lookout. One of the screws fell out of the front plate. He'd changed them for Northern Ireland ones that morning. So then it was hanging off. Instead of leaving it be, he tried to fix it, and was spotted by the worker in the exchange, who must've called the cops. When he heard the sirens, Brenno panicked. Next thing, we're hightailing it out of the North with the PSNI chasing after us.'

'For fuck's sake, Dean.'

'The plan was to leave the heavy machinery stashed in an industrial unit in Fermanagh, for a while anyway. I called a halt to the whole thing until we heard more and the heat had died down. I told Brenno to park the plans for now, but only for now. Bird probably thinks he's out of pocket, but he's not. It's just delayed. I told Brenno to pass that on to him. I had to steer clear of him for a while, in case the PSNI officers chasing us had got a look at me.'

'Do you think Brenno told him that the job was on hold and not cancelled?'

'Yeah. I think.'

'You think? Would Bird believe Brenno?'

'Who knows?'

'Why didn't you just give Bird his machinery back and let him have his share?'

'Well, I can't do fuck all now, can I? Here in a hospital bed.'

'Jesus, Dean, you should have done it before today. As a mark of trust or something.'

'The cops seizing his stuff last month hurt him like fuck. He's paranoid, thinks everyone is stabbing him in the back. How could I move huge machinery like that without drawing attention? Besides, we now know how long it takes for the PSNI to get to that currency exchange.'

'There's always a way around with you, isn't there?'

'Yeah, and Bird needs to remember that. What's wrong with him is he's itching to find a rat, and no one knows who it is.'

'Jesus Christ. He can't think it's you, surely?'

'I'd burn my own eyelids off before I'd peddle info to the fucking cops.'

'But does Bird know that?'

'He'd better.'

'What about the other jobs he'd backed you on?'

'Yeah, well, we got four done, but his cut was coming from the next few.'

'Did he know that was the deal?'

Dean stared out of the window.

Ged spoke through clenched teeth. 'I'm asking you a question, Dean.'

'Sounds like you're putting me through an interrogation.'

Ged put his face close to Dean's. 'This is no time to get smart, my son.'

'I'm not, Da, I swear. Bird is getting paranoid. He's snorting his own stuff and it's eating his brain.'

Ged straightened up. 'Jesus Christ, Dean. Us and them go way back, right to when me and his father raced pigeons together. Brenno could have told him about the other jobs, and that the money was there and hadn't been shared. You should have given him his cut after each job, the way it was always done, and not waited to pay out. Especially after him suffering the loss with the brown. It is a pisser knowing your special delivery is sitting in the cops' warehouse waiting to be destroyed.'

'I have my way of doing things, Da, and that's that.'

'Do you not think the way it was done all along didn't serve a purpose? It kept things ticking over between the two families. Especially since—' he glanced at Danielle — 'since they were in danger of falling apart all those years ago.'

Danielle's heart pounded. Were they blaming her for the rupture between the two families? *Jason* was the cheating bastard, not her. She'd lost a baby after some thug tried to shoot her. She'd had to flee to a different country. And now the conflict was her fault? She wanted to spit.

Ann was staring at her. 'You all right there, Dani, love?'

'Yeah, grand.'

'Not exactly the welcome you'd hoped for, eh?'

'It's fine, Ann. Don't worry about me.' *No one's been worried up to this point, so why be bothered now?*

Ann continued to stare. 'I just want to make sure you're okay, Dani. I don't know why you've got this attitude with me. I thought we got on better than that.'

Danielle exhaled. 'Yes, Ann, we did get on better — I mean, we do, and thank you for your concern. As you said, this is not the welcome I'd hoped for. I certainly wasn't expecting to end up in the hospital at Dean's bedside. It must have been a huge shock for you when you got the call.'

'Well, it turned out grand. There was I thinking Dean was dead, only to find out he's not. And then to arrive and find you here too, well, it made my day — no, my decade.'

'Did you not know I was coming?'

'No one knew, Danielle. Did you know, Ged? What about you, Dean?'

'No, Ma, I didn't.'

'Then how come Pat and Mark were there to, er, greet me?' Danielle said to Ged.

'A contact at the hotel you booked into,' Ged said.

'Really?'

'Did we ruin your surprise, Danielle?' Ann asked.

Danielle shrugged. 'I wasn't sure what kind of a welcome I'd get.'

'Well, you are welcome, Dani, love,' Ged said. 'We're so glad to have you back. You've got a great head on you. Maybe you can teach Dean a few tricks.'

'I don't need any lessons, Da. I'll sort this out myself.'

'Danielle has always been a quick learner,' Ann said.

'She can't hope to know the business after she's just breezed back after ten years,' Dean said.

'Trust me, she'll be fine,' Ged said. 'And leave this to me to sort out, Dean. I'll try to have a word with Bird. Do some mopping up.'

Dean sucked in air through gritted teeth. 'No. If it was him tried to take me out, why should you? Fuck him. There's only one way to answer something like that.'

'Steady on, son. You want to start a war? We have to be sure he's involved.'

'He must be. Do you think if Brenno Ahearne was involved that he could have done this off his own bat? Not a hope. Bird Flynn had the say, which means he fucking started it. He did, Da, not me.'

'You're right,' Ann said. 'He threatened our family and there's only one reply to that.'

'I still have the final word on this,' Ged said.

'Yes, but we don't take shit from the likes of the Flynns. Dean's right: if there is a war, he started it.'

'No. Let me talk to him. Then we'll decide what to do.' Ged fumbled with his phone, which slipped from his hands, clattering to the floor. 'Damn it.'

Ged and Danielle both bent down to retrieve it. She got there first. 'Don't worry, the screen isn't broken. Here.'

'All right, Ged,' Ann said. 'Go have your chat with Bird, but if that doesn't work, we'll have to take action. Do you want me to get my crowd up from Limerick?'

'No! Christ, not that.' Ged put his hands up.

Ann shrugged. 'Fine.'

Danielle's mind was spinning. Just what was going on? 'Wait a second. When did we start talking wars, hits, revenge? What happened to earning a bit of an income from providing a few betting shops with protection?'

Dean laughed. 'How long has it been, cuz?'

'Ten years,' muttered Ann.

'Ten? That's a lifetime in this game. You need to get yourself up to date.'

'Are you sure you want to be coming back now?' Ann said.

'No. I came to find out,' Danielle said.

'What do you mean "find out"? Find out what, exactly?' Dean said.

'If I'm safe, for a start. Whether there's a role for me in the family. Find out if there's any progress on the investigation into my shooting.'

'What? A decade on? Good luck with that,' Ann said. 'One of them detectives from the investigation retired. The other was murdered not long after.'

'I know.' Danielle's throat felt dry. She knew his name too — Gavin Kelly. Knew also that his wife, Saoirse, had also lost her unborn baby. Danielle had met her in the maternity hospital where they both went for a check-up just before she left for England. But they didn't need to know that. She looked around for something to drink.

Ann stepped closer. 'The rest of 'em couldn't even solve their fellow cop's murder. You think they'd give a shit about your near miss?'

'It was more than just a near miss. I was shot. Shall I show you the scar? I lost my baby, too. And me and Jason split.' Danielle's voice cracked.

'We know, love. It wasn't easy for you.' She put her hand on Danielle's arm and squeezed. It was unexpectedly gentle, comforting. 'I thought I'd lost Dean today. It was a terrible shock. But, you know, we lost a lot too, that time you left us.'

Danielle looked up. 'You told me I was doing the right thing by going, Ann.'

'Did I really?'

'Yes. You said it was for the best, men like Jason don't change. I had to go.'

'Yes, of course you did.' Ann let go of her arm and Danielle took a deep breath. She wasn't about to let them see her grief.

Ged put his arm around her. 'We know it was hard for you, going through all that.'

'Yes, it was. Then having to leave you all.'

'Pity you sent Jason packing though,' Ged said.

She pulled away from her uncle. 'I didn't just "send him packing". The two-faced bastard was cheating on me, and I'd just lost the baby.'

Ged shrugged. 'Ah, that's men for you. It was his loss, too. We men have a different way of coping to you women. It took a while before Bird and Jason were on speaking terms again. Nearly cost us a fortune.'

'Really?' Danielle asked. *Was that all that Ged had been worried about? The cost of it?*

'Bird was incensed that Jason fucked up and hurt you,' Ged said.

'Especially since you'd chosen his younger brother over him,' Ann added. 'Bird swore up and down that he'd never have treated you like that.'

'I wasn't attracted to Bird, that's all.'

'But he was attracted to you. The two of you could have been a very valuable union. But you didn't give Bird a chance, disappearing like that after Jason did the dirty on you. I mean, Bird could have grown on you,' Ann said.

Like a fungus, Danielle thought. 'No way.' She cleared her throat. 'Anyway, it's too late now.'

'Not necessarily. In fact, I think I know where you can help.' Ged abruptly left the room.

'Da always has a good plan,' Dean said.

'I hope so,' said Ann.

Ged was soon back. He marched into the room. 'Right, Dani. Grab your bag. You and I have a meeting to go to.'

'What about me?' Ann asked. 'You're just leaving me here, are you?'

'You've your baby boy to look after,' Ged said.

'But what if they hear he's not dead and come back to finish the job?' she said.

'The hospital will have rung the guards by now. They won't be far.'

'Fuck the cops,' Dean said.

'Don't let them in the room. Say you're too sick to talk to them. But make sure they stay in the hospital. Use them for protection. No one's going to chance coming in here with a gun when there's a squad outside, are they?'

Ann gripped her bag with both hands.

Ged groaned. 'Don't tell me you brought one with you.'

'Well, I had to make sure I was protected.'

'Jesus Christ. What if you'd been searched?'

'They're not going to search a grieving mother, now, are they?'

'So that was what all the drama was about. To divert their attention. Meanwhile, you were carrying a loaded weapon. It is loaded, isn't it?'

'I wasn't diverting their attention. I only realized it was in the bag when I looked for my tissues. Forgot about it, didn't I?'

'Fuck's sake, Ann.'

'Don't "fuck's sake" me, Ged Lewis.'

'Well, since it's here now, you can lend it to Dani.'

'Why would I need a gun?' she said.

'Keep your voice down,' Ann hissed. 'You won't need to use it. You'll be fine.'

Danielle turned to Ged. 'Where are we going, anyway?'

'You'll see. Come on.'

Danielle left the room with Ged, without taking Ann's gun. No point risking getting caught with it or, worse, having to use it.

CHAPTER 8

To Bird's disappointment, there were no lights on in the penthouse at Clonliffe View. The entire building was in darkness and there were no cars parked outside.

Sal coasted to a stop. 'Maybe they're all at the hospital, Bird.'

Bird's phone rang. It was Ged. 'Shit.' He declined the call, but Ged rang again. This time he answered.

'Ged. How are you?'

'Not great, Bird. We need to meet.'

'All right. Why?'

'There's something we need to discuss.'

'Sounds serious. Are you okay?' Bird said.

'Yes and yes.'

'Fine. Where and when?' He asked himself how come he was being so compliant. Surely it was he, Bird, who should have decided where they were to meet.

But the location Ged proposed was perfect for Bird, near one of his empty factories.

'Head for the Eastpoint Business Park, Sal. I have a meeting,' Bird said.

'Want me to pick Bosco up, just in case?' Sal asked.

'Nah. Ged sounded okay. I'm sure he doesn't suspect anything. The two of us on our own should be grand.'

'You're sure?' Sal asked.

'I know what I'm doing.' If he arrived with his lads, it would arouse Ged's suspicions.

They crossed Eastpoint Causeway and pulled into a vacant lot. Two of Ged Lewis's henchmen stood waiting by his car. As they drew to a halt, one of them opened the door and Ged stepped out. The two men met halfway between the cars.

Bird offered Ged a cigarette, took one for himself and lit them both. He cleared his throat, waiting for Ged to speak. Allowing him to choose the venue had been enough of a concession. They stood eyeing one another, wreathed in smoke.

'My son's in the hospital, Bird.'

'No! What happened?'

'Gunned down.' Ged pulled on his cigarette.

'Jesus Christ. Is he bad?'

'He'll live. You didn't know about it then?' Ged said.

'No, I heard on the news there'd been a shooting, but I had no idea it was Dean. I'm glad to hear he's okay,' Bird said.

Ged stared at him. 'You any idea who might be behind it?'

'Jesus, no. How the fuck would I?'

'Dunno. I thought you might know something that would help us find out more about it. Are you sure you don't know anything?'

'Of course not, Ged. Dean and me are just after doing a job together. I have a few quid coming my way from it. He took on the dirty work and I supplied the equipment. Him being out of action, even for a short while, won't help my profit line any, will it?'

'Hmm.' Ged's eyes narrowed.

'What are you trying to say here, Ged? Sounds to me like you're making accusations.' Bird took a stance, squaring his shoulders.

'I'm not accusing anyone.' Ged blew a stream of smoke into the air. 'I'm just letting you know what's happened, in case you can shed any light for me.'

'Fair enough,' Bird said. 'I suppose you're after a bit of a shock.'

'Yeah.'

'What else is it, so?'

'You and me are in business together, Bird.'

'True enough.'

Bird spotted movement inside Ged's car and, instinctively, his hand went to his gun. Ged's two lads reached for theirs.

'Woah!' Ged held up his hands. 'Calm the fuck down. We're only talking here.'

'Who's that in the car?' Bird said.

Ged stamped out his cigarette and nodded to Pat, who opened the car door.

Bird froze. Was it really her? They shouldn't be meeting in some scummy yard; she should be descending some opulent staircase . . . The others faded into the background, leaving just the two of them.

Ged's voice sounded in his ears. 'You remember my niece, Dani, don't you?'

Bird sighed. She was just as stunning, not even a single extra line on her face. Princess of the Lewis clan, and destined to be queen of Dublin, if he'd had his way. He should have been more persuasive. But no, Danielle had to fuck off across the water. He'd cut Jason off from all sources of finance and kicked him out of the house. It took him a year to forgive Jason for what he'd done to her, after he'd come crawling back to him, begging for work and a bit of cash. Bird had relented and given him work, but he would never again share a house with him. Bird had wanted to reach out to Danielle, find out how she was, but no one seemed to be able to tell him where in the UK she'd settled.

Bird had always assumed Danielle would choose him over his loser of a brother. After all, he was the older and wiser one, the one with a multimillion-euro plant-hire business. The two of them would have controlled the city, uniting the Flynn and Lewis families in one huge empire. Jason had claimed she left the country because he'd met someone else. Bird hoped the real reason was because she'd come to her senses and realized she'd chosen the wrong brother. For ten years, he'd lived in the hope that any day she'd come back for him. Maybe today was that day.

In a daze, Bird approached her. He took her hand and raised it to his lips, breathing in the scent of citrus and vanilla — that perfume she'd always worn. He gazed into Danielle's eyes for a long moment, until she looked away. Rejected once more, he squared his shoulders, jutted out his chin.

He managed a tight smile. 'Did you decide to return to your rightful place with your family?'

Danielle glanced at her uncle. Ged didn't offer anything.

'What? Can't speak for yourself? It's not like you to be timid, Dani. Did you leave that spark of yours behind in the UK, or wherever you ended up?'

'Not at all, Bird. When I have something worth saying, you'll hear it.'

Just to hear her say his name made him melt. She was a firecracker, for sure.

'That's my girl.' Ged smiled at her and stuck out his chest.

Jesus, how Bird would love to wipe that grin from his face. *My girl.* Danielle should be his, no one else's.

'Now, back to the issue at hand. My son landed in hospital, and I want to find out who was responsible. Someone needs to pay compensation.'

Bird spread his hands. 'Like I already told you, Ged, it had nothing to do with me. Still, I'll put my best men on to it and let you know as soon as I find them.'

Ged shrugged.

'What more do you want from me, Ged?'

'Nothing, I suppose. That will have to do.'

'I've promised my best, and that's what you'll get.'

'Okay.'

He turned and called out to Danielle, 'Will I tell my brother you said hi?'

'Not when I didn't.'

Bird got back into his car and told Sal to take him to Dublin's pedestrian shopping district, Grafton Street, and wait for him while he went into Brown Thomas. There, he threw down a few euro on two bottles of that exquisite perfume. One for his bedside and one for Marion, so he could close his eyes and imagine he was making Dani Lewis scream his name while he fucked her senseless.

CHAPTER 9

They drove away from the meeting with Bird in silence. Watching the world whip past from the front seat, Danielle snuck a peek at her uncle, who, like her, was staring out of the window. Pat, the man of few words, stayed true to his nickname. Muttonhead Mark sat quiet beside her uncle. Danielle finally had a chance to think. The escalation in danger, the threats, the hum of violence in the air had taken her by surprise. Had the violence increased, or had she chosen not to see it back then, a decade ago? There was always a certain amount of brute force in the criminal world, but she had never believed her family capable of actually killing. After she had been shot, Ged had vowed to pull out of their criminal activities, as things had gone too far.

Even slimy Bruce 'Bird' Flynn was no longer the same. She remembered him in overalls, nails black with grease, tinkering with some engine or other amid the dust and grime. That dust and grime had earned him a great deal of cash. Now he looked like a del-boy who'd just bought his first classy suit. Yet beneath the tacky veneer lurked the old Bird, capable at any moment of losing his shit and beating the crap out of anyone who looked at him the wrong way.

She supressed a shudder at the thought of his pleading gaze. He hadn't even asked her why she had returned.

She had hoped to be able to settle before announcing her return to the family. Instead, she had landed in the middle of a snake pit. She hadn't been left alone for a second. Pat and Mark had been watching her every breath. She had no alternative but to go along with whatever was expected of her for the time being, until she found a way to do what she came back for.

Ged kept playing with his phone, but he made no calls, sent no messages. In the ten years since she'd last seen him, he'd become an old man. Maybe it would be better to stay for a while. It seemed the family even had a contact at the hotel where she was staying. Even so, she hesitated to cancel it, in case relations with her family turned sour. So far, they had welcomed her return.

As if reading her mind, Ged said, 'The penthouse at Clonliffe View is yours, Dani. Make yourself at home there. It's quite secure. There are panic buttons in the kitchen, the bedroom and beside the front door.'

'Am I still in danger?'

Straight questions had always resulted in straight answers where her family was concerned. Not so this time, it seemed.

Finally, Ged said, 'I doubt it, but we can't take the chance. For a start, I wouldn't risk visiting your mother's grave.'

It wasn't likely, was it? The memory of that last visit was engraved in her brain. The bullet whizzing past her ear, the next one finding its mark. She had folded like she'd been gut-punched, spattering blood across Rosie Lewis's headstone. So much blood. She would have died but for the quick reaction of two officers who chanced to be nearby. Saoirse had told her that her husband, Gavin, had been on a special op with another detective. He heard the shots and went to investigate. She could still hear the crackle of the Garda radio coming to life when he found her, the urgent request for assistance — shots fired . . . an ambulance.

All that remained was a scar under her ribcage — and another in her brain. With time, the mark on her skin faded, but not the memory. Who the shooter was remained a mystery. Even the detective's death hadn't been solved. Gavin Kelly. The man who'd saved her life. His wife, Saoirse, and Danielle formed an unlikely bond in the midst of their shared grief.

Returning was never going to be easy, but it had to be done. She was still partly the Danielle she'd been ten years ago. And without answers, without closure, she could never be made whole. Knowing who was behind the shooting would go a long way to healing the rift within her.

At the time, she'd suspected it was retaliation for something stupid and reckless Dean had done, and the easiest solution had been to leave. Fleeing to West London without telling anyone where she'd gone had ensured her safety. But it couldn't ensure her peace of mind. For the first few months, all she could think about was how badly Jason had treated her. He'd been balls deep in another woman — a hooker — and she'd caught him in the act.

'I'm going back to the hospital,' Ged announced as they pulled up outside the block of apartments. 'Pat will drive me and Mark can stay here for your protection. Almost everything in the penthouse is remote or automatic, so you'll need him to show you. Right, off you go.'

Pat waited until they were inside and the gates had closed behind them before driving away.

Stuck with Muttonhead. Great. Mark walked ahead of her, muscular and broad. His head sat on his shoulders as if he didn't have a neck. There was a damp patch on the back of his khaki T-shirt. He'd one ear pierced and wore a small chain-link bracelet around one of his wrists, a sovereign ring on his little finger. No other jewellery. He was the sort who'd have multiple tattoos, yet his arms were bare. Maybe they were on his back or one of his calves.

They got into the lift and travelled up to the penthouse in silence. Outside the door, he handed her a set of keys and pointed to a keypad. 'Who do you appreciate?'

'What?'

'The code — two, four, six, eight, who do you appreciate.'

'Right. By the way, do you have any spare fags?'

'Aw, shit, I left mine in the car. I'll see if I can get some.'

She keyed in the alarm code and went in. Alone at last—

A loud knock made her jump. Mark was back, holding out a battered box of John Player Blue, four missing, with a lighter stuck inside.

'I thought you'd left them in the car.'

'I was wrong. They were in my pocket.'

'Right. Cheers.'

'You want anything else?'

'No, I'm good. You can head off now, thanks.'

'I have to stay put. That's what I was told.'

Would she never be allowed a bit of space? 'Do you really have to?'

'Look, I'll hang around outside for a bit. Shout if you need me.'

Danielle found the remainder of the bottle of whiskey, poured herself a generous measure and swallowed it neat.

She set about exploring the rest of the apartment. There were views from every window, the rooftops below or the mountains beyond.

She picked up the velvet throw from the bed in the master suite and wrapped it around her. Taking whiskey bottle and glass, she slid open the patio door and raised her face to the sky. The city's north side glittered below. Was she off her head to be doing this? No. In order to move on, she needed to know who had ordered the hit all those years ago, and why.

Back then, she visited her mother's grave regularly, never imagining it to be dangerous. Out there in the open, she was vulnerable and the graveyard offered plenty of opportunity for a quick exit. The shooter was obviously an expert. Two shots, and she went down when the second hit. Lucky for her the detectives were nearby — though not for one of them. Not long afterwards, he'd been abducted and murdered.

Danielle wiped her eyes. Told herself to toughen the fuck up.

CHAPTER 10

It took Dean three phone calls to identify the two lads on the dirt bike. Cousins Jake and Sean Brady, a couple of nobodies with ambition. Dean knew Jake's older brother, who owed two grand and was slow paying up. Dean had been on the way to see him for an instalment when the shooter struck. Dean still wasn't sure if the lads had intended to help him. Either way, they could be put to some use. He would just have to think where and how.

To his annoyance, the hospital insisted on rationing his supply of painkillers. Pat reckoned the nurse had copped on that Dean was adding a bit of drama to his expressions of pain. Accordingly, he sneaked in a few extra somethings to take the edge off. Pain or not, Dean was lucky the shooter'd had such a crap aim.

His ma had taken herself off somewhere to calm her nerves. He'd been trying to nod off when his da came back. Without Danielle.

His da began pacing the room again, and it was doing his head in.

'Da, it's grand, I've handled it.'

'Handled it? You're in no fit state to handle anything.'

'Don't worry. I slurred the fuck out of my words until they gave up and fucked off.'

'You mean the doctors let the guards in here to talk to you? And you off your face on drugs?'

'The doctors said they'd given me strong painkillers, so it was fine.'

'Fuck that. I should have told them you weren't to give a statement.'

'I'm the victim, Da. They need one from me.'

'Who was it? Did they leave a card?'

'That fella who used to work with Criminal Assets Bureau, Dave Richards. Had a new one with him. Smell of fresh-out-of-training off her. Teegan. Her full name's there, too.'

Ged rummaged in the locker beside Dean's bed and found the cards. He read the names out loud: 'Detective Sergeant Dave Richards and Detective Garda Sinead Teegan.'

'That's it. I knew it was something Irish.'

'Are you sure it was who you said?'

'You're just after reading me out their names, Da.'

'No, no, the fella who shot you.'

'I'm not a bit sure, now the drugs have worn off. I can't even remember what I said yesterday.'

'Fuck's sake, Dean. I can't cut decades of ties with the Flynns if you're *not a bit sure*. I met Bird and he was like an iceberg.'

'Huh?'

'Harmless on the surface, but a lot going on underneath.'

'You took Danielle, didn't you?'

'Yep.'

'That was it, then. He probably still has the horn for her.'

'Nah, it was more than that.'

'Well, anyway, when I'm clear about who it was, I'll let you know. If it is Brenno Ahearne, he might've been working alone. Maybe he was setting Bird up to look like he's behind it. I wouldn't be too happy either, if he were knocking off my ma.'

Ged scrunched up his face. 'Don't even put that vision in my fucking head.' He ran a hand across his scalp. 'Well, Bird wouldn't risk losing his split from the job you did together. Too costly for him, especially after last month's loss.'

'Yeah. Whoever shopped him better pray he doesn't catch up with them.'

'And what about his equipment?'

'I can get it back to him,' Dean said. 'Be worse if the cops took that too. I'll take it back in a few weeks — well, as soon as I feel right.' He shifted in the bed. 'Speaking of Ma, any sign of her out there?'

'No. She's probably getting a dart of coffee into her. Anyway, she was no good to us in here, all fretting and the like.'

'More like sorting her nerves through the end of a vodka bottle.'

The slap landed out of the blue. It stung. Dean's hand shot up to his cheek.

'Don't talk about your mother like that.'

'Sorry, Da.'

'Yeah, you'd want to be sorry.'

A nurse entered and checked the dressing. 'The doctor will be in to see you soon.'

'Right,' Dean said.

'Any news of him going home?' Ged asked.

'The doctor will be in soon,' she repeated and left the room.

'As soon as you're out, we'll organize a welcome-home party for Dani.'

'Really?'

'Yeah, be good to celebrate her return. A show of family strength.'

'Will Ma stay for that or fuck off back to Limerick?'

'She'll stay. Your mother loves a party.'

She does, doesn't she? Dancing on the tables until she falls off. Dean kept the thought to himself.

'Wait till I'm feeling a bit better. Ma's not the only one who likes to party.'

'Maybe you should learn to rest more,' Ged said.

'Nah, I'll be dead for long enough, Da.'

'The new place we bought. The pub. It would be perfect for a celebration,' Ged said.

'Yeah. What's your plan for Dani? Can't let all her skills go to waste. What was she at in London?'

'A beautician. She built up her own business, which is a good thing for us. She can take on the knocking shop on Berkley Street while the bar is being renovated. Then she can sprinkle her magic there too, bring a bit of class to it.'

'Wait. The pub? I thought I was getting that.'

'But you're out of action now, Dean.'

'Not that much.'

'Give yourself a chance to recover.'

'Sounds like you're shoving us all out of the way to accommodate Danielle, Da.'

'No, I'm not.'

'You are. What about Hazel? Won't she be put out that Danielle's taking over?'

'Nah. She's about to pop any day now.'

'What? I thought she was getting rid of it.'

'So did I. But no. Nothing I can do now, it's my flesh and blood. A girl.'

'A baby sister, eh?'

Ged pointed a finger at Dean. 'Never say that out loud, you hear me? And never in front of your ma.'

'Course, Da, course. Not a word.'

'You have a point though. Hazel will be pissed off that her earnings are gone. But there is a house all lined up for her and the new baby.' Ged waved a hand. 'It's kitted out with the best stuff. She'll have little to complain about, I hope. If she does, she can go and moan to someone else. Anyway, all she'll be worried about is getting her figure back.' He stared at Dean. 'Not a word to Dani either. She might be good at keeping her trap shut, but she has time for your ma. I don't want anything slipping out. Understood?'

'Yeah, course. What about security?'

'Hazel'll be looked after. I'll have one of the lads keeping an eye on her and the baby.'

There was a murmur of voices outside the door. The doctor marched in, followed by a group of about six others, along with the nurse.

'Can you excuse us, please?'

Ged stood where he was.

'Please, Mr Lewis. Let the doctors do their work.' The nurse led him to the door.

Dean watched his father leave the room and turned his attention to the doctor.

'Can I go home, Doc?'

'Not yet, and when you do, you'll need to return to outpatients the following week to have your dressing changed and your wound examined.'

'I can do that. Can I go now, so?'

Meanwhile, the doctor was busy probing the wound. 'You're healing well, but I would still like to review you in another twenty-four hours, just to make sure you're ready to continue your recovery at home.'

'So I'm here for another night then?'

'Yes.'

'What about the bullets, Doc?'

'The one that damaged your shoulder went right through, hence the dressing front and back. The one in your buttock was removed.'

'Can I keep it as a souvenir?'

'That's not our policy, Mr Lewis. Besides, the police will need it.'

'But it's mine. It came out of my body. Do I not need to give permission or something?'

The doctor ignored the question and left, passing Ged on his way back in.

'I'll be out tomorrow,' Dean said. 'I just have to be back to get my dressing changed, then physio.'

'Great news. What's with that look?'

'The bullet. I wanted to keep it.' Dean winced. 'Will you get me the bottle of orange juice — there, beside my shave bag.'

Ged started to take the lid off.

'No, pop the bottom for me, will you, and get out what's inside?'

Ged did as his son asked, pulling out a tray of blue tablets wrapped in foil. 'Oxy? Dean, really! Can you not stay away from the opioids?'

'I need them, Da.'

'The medics will know you're out of it, Dean.'

'Better than the pain.'

'Go on, what were you saying about keeping the bullet?' Ged asked, handing him a pill.

'Fucking cops have it.'

'Can they do that?'

'They need it for the investigation, apparently. They probably have the other one too, from the scene. Place was swarming with cops.'

'Anyone talking?'

'No one, Da. They know better.'

'At least getting out tomorrow means they can't come back to get a statement from you.'

'Yeah, but they'll call to the house, won't they?'

'I suppose.'

'What'll we do?'

'Did they leave you a card?' Ged asked.

Dean stared at his dad for a beat. 'Yeah. You had it in your hand when the doctor came in.' What was up with his da?

'Where is it?' Ged patted his jacket pockets and eventually found it. 'Oh, yeah, here it is.' He read the names out again. 'Do you know them?'

'Da? Are you okay?'

'Yeah, yeah. It's the stress. Has me addled. Don't mind me. Yes, I remember now. Richards. Were they convinced you weren't in a fit state to talk to them?'

'Yes.'

'Dozy bastards. Here. Call them. Tell them to come in.' Ged handed the card to Dean.

'What?'

'Go on. And get them to put it on record that you're making no complaint. I'll be here and I'll get our brief in here, too.'

'They're only allowing one visitor at a time, Da.'

'Fuck them. Let them try to stop a solicitor.'

'What if they push it? You know these places. They have rules.'

'When did rules ever stop us?' Ged sighed. 'All right, tell them to call at your place. There's nothing there?'

'No, I never keep anything at the house.'

'No piece? No spare gear?'

'No, Da. Look, I'm the victim here — they won't land in with a search warrant. They'd have no grounds, and if they did, we'd set the brief on them.'

'Right, invite them then. We can always ask them to leave. Look to be cooperating, all right? Say you don't remember a thing, you blacked out and you won't be putting anything in writing.'

'Will do.'

'And say if you hear anything you'll let them know. Who's that yoke anyway?'

'You've just read that card, Da.'

'Here, you read them. I forget with everything going on.'

'You haven't been drinking this morning, Da, have you?'

'Don't be cheeky, son.'

'Right. Sorry. It's Detective Sergeant Dave Richards and Detective Garda Sinead Teegan.'

'What was she like?'

'Looked to me like she was fresh out of the brainwash farm — Templemore training college, or whatever they call it.'

'Fucking Richards. He's well in with that Cashman.'

'Oh, you mean as in that head Criminal Assets Bureau fella. He was in charge the time Ma's sister's place got raided, along with cousin Martin McCarthy's farm in Adare.'

'The one and only. Sure, Cashman moved, but them bastards never forget. What's more, they pass the information around.'

All at once, Ged was overtaken by a fit of coughing. His face turned bright red.

'You okay, Da?'

'Course I am,' he gasped. 'It'll take more than the thought of them bastards to kill Ged Lewis. Now try and remember. If it was Brenno, and only if, we need to make sure he was working alone.'

'I get it,' Dean said. 'I make a mistake and we're heading for disaster.'

'Yes, you remember that. We don't want to start a war.'

'I hear you, Da. I hear you.'

To Dean's mind, a war was just what they needed. Something to clear away the old has-beens like the Flynns. Get them out, and Dublin would be Dean's to run as he liked.

CHAPTER 11

Danielle shot upright. Where the fuck was she? It was pitch black. Then she realized her false eyelashes had stuck together. Bastards of things. She prised them apart to find the sun rising above the neighbouring buildings. She'd fallen asleep on one of the loungers on the balcony.

She squinted at a distant view of Fairview Park and the Tolka River, past the upper stands at Croke Park. The stadium was eerily empty, a tattered newspaper blowing across the pitch. She recognized the yard where yesterday they'd met that creep Bird Flynn. A pigeon was grooming its feathers on the railing. Dirty yokes. Bird's father used to keep hundreds of the things.

She wondered if Bird had carried on the tradition. Tommy Flynn had treated them pigeons better than his kids. Bird's father, also known as 'Feather' Flynn, had been a champion featherweight, and later a great trainer, but a shit father. Ged and Tommy Flynn had become friends through the boxing. Ged, she remembered, also had in interest in the pigeons, and back in the day, he and Tommy had bonded over the care and racing of them. That bond had carried over to the next generation, but it looked like it would be coming unstuck if Bird really had been behind Dean's shooting.

It might be July, but it was fucking skinning cold. She pulled the throw tighter around herself and lay back down with nothing on her mind now but a fag and coffee. Voices reached her from inside. *Fuck.* What must a girl do to get herself some space? She turned and looked back through the window into the living room. Nope. She was still alone. The voices had come from passers-by on the path below.

Maybe a strong drink would sort her . . . No, she needed focus.

She cleared her throat. The pigeon fucked off. She raised the blanket and looked down at herself. At least she still had her clothes on. The empty glass had fallen over on its side, fag butts on the ground beside it. She tugged at her hair. Some of the extensions had knotted.

Finally, she got to her feet and headed into the living room, trailing the throw behind her.

Her head rested on her shoulders, heavy as a bowling ball, and her brain was foggy. Yet again, she wondered if she should have stayed in London. At least she could have given more consideration to what she would do once she got here.

'Morning.'

She jumped, looked around for whoever had spoken. A head appeared over the back of the couch.

'Jesus Christ, Mark. You frightened the shit out of me. I thought there was no one else here. Why didn't you sleep in one of the bedrooms?' she asked.

'Oh, sure,' he said. 'What good would I be to you there if someone came in the front door? At least here, I'd get to them before they found you.'

'Anyway,' she said, 'I'm heading for a shower. Will you make us some coffee, please?'

'Okay. Take your time,' Mark said.

* * *

The buzzer went just as Danielle had finished dressing. A camera on the wall showed a man she didn't recognize standing at the door. He must have known the code or had a zapper, since he'd got through the gate. Her phone vibrated with a message. It was from Uncle Ged.

Visitor this morning. Early. With a package.

The buzzer went again. She released the door to the hallway downstairs. A few seconds later, someone knocked on the door to the apartment.

She recognized the gaunt, grey-haired man, but his name escaped her.

She let him in and he strolled into the kitchen as if he lived there. He was carrying a gun, which he placed on the kitchen counter. She stared at it. Meanwhile, Mark was busy pouring the coffee, his back to them.

The guy nodded towards it. 'For you. Keep it safe. We can't always be around.'

'Me? Do I really need one?'

'Well, what if you did?' Mark asked.

It hadn't been part of the plan, but after yesterday, having one didn't seem such a bad idea.

'A nice little Beretta,' the visitor said. 'Small enough to fit in your handbag.'

'You might need a few lessons,' Mark added.

She didn't answer. She knew how to use one. It was an APX Carry. She ran her fingers across the grip. The security it provided. The damage it could inflict. She aimed it out on to the balcony, at the pigeon who'd just settled back on the rail.

'Not a good idea,' the man said. Jeez, what was his name?

'You're right.' She left the Beretta where it had been on the counter. Her stomach rumbled. 'I suppose you didn't bring food with you as well?'

'No, I didn't.'

'Can you go to the shop and get something?' she said to Mark.

'They weren't my instructions.' Mark really was a muttonhead.

The other man slapped his arm.

'Job done. I'm off.'

'Stall a second, Ritch,' Mark said.

Of course! The legendary Ritchie Delaney. He'd been Ged's shadow when they were younger; they were always knocking around together. Ritchie was the same age as Ged, but had aged much better. They had had a big falling out at some point, lasted a few years. Well, they must be reconciled if Ged had him delivering weapons. Danielle looked at him more carefully.

'Can't. Boss needs me at the factory.'

The factory? It couldn't be the same place? Could it?

Mark watched her, noticed her surprise. 'You go on ahead,' he said to Ritchie. 'I'll join you in a minute.'

Ritchie went out, slamming the door behind him.

'I can run to the Maxol,' Mark said. 'Get you sorted. Any preferences?'

She shrugged. 'I'm not sure. Bit of fruit maybe?'

Grinning, he went to a door on the other side of the kitchen, opened it wide to reveal a pantry stocked with supplies.

She smiled. 'Jesus. I'll surely find something in there.'

'I have something else to show you.' He beckoned to her and she followed him across to the coffee table in front of the sofa where she'd had drinks with Ged the previous afternoon. 'I was going to show you last night, but you were fast asleep on the balcony by then.'

It was strange to think that he'd been there and she hadn't known. Did he just take a glance at her, see that she was asleep and go straight to the couch, or did he stand there watching her for a while? She'd never know, would she?

He sat down and patted the seat beside him. She sat. He pressed the side of the table just under the glass top. A screen rose up in front of them. On it, the hallway, the door and the lobby beyond. 'There you go. Never open the door blind again.'

'I didn't—'

He sighed. 'Look. All this stuff is designed to keep you safe. Ged wants to make sure you have nothing to worry about. He would like you to stay on in Dublin and not be rushing off back to London.'

'Right, okay. Thanks.'

'He considers you an important part of his family.'

'That's good.'

Mark nodded. 'It is.'

He held her gaze for a moment as if he had more to say, but remained silent.

'Thanks. It's all very fancy, I must say.' She played with the thing for a while, flipping through different views of the building. 'What about in here?'

He shrugged. 'Just watch your back, Danielle.'

'What do you mean?'

He left the room, and her question unanswered.

She found some crackers in the press. They'd do until she could get breakfast together. Her mind racing, she headed out to the balcony and smoked two cigarettes in quick succession. That fucking pigeon again. Persistent little fucker. She ran in, grabbed the gun and aimed it at him but he'd taken off.

It had to be Bird that had ordered the hit on her. Why? Heartbreak? Jealousy? Couldn't stomach that she'd hooked up with Jason instead of him? After he found out about the pregnancy, he drove one of his machines over Jason's motorbike. She was afraid they'd kill each other. Even after Jason did the dirt on her, she was still glad she hadn't chosen Bird. Not with his temper. He had a nasty streak. Nasty enough to take her out, so that no one could have her if he couldn't? But the hit on Dean had her thinking. Things had got rough. Someone was making moves against the Lewis family.

First, she needed proof that Bird really was behind it all. Would she need to get close to him in order to find out? She grimaced. There had to be another way.

Pat and Mark knew a lot more than they were letting on. But they weren't around a decade ago. If she found out that Bird was indeed involved, then fuck justice, he'd be thrust into the next life begging for mercy.

CHAPTER 12

Ann Lewis kept poking at Danielle's chest and slurring, 'Greata see you, love.' Meanwhile, Ged was busy pawing the preened and painted younger versions of Ann as he made his way to the bar. There he held court, sipping whiskey, laughing and giving the odd wave in her direction. This bar was one of two places he'd invested in recently.

'You'll be running a beauty and massage parlour for me, Dani — well, for yourself, really,' he'd said in the car on the way to the pub. 'Hazel will get you trained before she heads off for some rest.'

They pulled into the well-lit yard to the side of the pub. The gate slid closed behind them. Mark and Pat got out first and began poking about — investigating nooks and crannies, peering behind a stack of barrels — before indicating to the rest of them that it was safe to get out. They made their way in through the back entrance.

The pub, which looked pretty grotty, had musical instruments propped up in the snug, ready for a good old singsong later. As well as overseeing here, she would also be running a second bar on Hatch Street, close to Dublin's city centre, once it had had a makeover. Danielle was to earn a percentage of the profit. Not bad.

A tour of the other bar, as well as the place on Berkley Street, had been organized for the following evening, and this Hazel woman would show her around. Danielle had been warned not to mention her in front of Ann. Ged seemed to be more worried about Ann getting to hear about Hazel than about the fact that the pub he was running lay directly opposite Harcourt Square, home to the Criminal Assets Bureau.

Dean hobbled in to a wave of loud cheers and claps. His arm was in a sling and one leg dragged behind him. Neither of those things hampered his movements, though. Less than a week since the shooting, he'd improved quite remarkably — most likely due to all the non-prescribed drugs he was taking. He claimed he didn't really need the sling, but it was handy for hiding things in.

A tray with a round of shots landed on the table in front of her and Ann. Danielle was tempted to knock them all back, if only to block out the shrill bleating of her companion. There was surely a dent where her aunt kept jabbing a finger into her chest. No wonder the others had offered her the comfortable seat, while they perched on stools well out of range. Danielle had forgotten how annoying Ann could be when she got hammered.

Someone brought Dean a fireside chair. He was the first to pick up a shot glass.

He raised the glass in the air. 'Here's to Dani's return. Welcome home, cuz. And cheers for surviving those bullets. Fuck whoever tried to do you in. May the bastards die screaming.'

'May the bastards die screaming,' echoed around the table.

Dean raised his finger. 'More shots here!'

'Excuse the pun!' shouted a lad.

Everyone laughed but Danielle. It was hard to find anything funny about taking a bullet. How could they be celebrating what she had gone through? And what about her lost baby?

She'd dearly love to get pissed, but it was too risky. She needed her wits about her. She gripped her handbag tighter.

The Beretta weighed almost nothing. Maybe next time she would wear something that allowed her to carry it on her person.

'Right, Dani. Do your worst on the karaoke!' Uncle Ged shouted from the bar.

Jesus Christ. Karaoke? He must be joking. She stood, tugging at her skirt, and pointed to the ladies.

'Don't be long. We'll have the mic warmed up,' he shouted.

Ann, gold bracelets jangling, landed a hand on Danielle's arm. 'You going for a fag, love?'

'No, toilet,' Danielle said.

'Fine. I'll join you. We can head for a ciggie after.' It took Ann a few moments to hoist herself off her seat. She stood and swayed, her dress bunched up at the top of her thighs.

'Let's not be showing it for free, eh?' Danielle muttered.

'Oh, fuck. Cheers, love.'

Slowly, Danielle guided her drunken auntie to the toilets.

Ann took her time inside the cubicle, making a noise like she was building a bridge in there.

'Are you all right, Ann?'

'Yeah, yeah. Grand. Be out in a sec.'

At last, Ann bundled out. After a rummage through her bag, she extricated a pack of Major and a scuffed gold lighter. She stuck the cigarette in her mouth and tried to light it. Nothing happened.

'Jesus Christ, Auntie. What are you doing? Come on out to the back yard.'

'Fuck that.'

'You'll set off the alarm. Come on.'

Danielle ushered Ann out to the smoking area, where again she flicked unsuccessfully at the lighter. Danielle took it from her and lit both cigarettes.

'Give it here.' Ann held her hand out.

Danielle glanced at the lighter. It was inscribed with the letters *GK*.

'Come on, give it here.'

'Where did you get this?'

'Aren't you the nosy one?'

Danielle shrugged. 'Just wondering.' She held it towards Ann, who snatched it from her.

'Bird, that's where I got it, if you must know.'

'Oh, right.'

'He gave it to me to light up one night and I slipped it into my pocket. I call it my little trophy. It probably needs refilling by now. It's ancient.'

Danielle's head pounded. Little trophy? Ann had sounded proud to be the possessor of something taken from an innocent murdered man. Gavin Kelly, the detective who'd saved her life and later paid with his, it had to be. She eyed the back gate. A man wearing a puffa jacket stood in front of it, leaning against an empty keg — the security guard. There was nowhere to run.

'Are you all right?' Ann said, peering into her face.

'I'm fine,' Danielle said, looking away. She had come that close to falling apart in front of Ann. If nothing else, this was a wake-up call.

Ann was examining her, squinting against the smoke from her cigarette. 'Hmm. You've gone skinny, Dani, love, that's not good for you. Did you not look after yourself over there?'

'I was busy, but yes, I did.'

'What has you back now?'

Danielle glanced at her. Suddenly, Ann was no longer slurring.

'I missed my family.'

'Family wasn't top of your list when you left, was it?'

'It was safer for everyone that I went. You know that,' Danielle said.

'My boys needed you.'

'I needed to stay alive.'

'But you could have stayed. We could have done something,' Ann said.

'Like what?'

'Increased your security or something. I dunno.' Ann shrugged. 'Something so that you didn't have to run out on the family.'

'I wouldn't call it running out. You seemed to have forgotten that you encouraged me to go. And it did take me ages to settle, as well as getting quite homesick. Any of you could have visited me too, you know.'

'You never invited us.'

'I didn't think I needed to.' Jesus. What did she expect?

'Should we just call it evens, so?' Ann said. 'You didn't come back, we didn't go over, that's all there is to say.'

'All right, agreed. Time does pass quickly, though.'

'That's for sure. Are you not worried that there's still a threat?' Ann asked.

'Should I be?' What did Ann know that she wasn't saying? 'Did you hear something?'

'No, no, I'm just talking it out. Did you ever find out who did it?' Ann said.

'No, you said it yourself at the hospital: what with one thing and another, the cops met loads of dead ends.'

'Useless bastards. Did they even let you know how the case was going?'

'No.'

All at once, screams were coming from inside. Danielle ran back in, Ann at her heels. There they found tables upturned, beer running on to the floor. One of the windows had been shattered. In the middle of the floor, a lone rock. A bottle came flying through the broken window, the rag stuffed into its neck alight, smoking, landing on one of the chairs where Danielle and Ann had been sitting. The seat burst into flames. The barman scrambled over the counter hefting a fire extinguisher, which he directed at the blaze. Danielle grabbed Ann and forced her back towards the smoking area, along with a crowd of panicked drinkers.

Ann freed herself and made for the exit. In her haste, she dropped her handbag, spilling the contents. Danielle helped her pick everything up and they ran again. Out in the yard, a stand of empty beer kegs blocked the exit to the lane. A man emerged from the melee, pushed them aside and ushered everyone out into the street.

Just outside the gate, Danielle hesitated. Which way should they go? What if whoever threw the petrol bomb was out there somewhere, waiting to attack?

Suddenly, Mark bowled through the crowd, grabbed Danielle and Ann, dragged them to a waiting car and pushed them roughly into the back.

Pat had the engine running, and as soon as they were inside, took off with a squeal of tyres.

'What about Ged?' Ann said.

'Don't worry, Ritchie has him,' Pat said. 'We'll meet him at Clonliffe View. It's the safest place, there's cameras everywhere. And it's close by.'

Danielle sat back and fingered the lighter she had pocketed when Ann dropped her bag. If it had belonged to Gavin Kelly, it would link Bird to him, and maybe his murder.

If Ged had believed that meeting Bird Flynn would keep him sweet, he'd been wrong. That fireball had to have been for her. Once more, she was a target. Maybe she always had been.

CHAPTER 13

That night, nobody slept. Coffee and lines of coke kept most of them alert. Avoiding the drugs, Danielle retreated to the bedroom. The others looked at her askance. One or two of them raised an eyebrow. Once again, she was running out on the family. Ann spent most of the night on the balcony, smoking cigarette after cigarette. Dean was nowhere to be seen.

Names were tossed about, various people discounted until, one by one, they began to nod off.

* * *`

Come Monday, they were all still there when, in the early hours of the morning, the buzzer jolted them awake.

The visitor was the bar manager, Rob, escorted by Mark. He told them the guards had questioned him. 'I gave them no names, Mr Lewis, not a one. They don't know who was there. I told the cops I was cleaning up when it happened and I didn't see a thing. They wanted to know if there was a party and I told them no. The food hadn't arrived by then, so they've no way of knowing I wasn't telling the truth.'

'Good, good. What's the story with it now?' Ged asked.

'Forensics are going over the place,' Rob said.

'What about fingerprints?' Danielle asked.

Ged nodded, scratching his chin. 'Good point. Which of you is on file?'

Mark and Pat both shook their heads. From the balcony doorway, Ann shrugged, then disappeared again.

Danielle cast her mind back. Had they taken her prints for elimination purposes after the shooting? Probably. She tried to remember where in the bar she had been, what she had touched. Those shot glasses? No, she hadn't participated in the toast. The toilet door? Yes, but so had countless others. The chair she'd been sitting on? It had been burned. Where had she tossed the cigarette butts? Down the drain.

'I am, but it's so long ago now they surely have them lost,' Ritchie said.

'You only picked us up, so you won't have left any prints.'

'Most of the glasses were broken and I kept wiping the bar down,' Rob said. 'I don't know about the jacks, but good luck to them in there.'

'Good, good, we might be okay, so,' Ged said. 'Right, off you go. Keep an eye on what's happening and let us know.'

Pat saw him out.

Danielle turned to Ged. 'I meant fingerprints as a means to finding out who might be behind this. Why are you so worried about the guards knowing who was there?'

'We have enemies everywhere, Dani,' he said. 'Everywhere.'

'What if that petrol bomb was aimed at me?' she asked.

He shrugged and said nothing.

'Well, who could it be?' Danielle asked.

Ged sighed. 'It could be anyone, Dani,' Ged said. 'They're everywhere, I tell you. I wouldn't even trust the cops.'

While the others dispersed to drink more coffee, make a snack or just snooze, Danielle tried again.

'What are you not telling me, Uncle Ged? I mean about the guards.'

'If they can't solve the murder of one of their own, what does that tell you?'

Ged's phone rang. He checked the screen and went out into the hallway to take the call. Almost immediately, he was back.

'Pat. Mark. Car. Now. Ritchie, you look after my girls.'

'Will do, boss,' Ritchie said.

After they had gone, she watched Ritchie head out to the balcony to join Ann, who had remained there while all this was going on.

Danielle still didn't know if Ged was paranoid or whether there was something behind what he was saying. She needed to pump him for more information.

CHAPTER 14

Dean tapped the steering wheel in time to an old nineties rave tune that blasted from the radio. His sling was beside him on the passenger seat, ready to slip on if occasion arose. The loud music took his mind off Friday night's arson attack. Avoiding his da's endless speculations about who might be responsible, he'd made himself scarce over the weekend. Instead, he'd decided to check on Bird's machinery and the stash from the previous ATM robberies. It was a fine way to spend a bank holiday Monday.

He'd caught the news over the weekend, some local who lived near the scene of the arson attack being interviewed by a reporter. Stupid woman. Imagine thinking that the sound of glass smashing and a pub in flames was a group of drunks singing, and not bothering to even look out the window, let alone ring the cops.

Hang on. Maybe she *did* look out? Maybe she saw the person who threw the petrol bomb, but just wasn't saying? Someone should pay her a visit.

Dean waggled the gear stick. He wasn't used to driving a van this old. It was a heap of shit, but it was all taxed and insured with a Louth licence plate, which made it less likely to draw attention. He could do with it being more comfortable, though. The painkillers were doing the trick but he couldn't take too many. He couldn't afford to get pulled off the road.

His phone was on his lap, Google Maps on the screen. The text message he'd received provided a set of coordinates along with a passcode, nothing more. He'd taken the main road through Monaghan and into Fermanagh without running into any checkpoints. No one was following him; he'd made sure of that. Everything looked as it should. He sang along to the radio.

Hedges brushing the sides of the van, the wing mirrors catching briars, he circled around Dummy's Lough. He took a right, passing Summerhill Lough, then another right into a boreen. The grass in the middle of the single-track lane stretched like a mohawk ahead. At last, a pair of steel gates rose in front of him.

He keyed in the four-digit code and the gates opened. With a quick glance at the surrounding shrubs, Dean drove slowly inside.

In the centre of a pitted concrete yard stood a huge steel shed. He pulled up close to a small door to the side of the large roller entrance. A cobweb stretched from the handle and across the lock and clung to his fingers as he slotted the key in the lock. The sound of the hinges creaking reverberated around the vast — empty — interior.

'What the fuck?' But for a pile of tarpaulin in the far corner, the shed contained no machinery, no equipment, nor the haul from the recent ATM machine robberies.

What the fuck had happened to it all? Bird would lose his shit. No way could he tell him. He'd have to find it fast, but where the hell to look?

CHAPTER 15

The wailing cry of an infant issued from the ward at the National Maternity Hospital on Holles Street. Ged had come to visit Hazel and their new daughter, born two weeks before Hazel's due date.

Hazel was still slick with sweat.

Ged wasn't the comforting type. He hadn't been there when Dean was born, either. Someone else could deal with all the blood and shit, thank you very much. He preferred to meet his offspring when they were all clean and powdered.

'The house is ready for you,' he said to Hazel. 'You'll have a nanny and plenty of help. Our daughter will want for nothing.'

'Will you be there with me, Ged?'

'You know I can't. Not yet. Ann would take me to the cleaners, and there'd be nothing left for us. This way I can pay for you to live in luxury like you deserve. But I'll be there when I can.' He kissed the baby's forehead. 'Here, give her to me for a cuddle.'

After a moment's hesitation, Hazel handed the baby over. Ged gazed down proudly at the button nose and the tiny lips that would one day say his name. She had her mammy's big brown eyes. He remembered holding Danielle for the first time after his sister had brought her home. He felt a stab of guilt at the way she'd been treated, left to wallow away in England for so long, without her family's support. According to Ann, that was the way she'd wanted it, but it still didn't make it right. The baby in his arms represented a second chance for him. To make good the harm done to Dani.

'It's not about the luxury, Ged. I don't care how much money I have. It's about you and me. This is your chance for a fresh start — with me, with the two of us. A new family, away from your old life with Ann. I love you, Ged. The baby and I need you. She needs her daddy. Please.'

Ignoring her plea, Ged asked, 'When are you getting out?'

'You make it sound like prison.'

'Discharged, whatever. You know what I mean.' He grinned at her.

Hazel's eyes filled with tears. 'Have you really nothing to say in response to what I've just said?'

Jesus Christ. That was the last thing he needed, a begging and bawling woman. It was enough for the baby to be at it. Besides, guilt trips didn't work on him.

'Look, don't get upset, please. I have a good reason for keeping my distance for a while. It's not safe. You'll need a bit of protection.'

'You'll protect us.'

'Dean was shot last week, Hazel. He might have been killed. And there was a petrol bomb attack on one of my pubs on Friday night. Until we know who's behind it and why, the people I care about are safer away from me.'

'Will you be sending all the others away into fancy houses, too? What about Danielle?'

'She knows how to look after herself, but yes, some of my boys will have to keep a close eye. I have her set up in a nice apartment, and she'll look after the businesses you run until you're ready to go back to them.'

'Aw, Ged, don't take them from me. I'll have nothing then.'

'I'm not. This is a temporary measure. We don't know which place they'll be targeting next, and we must keep the money flowing in. Besides, you don't have nothing. You have a beautiful daughter to look after.'

He handed the baby back to her. 'What did you call her?'

'Nothing yet. I was waiting for you.'

He shrugged. 'I'll go with whatever you want, love.'

'She's your daughter too,' Hazel said. 'Help me choose, please.'

'All right, all right. Nothing comes to mind right now, but I'll think about it.'

'Thanks, Ged.'

He stood up to go. 'Do you need anything?'

'You're heading off already? You've only just got here. Stay a bit longer, please. Look at how well she settled in your arms. She loves you already.'

'Didn't you hear what I said, Hazel? Someone's threatening me and the family business. This is serious. I can't be too long in one place. I'd be a sitting target.'

'But no one knows you're here. I certainly didn't tell anyone.'

'You never know, love.'

'Ged, don't go yet, please. I'm begging you.'

'I have to.' He kissed her and the baby. 'I'll have one of the lads nearby. You get the slightest hint of anything dodgy, you ring.' He rooted in his pocket and took out a burner phone. 'Mine is the only number on it. Ring this and we'll know you need us immediately.'

'But I need you immediately now, Ged.'

'Don't be a cling-on, love. You know I hate that.'

The tears flowed down Hazel's cheeks, landing on the baby, who set up a wail again. Hazel put her in the cot and eased herself off the bed, wincing.

'What are you doing? You've just given birth, for heaven's sake. Get back in that bed.'

'I'll get down on my knees if I have to.'

It was the last straw for Ged. 'I don't have time for this,' he muttered, and stormed out of the room.

Pat was waiting for Ged with Mark at the hospital door. Their departure was held up by paramedics loading a baby on board an ambulance. Finally, it drove away.

'Where to, boss?'

'Head back to the apartment.'

Pat spun the car around and roared away.

Ged stared unseeing through the window. Would his kid be safe? Not just from whoever was threatening them, but from her own mother? He'd put Pat in charge of their security, but also keeping an eye on Hazel in case she went doolally under the pressure of her new responsibility. Fuck's sake. Ann had had a spell where she cried all the time. He'd had to tell her to cop the fuck on. After that, she'd headed to her sister's place in Limerick for a bit, returning a brand-new woman. Good job too, or he'd have turned her out. Well, he wasn't about to tolerate that kind of shit from a bit on the side.

He noticed Pat eyeing him in the rear-view mirror.

'You've something on your mind, Pat?'

'Was everything okay, you know, back there in the hospital?'

'Yeah, yeah. Baby girl, beautiful.'

'Congrats, boss,' Mark said. 'What'd she call her?'

'Nothing decided on yet,' Ged said. 'She'll need minding, both of them will, especially with the increased threat.'

'All the alarms at her new house are working, cameras and everything sorted,' Pat said.

'It's at the end of the cul-de-sac, yeah? The detached one?' Ged asked.

'Exactly, and we have lads in the houses leading up to it.'

'Grand,' Ged said. There were more important matters to deal with now. He took a deep breath that ended in a fit of coughing.

'You okay?' Mark asked, turning around to look at him.

'Yeah, yeah, give us a fag, will you?'

Recovered, he went over the events of the past week or so. Dean's shooting, Bird Flynn swearing he'd nothing to do with it, yet his expensive equipment hadn't been returned, his drugs were gone, no share from the previous hauls as yet forthcoming. He'd surely arrange a sit-down talk instead of lashing out like that, wouldn't he? Then the petrol bomb. Attempted murder, that's what that was, pure and simple. Whoever did it had them all running scared, hiding out in the apartment complex. Fuck that. They needed to get out there and show face, and Danielle was going to help. And his crew better start coming back with answers too, quicksmart.

He'd already rung ahead to tell Dani to be ready to accompany Mark and Pat on a few collection runs. There was strength in numbers. Right now, they needed to show the world that they weren't afraid of anyone. Dani was a good girl; she didn't complain or question his decisions. Maybe she could teach Hazel a thing or two. Maybe she could even keep an eye on Hazel, report back if it looked like the baby might be harmed.

He left the lads in the car and met Danielle as she was coming out.

'You got your protection?' Ged asked her.

She patted her jacket pocket.

'Good, good. The boys know where you're to go, just follow their lead and keep safe.'

'Yes, Uncle Ged.'

'Right. Off with you now.' He put his hand on the door and stopped. 'Oh, and you'll have the place mostly to your-self when you get back. We're going home. Fuck this hiding out.'

'Okay, but will I be safe here?'

He went back to her and took both her hands. 'You went away because you were scared for your life, Dani. For a decade, there was an empty space in this family. Well, now you're back, and nothing is going to scare us into hiding ever again. You hear me?'

'I do, Uncle Ged, I do.'

'Right, good girl. Off you go then.'

He stood and watched them go.

Ann was waiting, holding her usual glass of whiskey.

'Where the fuck have you been? You just disappeared and left me. Took the two boys and all. What the hell, Ged?'

'I had business to attend to. Besides, Ritchie and Danielle were with you, so you weren't exactly left on your own.'

'Couldn't do without your whore for one day, eh?'

'No, Ann, it was business. I'm breaking my bollocks trying to keep us all safe, so until you're willing to put yourself out there like the rest of them, just shut the fuck up.'

The glass just missed his face, shattering against the wall behind him. 'You crazy bitch.' He took a step towards her, his fists clenched.

'Go on, I dare you,' Ann said.

Ritchie stood watching them from the balcony door.

Ged's shoulders slumped. He took a step back.

'That's better,' Ann said. 'Lay a hand on me and my family will be up from Limerick in a flash. And you know what that means.'

Hesitantly, he touched her shoulder. 'Look, Ann, love, just trust me, would you? I'm trying to keep us all safe. I should have told you I was going. All right?'

'It's just that Friday night was so terrifying, Ged.'

'I know, love. Let's head home and show them they can't fuck with us, shall we?'

CHAPTER 16

Remnants of blue-and-white crime scene tape wrapped around a thirty-kilometre speed limit sign flapped in the breeze as they pulled into an estate near Luke Kelly Bridge. Pat got out of the car and headed towards one of the houses. He was moving stiffly, and Danielle noticed the extra bulk at his chest. He was wearing a vest. So where the hell was hers?

'Are you wearing a vest too, Mark?'

He made no response.

'What the fuck's the matter with you? Stop being a dick-head and answer me.'

He snorted. 'Vests are for pussies, like Pat there.'

'Is there a spare one, in the boot or something? Think I'd feel more comfortable,' Danielle said.

'We can get you one, so, but no, there's no spares,' Mark said. 'Pat can stand in front of us if anyone starts shooting.'

Danielle looked around in alarm. 'How likely is that?'

'What? That Pat would defend us?' Mark asked.

'No, that we'd get shot.'

'I'm not expecting that to happen,' Mark said.

'But Dean didn't expect it either the other day,' Pat added.

'That was here?' What the hell were they thinking of, bringing her to this spot? Were they setting her up? She scanned her surroundings, looking for a likely escape route. 'When Ged said he wanted me to accompany you two on your rounds, did he say we were to come here?'

Neither Mark nor Pat offered an answer.

'I'd assumed we wouldn't be going back to where Dean was shot,' Danielle said.

'Why would you assume that?' Mark asked.

'I don't know. It's just a bit weird, that's all. It makes me uneasy.'

Ahead of them, Pat said over his shoulder, 'Dean didn't make the rest of the collections, for obvious reasons. We can't let the people owing us money get away with it just because one of us is injured. It wouldn't be good for business.'

'It wasn't exactly good for business for Dean to get hit either,' Danielle said.

'True. So let's hope it's also true that lightning doesn't strike twice,' Mark said.

'He was on his own the day he was shot, wasn't he?' Recalling Dean and Ged's conversation in the hospital, Danielle was interested to hear Pat and Mark tell their version of events.

'Yes,' Mark said.

'Should one of you not have been with him?'

'We both were,' Mark said.

'Till Ged rang and sent us off to collect you,' Pat said. 'We did as we were told.'

'Dean even told us not to hurry back,' Mark added.

'Really?'

'What do you mean, "really"?' Pat asked, coming back to the car.

'I just mean that if you usually go with him, why would he be happy go it alone on that particular day?'

'Because he was familiar with the area and none of us suspected that he might be a target,' Pat said.

Danielle thought for a moment. 'And who were the lads that came to his rescue?'

'What? I heard nothing about that. Did you, Pat?'

Pat took a wad of cash from his pocket and handed it to Mark, who stuffed it in an envelope and put it in the glove box.

'Look,' Pat said, 'we have a few more houses to do, so if you want to continue your interrogation, you'd better get your arse out of the car and come with me. Not that I'll have the answers you're looking for.'

'Fine,' Danielle said.

Not far off, the tinny rasp of a motorbike could be heard. It came closer, a white dirt bike heading straight for them, two onboard. The driver wore a helmet, the other just a baseball hat with a hoodie pulled up over it, a snood covering his mouth.

'That's the little fuckers that crossed in front of us the other day and drove off,' Pat observed.

'Yeah, nearly drove me through the seats, the bastards,' added Mark.

That looks like the bike Dean described in the hospital, Danielle thought. *The lads who helped him.*

Pat took his gun out and laid it on his lap, finger on the trigger. Mark did the same. Danielle followed suit.

The bike reached the car and skidded to a halt. The passenger hopped off. Pat jumped out and pointed his weapon at them. The two riders put their hands up.

'Woah. We just want to talk, mister,' the guy with the hoodie said. He nodded towards the gun. 'Can you not put that away?'

Pat regarded them for a beat and then lowered his weapon. 'You can put down your hands,' Pat said, 'but keep them where I can see them.'

'Okay, mister.' The lads looked at one another and nodded. 'Meet us at the yard on Esmond Avenue,' the driver said.

Danielle stepped out of the car. 'How do we know it's not a trap?'

'It's not, miss, promise,' the driver said. 'Dean would have a bullet in his head only for us.'

'Please trust us,' the other said and glanced around. 'There's too many eyes and ears here.'

Pat looked at Danielle, who nodded.

'Okay, you lead on,' she said. 'Any sign of bother and you're both dead, you hear me?'

They looked at one another, eyes wide, then back to Danielle. 'Yes, miss.'

She got back in the car.

'Are you sure about this?' Mark asked as he, too, got in.

'I am,' she said, although her heart was pounding.

They followed the bike out of the town, past the houses and into the wasteland of half-empty yards and self-storage units. Just past a graffiti-covered hoarding, they turned left into a narrow lane. The motorbike had vanished.

A car was coming towards them from the opposite direction, moving slowly. Danielle noted the blacked-out windows and was gripped with a terrible foreboding. A white van was stationed across the top of the road, almost blocking it.

'Er . . . I'm not too happy about this, lads. You see the van?' she said.

'Yes,' Pat said. 'It was behind us at the junction.' He glanced at Danielle. 'Look, this is our territory. Hold tough.'

Ahead of them was the yard where they were to meet the boys.

They slowed down to turn, while the car with the blacked-out windows sped past them and disappeared from view. At the same time the white van pulled away.

'Don't drive into the yard just yet,' Danielle said.

'Why not?' Pat asked.

'I'm still not sure about that car and the white van. Something about them just wasn't right,' Danielle said. 'Go to the end of the lane, then turn and come back. I want to see if the car that passed us has really fucked off.'

With a shrug, Pat did as she asked.

'Slow down, Pat, that car is just ahead,' Mark said.

Danielle had been right. The car's reverse lights were on. It careened backwards, heading straight for them.

'What the fuck?' Pat yelled.

The car swerved past them, slid left in a handbrake turn and disappeared into the yard.

Danielle counted seven shots before the car screamed out of the yard.

This time it did disappear, turning at the junction in the same direction as the van.

The driver of the dirt bike, still wearing his helmet, ran out into the lane and stopped, panting, beside their car. He tugged frantically at the rear door, which was locked.

'Get the fuck away. This was a setup.' Pat pointed his gun at him.

'Please, let me in. They could come back, you have to get me away.'

'What about your buddy?' Danielle asked.

'Fucked. His brains are all over the yard.'

'How come you're not hurt?' Mark asked.

'I hid behind a skip.'

'Let him in,' Danielle said. 'Let him the fuck into the car. Now.'

Pat shrugged. 'All right. But be it on your own head.'

'I'll take full responsibility.' The door lock clicked and the lad fell in beside her.

'Take off your helmet,' she said.

He did. Danielle saw a boy who couldn't be more than fourteen or fifteen. He was shaking uncontrollably.

Danielle wanted to put her arms around him and tell him everything would be all right. She didn't, though, conscious of Pat's eyes on her in the rear-view mirror.

Pat drove to Alfie Byrne Road and the all-weather pitches, where he pulled in. He got out, hauled the boy from the car and shook him. He aimed his gun at the kid's head. 'You have five seconds to tell us who you are and what went on back there.'

Danielle watched, helpless to intervene.

'Sean's my name, Sean Brady, and I swear on my ma's life I don't know.' The kid cowered, one arm across his eyes. 'We spotted you doing the calls, like you do with Dean, and we wanted to ask how he was and if he had any more work for us. We thought he might, seeing as, you know, we helped him.'

'How? How did you help him?' Pat demanded.

'He would have got it in the brain if we hadn't thrown down a few black cats. The shooter thought it was bullets. It gave Dean a chance to roll away.'

Mark muttered to Pat, 'That's where they were coming from when they drove out in front of us while we were on our way back from the airport.'

'But why get us to come to the yard?' Danielle asked. 'Was the hit intended for us?

'Me and Jake wanted to talk business, but not in front of everyone on the estate,' Sean said.

'Who knew that you were looking for us?' Pat asked.

'No one,' Sean said.

'You mean them shooting you was just random?' Pat asked.

Sean shrugged. 'Must've been.'

'Come on. They didn't kill your mate for nothing,' Pat said.

Sean gulped. 'One of my cousins — well, he owes Dean a few quid. Just a couple of grand is all. And another few quid to Brenno Ahearne. Maybe they sent those men to kill us.'

'No way Dean would do that when you helped save him. And Brenno? Doesn't seem likely.'

'I dunno.' The boy's jaw quivered.

Danielle stared at him. 'You said *more* work. What had you done for Dean before?'

'I can't say.'

'Right. Who was your friend, then?'

'Jake. My cousin and best buddy. It's Jake's brother who owes the money.'

With a quick glance at Danielle, Pat raised his gun and took aim.

Danielle touched his arm. 'No,' she said quietly. 'We can use him. He'll be hungry for revenge. Let his anger work for us.'

Pat lowered his weapon.

CHAPTER 17

Dean sped away, bringing his fist down on the steering wheel. 'Fuck fuck fuck.' Who could have taken that equipment?

Crossing into Monaghan, he spotted a Garda check-point and was waved through. As soon as he was out of their sight, he put pedal to metal again, anxious to get back to Dublin.

He called Pat on his mobile. 'Christ, why did it take you so long to answer?'

'Dean. What do you need?'

'Answers, Pat, that's what I fucking well need, and now.'

'What do you mean?'

'Are the lads taking the piss out of me or something?'

'Dean, honestly, I'm not sure—'

'I got to the place and what greets me?'

'I don't know. What greeted you?' Pat asked.

'A great big fuck all, that's what.'

'You mean there was nothing there?'

'That's exactly what I mean, Pat.'

'We shouldn't be talking on the—'

'We shouldn't be doing a lot of things. Ritchie should have overseen the delivery of the packages to the location up here, but no, he couldn't even get that right.' Dean moved the phone closer to his mouth. 'He's dead, do you hear me? Dead.'

He veered back on to the road causing the driver behind him to blow his horn. 'Bastards!' he shouted. 'Keep your horn for your wife.' He turned back to his phone. 'Pat, are you still there?'

'Yes.'

'Get hold of Ritchie, now. I don't have his number in this phone.'

'Ritchie was overseeing the other job at the house in Clontarf,' Pat said.

'Who looked after this one, so?'

'Not sure.'

'Well get sure,' Dean growled.

'Right. I'll find out what the deal is. Use the other number for anything else to do with this. As soon as I get the background on what's happened, I'll ring that one. There could be a reasonable explanation.'

'Unless they all dropped dead en route, there's no excuse for sending me off to a whole load of nothing. They're making me look like a bollocks.'

'Leave it with me. I'll see what the story is,' Pat said.

'You do that.' Dean ended the call and slammed down the mobile, causing the van to swerve. The motorist behind leaned on the horn again.

'Bastard,' Dean muttered. He jammed on the brakes and this time, the vehicle behind rear-ended him. Both vehicles came to a halt. 'That'll show them to blow their fucking horn at me.'

Heavy footsteps approached his side of the van. Reaching behind the passenger seat, he found the aluminium baseball bat. He glanced in his wing mirror. *Shit.* Was it the man from the checkpoint? No, this man had a beard. Quickly, Dean pushed the bat out of sight. Then he slumped back against the seat, his hand at his chest.

'What the hell are you doing, stopping up like that?' The man's voice, through the closed window, was muffled.

There was a tap on the window. The man peered in and his eyes widened. 'Do you need an ambulance?'

Shit, no. Not an ambulance. That would bring the cops. Dean shook his head. The man glanced back along the road and stepped back as Dean got slowly out of the van. Letting out the odd groan and moan, he bent forward. The guy put his hand under Dean's arm, supporting him as he straightened up. Dean patted him on the back in thanks.

The man took a mobile from his pocket.

'Who are you calling?' Dean asked.

'The guards? An ambulance?'

'I don't need an ambulance. No need for guards either. Turn that off and put it back in your pocket.' Dean closed the space between them.

'But don't you . . . ?'

'Unless you want to get done for rear-ending me.' Dean stared at him.

'You stopped dead in front of me,' the man said, having caught on that Dean had been acting.

'Don't matter.'

'What?'

'You were too close. Your fault. Have you a dashcam?'

'Yeah, I have. And it will show you driving erratically, slamming on the brakes and stopping suddenly right in front of me.'

'And it will also show you failing to brake on time and landing up my hole. One hundred per cent liable, my friend. Not only that, my neck and back aren't right.'

'What do you want to do, so?' the man said.

'Let's have a look at the damage.'

They walked back and stood looking at the smashed-in grill of the man's Audi and the light dent on the rear bumper of the van.

'Now, put the phone away.'

The man slipped it into his pocket.

'No, throw it into the car and close the door.'

'Why?'

'Can't have you making any recordings now, can I?'

The man hesitated for a beat, but did as Dean had instructed.

'Right. This is the way it is. You came off worse there, bud. No point costing you more in a big injury claim, what with my back and neck killing me.'

The man opened his mouth to speak but Dean continued. 'We can go back there to the checkpoint and report it to the guard. But if we do that, he'll be calling an ambulance for me, what with how weak I feel. I'll have dropped to the ground, howling like an injured animal, before you've ended the call.'

'Or?'

'Or I can take my van to my local bodywork shop. I know they'll do a good job. You can pay them direct. They'll do cash in hand.'

'What?'

'What you can do now is check that your car is drivable and both of us can get the fuck out of here and carry on with our day.'

'How do I know you won't still make a claim?'

'I didn't make a note of your reg plate. All I need is your number. I'll text you the garage details and you can sort it out with them.'

The man sighed. 'Fine.' He gave his number to Dean. 'Let's take these into the hard shoulder. I'll see if this yoke will get me home.'

With a crunch and a scrape, Dean drove the van slowly forward. He hopped out and kicked the smashed glass to the side. 'Well?'

'It's driving.'

'Good.'

The man picked up the bumper and the grill and threw them into the car.

'You can tell anyone who asks that you hit a bollard or something.'

'Whatever,' the man said, and shook his head.

'One more thing,' Dean said.

'What now?'

'The dashcam SD card. Give it here.'

Muttering 'Jesus Christ', the man handed it over.

Dean slid open the side door, reached for a hammer and brought it down close to, but not on, the small square piece of plastic.

'There now.'

'Wait,' the man said. 'I didn't get your name — you know, for when I'm paying the garage.'

'Oh yeah. It's Martin McCarthy.'

'Right.'

The man drove slowly away.

Dean put the intact SD card into the glove box, on top of the man's card case containing his driver's licence and bank card. Lifting it had been a cinch. Now Dean had insurance, should the guy turn out to be brainless enough to report the accident.

CHAPTER 18

They'd left Sean Brady at the edge of the road by the all-weather football pitches, but not before Danielle made sure he'd called someone to come and get him.

Castle Avenue, Clontarf consisted of identical detached houses with identical manicured lawns. Ann and Ged's house was no different. Ritchie answered the door and ushered them along a hall to a vast kitchen. There, they found Ann sitting at the table, Ged pacing back and forth, his shoes squeaking on the porcelain tiles.

'Where the fuck have you been?'

Danielle opened her mouth but Ged wasn't looking for an answer.

'Don't mind that, you're here now. We've to discuss a shipment coming into Belfast.'

'That's next week, isn't it?' Pat asked.

'It was, but they moved it to tonight,' Ged answered. 'We're to meet them at midnight just outside Downpatrick near the racetrack. Tableware, linens, cotton duvet covers and pillowcases. Collect them — I have two vans lined up — then take the back roads towards Newry, then on to the motorway to a location I'll let you know about in an hour or two.'

Ged stopped pacing. 'Mark, I was going to get you to drive one of the vans, but I've another fella in mind for this. Pat, you're not going on this one either. I need you here.' Ged glanced out of the kitchen window for a moment. 'Ritchie, you can drive the other van.'

'Who'll be with me?' Ritchie asked.

'Take Dean.'

'But what about his injury?'

'He'll be grand. Be good to get him active again.'

'I think he's heading to check on Bird's equipment,' Pat said.

'Jesus Christ, is that not sorted yet?' Ged asked. 'He needs to return it, or pay him, or something, and get Bird off our backs.'

'It's too hot to move right now,' Pat said.

'Right.'

Danielle had been listening to this exchange. She decided she'd find out more if she was hands-on with them and said, 'I can help with tonight's run, if you want someone. I mean, if it's only household stuff, what's the risk?'

No one answered. Pat looked at her and sucked on his teeth.

'Oh, I see. It's not just linens and tableware,' Danielle said.

'Took you a minute there, didn't it, Danielle?' Ann said.

Danielle sighed. 'I could still help.'

'No,' Ged said, 'I'm showing you the ropes at the business on Berkley Street. I need someone there pronto. Linda's grand, but she can panic and needs support. She's better on books and computers and all that, and it needs solid leadership. The girl in charge went into labour early, and it's a plane without a pilot at the moment. I need you to handle something else there, too.' He glanced at Ann, who seemed to be examining her nails. 'I'll fill you in later.'

'Right. Whatever you need me to do,' Danielle said.

Ged turned back to Ritchie.

'Now, there's over five million's worth in this load. Don't fuck it up.'

Ritchie nodded.

'Pat, keys. Danielle, you right?'

'Just need to powder my nose.'

'Don't be long,' Ged said. 'Third door to the right off the landing above.'

Danielle climbed the stairs and went into a large tiled bathroom. She was thinking about the young lad left lying dead in a scummy yard. Everyone had bailed out on him — including his cousin and best mate, for God's sake. What if that child could have been saved? What if all he needed was a bit of first aid? If not, then some kind words in his ear, someone to watch over him, if there was no hope. Jesus Christ. Should she have called an ambulance? No, that would place them there, drag them in as witnesses. There'd be too much explaining to be done.

How could she have failed to realize she'd be facing this level of violence, and the effect it would have on her? She'd returned for a reason, but circumstances were taking her away from what she'd been planning for so long. She must remain focused.

She splashed water on her face and refreshed her make-up. Powder and paint. Shields. Protection.

Downstairs, Pat had the car running. Ged was sitting in the front seat; Danielle slid in behind.

'Go by the Howth Road.'

Ged's phone was ringing, but he kept cutting the call.

'Pull in here for a second,' Ged said, as they approached the Applegreen service station.

He got out and began to speak on his mobile. He rubbed his forehead and stared at the ground. His expression was grim.

He got back into the car. 'Hazel's nephew, Jake Brady, has been shot dead in cold blood in a yard on Esmond Avenue.'

'Who's Hazel?' Danielle leaned forward between the seats.

'The manager you're taking over from,' Pat said.

Pat glanced back at Danielle and swallowed.

'We were there, Uncle Ged,' she said.

Ged turned around and stared at her. 'What the fuck? We didn't do this, did we?'

'Of course not.'

'Well, explain then, and fast.'

'We were doing the collections when two lads on a scrambler approached us. They said they were the two who helped Dean and they wanted to talk somewhere private. We followed them to that yard, and a dodgy-looking car came by. We thought it was for us. The car turned into the yard. We heard shots. Then the other young fella legged it out and flagged us down for help.'

'And did you . . . help?'

'Of course. He said the lad inside the yard was his cousin. He got away because he hid. He was in bits.'

'At least you didn't leave him there for the cops to get dug into him. Will forensics show any of you there? Anyone get out of the car, any cameras?'

'No.' Danielle wasn't fully sure about the cameras, but Ged didn't need to know that.

Ged looked to Pat. 'Well?'

'I'm pretty sure there wasn't, boss.'

'And what? This fucker was just sitting around in his car all day outside a yard in the middle of nowhere, waiting for these kids to show up so he could shoot them?' Ged asked.

'They might have come across them by chance,' Danielle said. 'Maybe they knew the lads ride around on a scrambler together and spotted them going into the yard.'

'Why Jake, though?'

'He said Jake's older brother owed money to Dean. And to Brenno Ahearne. He couldn't think of any other reason.'

'Fuck's sake. I can't see Bird Flynn giving the nod to Brenno to carry out a hit on a boy that age. Surely not.'

'Could Brenno be acting on his own?'

'He'd want some balls on him to disobey Bird, or any of the Flynns, for that matter. As far as I know, Brenno is a quiet lad. He's only drawn into the violence because Bird is with his ma.'

'The boy, Sean, also said that he hoped to get *more* work from Dean,' Danielle added.

'So Dean sent the boys on jobs for him?' Ged asked.

'That's what the kid said, but he wouldn't go into specifics.'

Ged sucked in air through his teeth. 'I think you can help us on this one, Dani.'

'What do you mean?'

'Use your womanly wiles.'

'How? On who?'

'Jason. Bet he still has the horn for you. Could be worth tapping him for some info.'

'But we broke up after what he did to me. He might not even talk to me.'

'It's worth a shot. Have a think, Dani. For the sake of the family. Either him or Bird. I saw the way he looked at you when we met the other day.'

Danielle made a face. 'No fucking way am I letting that creepy bastard anywhere near me.'

'Then Jason it is, so.'

'He's surely heard by now that I'm back. He'd have got in touch if he wanted to, or come to the pub the other night.'

'Pride, my girl, pride. Most likely that's what stopped him,' Ged said.

Danielle pushed herself off the seat backs.

'We're not asking you to do anything more than recon- nect, Dani — unless, of course, you think more is needed. But I'll leave that up to you.'

She squeezed her lips shut. How the hell was she going to get out of this one?

CHAPTER 19

Bird had chosen well. Marion couldn't keep the huge smile from her face as she tore the ribbon off the gift wrapping and pulled out a bottle of Coco Chanel Mademoiselle. She liberally sprayed her neck with the perfume, then her new boobs and each ankle.

'Everywhere a girl wants to be kissed,' she said, with a quick squirt at her crotch.

She was just about to show her appreciation when the front door banged.

'Shit, it's my Brendan.'

Little fucker. Although, in a way, it was a pity Brenno hadn't walked in on them while they were at it. He'd have soon found out where he stood in his mother's list of priorities.

'I'm busy, hun,' Marion called. 'Go into the front room and I'll be out in a sec.'

There was no reply.

'When's he moving out?' Bird said, zipping up.

'But then I'll be here on my own.'

'I can't keep listening out for him whenever I come round.'

'But he's only twenty. Where would he go?'

'Yes, twenty. Big enough to fend for himself. I pay him enough, for Christ's sake.'

'And I'll be sitting here waiting for you to visit. It's lonely here at night.'

Bird sucked in his bottom lip.

'I can fix him up in a place. He'll be grand out.'

'But—'

'It's me or him. No more gifts, no more trips away, no more cuddles. No more money.'

She bit on her thumbnail. 'We could move in together. I could come to your place.'

'Not yet. I want us to have someplace nicer. In the meantime, Brenno moves out. It gives us a chance to see what it's like, just you and me.'

'Just you and me.' She smiled. 'Really? You know, we haven't been away in ages, Bird. If I tell him to find another place to stay, can we go somewhere nice? Will you whisk me away like you used to?'

'Sure we can.'

'And you have a place for him?'

'I do.'

'And he'll be safe?'

'Yes, yes.'

'He's my only baby boy.'

He reached for her and pulled her close. That scent. He pictured Dani wearing nothing but that perfume — and maybe a lacy see-through bra.

'Yes, I know.' Things were stirring again. 'Now, come on upstairs with you. We've something to finish.'

Her bedroom was right above the living room, where Brendan would be sitting. He made sure the bed creaked as they continued what Brenno had interrupted when he came in. The headboard banged. There were chips in the plaster by the time Bird was done.

With a brief glance at her, all drowsy and contented, he got out of bed and headed for the shower.

Marion's home was adorned with mermaids and unicorns, glitter and feathers — the gaudier the better. Her bathroom was done up in a vomit-inducing pink. He stepped into the shower and closed his eyes.

'Are you okay?' Marion called out.

Having dried off, he got dressed quick.

'Are you not getting back in?' She patted the bed.

'No. I'm nice and clean, and those sheets are a mess. I'll go down,' he said.

'Be there in a second,' she called after him, as he left the room and headed down to the kitchen.

She could stay put, for all he cared.

Upstairs, the shower began to run. There was no sign of Brenno. He'd have sworn they'd heard the door closing and someone coming inside. The sound of him banging Marion must've been too much for the little fucker.

He sat, legs spread, taking up most of the couch, letting his mind wander as he waited for her. As usual, his thoughts drifted to Danielle. Why had she returned now? It had to be for him. He had to work this right. There'd be no missed opportunities this time.

Marion wandered in after about an hour. The tight red dress did look the business on her, no sags or bulges. She wore her age well.

'You look great, love.'

'Thanks, Bird. I got this dress the other day with the money you gave me. Glad you like it.'

'I do. You picked well. Right, so you'll get him — your Brenno — to move out soon as?'

'You mean Brendan? He was christened Brendan, you know.'

'Yes, yes, Brendan.'

'I will, Bird, I surely will.'

He patted her on the knee and kissed her forehead.

'Do you want something to drink?' She stood up and headed for the cabinet.

'Go on. I'll have a Jameson, on the rocks.'

'I've only got Powers.'

'That'll do.'

Ice cubes clattered into the glasses.

'Not too much for me, love. I've business to conduct later and I'll need a clear head.'

His phone buzzed. It was Sal, saying he had the car parked nearby, whenever he was ready to go.

Bird finished the drink in three swallows and got to his feet.

'Got to go, love.'

Marion looked at her glass, the gin and tonic hardly touched. 'Already?'

'We talked about this. It's a crucial time for me. There are deals going on all over the place and I need to be there. A business like mine can be, er, complicated. It runs best when the boss keeps a close eye. I can't have what happened last month happening again. All that money gone, the thought that someone went behind my back and tipped off the guards. I'm still gutted over it.'

'Are you sure someone did grass on you?'

'They must have. Them guards are thick. No way would they have found out for themselves.'

'Would they have been watching you?'

'What do you know?'

'Nothing, hun.'

'Well, stop. Unless you can tell me who the rat is, then button it.'

'Of course, Bird. Whatever you need from me. I'm always here.'

Of course she was. To hand, like a dishcloth. He was already making his way to the back door.

'Do you fancy coming by later? You could stay the night. Brendan will be at a friend's place.'

She persisted in asking more of him than he was willing to give. Better to say nothing. He shut the door behind him, leaving her question unanswered. That perfume, so reminiscent of Danielle Lewis, still clung to his clothes. He turned the corner and spotted Sal. As reliable as ever, Sal had the car running.

'Where to, Bird?' Sal took a slug from a bottle of Coke resting in the cup holder.

'Back to my place.'

The whiskey had gone down well. He settled back in his seat, picturing Marion sitting on her sofa with her gin and tonic, thinking about him and waiting until his next visit. So it came as a bit of a surprise to see her with her jacket on, bag over her shoulder, almost running out of the estate. No longer in her sexy red dress, Marion was wearing trousers and a pair of flat shoes.

'Will you take a look at this?' Sal said and pointed to the right. 'The fire brigade wouldn't be in that much of a hurry.'

'Hmm. Slow up a bit and let's see where she's off to.'

Sal pulled the car into a lay-by a few yards away from Marion. She crossed the green, passed Buttercup Park and stood waiting at the bus stop on Priorswood Road.

'You want us to stay with her, Bird?'

'Yeah.'

The bus trundled along. When it got to Hawkins Street, Marion jumped off and headed towards Townsend Street.

'Fuck's sake, Bird. She's not heading to the cop shop on Pearse Street?'

'She'd better not be, the dozy bitch. Anyway, she's nothing to tell them, other than what a great lay I am.'

As she hopped on the Luas tram outside Trinity College, Sal had no choice but to drive ahead, as the traffic was building up behind him. They followed the route around the side of the college and along Nassau Street. It was usually busy with tourists en route to the National Art Gallery or shopping for authentic Irish knick-knacks or wool jumpers. But at this hour of the evening, there was only a smattering of people, most likely looking for a decent restaurant or bar.

'Will I keep ahead of it?'

'Yes. Make sure she doesn't spot us. Turn up on to Dawson Street and we'll drive around, then down Kildare Street. If she gets off somewhere there, we'll still see her.'

She stepped off at the Lincoln Inn stop, which was only minutes from where she got on in the Luas. She hoisted her bag more firmly on her shoulder, glanced around and proceeded towards Merrion Square. Sal had to follow the traffic around to Lincoln Place.

'Pull in here and let's wait for her to go across,' Bird said.

Sal did as instructed and pulled in by the Davenport Hotel. Sure enough, Marion trotted across the street and continued straight ahead. Sal pulled out and rounded the corner.

'There, land in that spot.' Bird pointed to a gap between two small cars.

They waited to cross, the indicator ticking like an irritating drip.

'Some prick better not steal our space,' Bird said, his eyes darting from the parking spot to Marion and back again.

Sal got the nod to cross the traffic from another driver coming from the opposite direction and eased the car into the free space.

'Go after her. She's less likely to spot you than me,' Bird said, watching her turn into Holles Street.

Sal got out but had to wait to cross. Bird saw him stand and gaze along the street for what felt like ages, before he turned and headed back to the car.

'Well?'

'She's gone in the maternity, of all places.'

'What?'

'Yep. She did a right scope around her before going in. I hung around for a minute or so, to see if she came back out again, but she didn't. She's hardly up the pole, is she?'

'I don't think so.' Bird swallowed. 'She'd have said.'

'Anyway, you'd never get caught like that.'

'Christ, no.' *Shit. But what if she is?*

'Unless she's visiting someone. Anyone belonging to her popped a sprog lately?'

'Don't know, Sal, but I aim to find out. What the hell is going on with her?'

103

CHAPTER 20

Pat led Danielle up to the front door of a red-brick Georgian-style house on Berkley Street. He gave his name and was buzzed in. They had to pass through an endless number of doors, all with similar intercoms, before they finally reached the entrance.

Inside, they were met by a tall redhead in a bodycon black dress, her plumped-up breasts almost spilling out of the top. She stepped out from behind the reception desk and greeted them with a big smile.

'Welcome to Georgian Beauty, Tanning and Massage Therapy.'

Danielle looked around. There was nothing in the reception area to indicate that they were in a therapy centre for men. This wouldn't do. If Ged wanted the place to look legitimate, they'd have to do better than that.

'This is Linda. She stepped in at the last minute,' Pat said, his hand on the woman's waist. 'Linda, meet Ged's niece, Danielle. She'll be running the place for a bit. Could you show her the ropes, give her a tour?'

Linda's smile faded. Looking Danielle up and down, she said, 'Of course I will, Pat.'

Danielle wondered if Linda was usually this apathetic. The way she dressed needed to change, too. For a start, if a beautician wore a dress like that, her boobs would fall into the wax pot. She knew exactly what kind of beauty treatments they offered here. Not like her business in London — which had been booming when she left. Hers dealt strictly in beauty therapy, with no added extras.

They heard raised voices coming from a room on the floor below. Linda clattered off.

'Go and see how things are handled,' Pat said.

Danielle followed the sound of Linda's spiky heels into a room where she was confronted with the sight of a burly guy holding a half-naked man by the scruff of his neck.

Linda stood in the doorway, her hand to her mouth. Danielle pushed past her and into the room. There, she saw a girl, who had to be no more than eighteen, crouched on the floor nursing a bloody lip and with a red welt on her cheek. Danielle helped her to her feet.

'Take her out of here and get her some ice,' Danielle said to Linda. She turned, picked up some briefs and size eleven shoes and went to where the burly man — obviously the security guard — held the other pinned, whimpering, to the wall. She knew who he was. That dimpled chin, the little mole on his cheek by his ear, gave him away immediately. He was an auctioneer at Holton Properties, his family's business, which had made a fortune during the 'Celtic Tiger' period. What was his name now? Ah, yes. Darren Holton. He'd aged since she last saw him.

'Right,' Danielle said. 'That will be a €5,000 fine for the assault.'

'What? Five grand? She's not worth a fraction of that,' Holton said.

Burly Security Man tightened his grip.

'Look, she fell. That lip had nothing to do with me.'

'Do you want to be barred as well?' Danielle said.

He shook his head. 'I don't have that kind of cash on me.'

She glanced at his wrist. 'Fine. Your Omega can stay here until you return with it.'

'You can't do that.'

Danielle raised an eyebrow. 'Well, I can always send our girl to accident and emergency, where she can report an assault, and maybe more. I'm sure there is plenty of forensic evidence on her body to convince an investigating officer that she's telling the truth. Your choice.'

He gulped. 'Okay, okay.'

She nodded for him to be released and threw the briefs at him. He put them on, squaring his shoulders and glaring at her. Then he loosened the strap on his watch and handed it over. 'I'll get it back, right?'

'Of course. When you return with the compensation.'

She stood with her hands on her hips while he hopped about, putting his legs into his trousers, his shoes on his feet.

'Does he owe anything else?' she asked the burly man.

He shook his head.

'Good. Off you go.'

Holton was guided, none too gently, to the front door.

She went to the back of the house, where she found the young girl, still in her underwear, shivering.

'Get something to cover her up, Linda, please.'

Linda left and returned with a dusky pink satin dressing gown, which Danielle draped around the girl's shoulders. The girl bent over, holding her stomach.

'You okay?'

The girl gave a shaky nod.

'He hit you?'

The girl nodded again. 'He gets off on the rough, but he's never thumped me before.'

'It won't happen again,' Danielle said.

The girl looked taken aback. 'But he's a regular.'

'We'll see. Take a break, get a coffee or whatever and then we'll have a chat. Okay?'

'Okay.'

'Right. Wait, what's your name?'

'Cheryl.'

Danielle headed out to the front desk, where Pat joined her.

'Nicely played,' he said. 'Do you think we'll see him again?'

Danielle held up the watch. 'You see this?'

'Yes.'

'This is worth over twenty grand. There's no way he's going to leave it behind for the sake of a fraction of its value.'

'What if he says he was robbed?' Pat asked.

She smiled. 'Let him try. He'll find that our Cheryl has departed for A & E.'

The buzzer went just as Danielle was about to start examining the accounts. Holton had been quick.

Back in reception, he counted out the money in €50 notes. He tossed the last two fifties down.

'There. Your bloody fine is paid.'

She handed him his watch. 'You treat any of my girls like that again and you'll have to pay more than just a fine.'

'So, I'm not barred?'

'Think of it as, say, a two-week suspension.'

Disgruntled, Holton left.

Cheryl joined them, barely recognisable in her jeans and top. She looked even younger with her clothes on.

'Here.' Danielle held out part of the cash Holden had just given her.

'What's this?'

'Compensation for your injury. The customer sends his apologies.'

Cheryl beamed. 'Really? He said he was sorry?'

Danielle forced a smile. 'Oh yes.'

Pat waited until Cheryl had left. 'He didn't, you know.'

'I know that, but let her believe he did. It'll make her more inclined to deal with him again.'

'That's a relief,' he said.

'What is?'

'I thought you were a softie there. Those girls will fuck you over, given half a chance. How much did you give her?'

'Two hundred quid.'

He smiled. 'I think this place is in good hands.'

He had a nice smile. She should try and make him smile more. 'Believe me, Pat, I know what I'm doing.'

'I never doubted you, Danielle. After all, you are a Lewis.'

CHAPTER 21

The nurse had a scowl on her enough to sour milk. She bounded in and at once went at the dressing on his shoulder.

'Ow!' Dean jerked his shoulder back. She sighed and went at it again.

'That'll leave a right dirty scar,' Dean muttered. 'I should sue you lot for stitching it all over the place, messy and ugly is what that is. Ruining my physique.'

'Can you spell that?' she said, gauze held aloft. 'Turn over and drop your trousers. I've to change the other dressing now. I'll step outside while you get yourself sorted. Call me when you're ready.'

He grinned. 'Are you not going to help me get my jeans off?'

'No,' she said, and whipped the curtain shut behind her.

Dean struggled with his jeans and rolled on to his stomach.

'Right, I'm ready for you.'

She got to work, while he peered over his shoulder trying to catch a glimpse of the wound.

'Stay still.'

'Getting a good view, are you?'

'At the wound, yes. It's healing nicely, no sign of infection. You must be following instructions.'

'Yeah, I'm a good boy, me . . . Ow, what the fuck? Go easy, would you.'

'Go easy yourself.'

'Bitch,' he muttered.

'Any more abuse from you and you're out, mister.'

'Abuse?'

'I heard what you said.'

'No, no, I said "the switch". You know, to turn the pain off.'

'Sure.'

'Besides, I should be entitled to home visits.'

'Really?' She looked at the name on her clipboard. 'Jesus Christ. Dean Lewis, will you just stay still so I can get you sorted and out of here.'

'You've a Limerick accent,' he said.

'I do, and what of it?'

'My ma is originally from Limerick,' he said.

'Yeah. I knew her before she was a Lewis. Ann McCarthy, isn't it?'

'Really? You knew her?' He looked at her name tag and saw she was called Renee.

'We worked in Zackary's chipper together when we were teenagers. Your dad, he met your mam when he was down to see my brother. I remember you in short pants coming to Limerick on your summer holidays. A right little cheeky sod you were then. I see not much has changed. So, lay the hell down on your stomach and let me do my job. You're not the only patient needing treatment, you know, but you are the one causing me the biggest headache.'

'Sorry, Renee. I meant no disrespect. I had a bad day yesterday. Some fella acting the bully on the road, taking it out on me. And all this getting shot. Jesus, I'm good for nothing after it all.'

'You're all right. It wasn't a nice thing to happen to you.'

'I thought it was lights out.'

Following this exchange, he remained quiet while she worked on the wound.

'There you are now. Not quite as new, but good enough.'

'Sound, Renee.' He nodded. 'I'll say it to Ma that you looked after me.'

'You can.'

'Right. And, look, sorry again, it's the pain getting to me, you know.'

'Yeah? Well, the wound is healing and the ache will settle, trust me.'

Dean got his jacket and limped out to where Mark was waiting.

'Where to?'

'Berkley Street.'

'Danielle has taken over,' Mark said.

'Really?'

'Yep. Pat took her there yesterday to show her around. She ended up sorting a bit of hassle and saw the day out there. Getting rightly stuck in.'

Dean nodded. 'Good for our Danielle, so.'

'I suppose.'

'Do you know what the hassle was?' Dean asked.

'No, just that there was one,' Mark said.

'Then what the fuck are you giving me half a story for, so? Jesus Christ.'

Mark drove up to the front door, cutting in front of a cyclist, who gave him the finger.

'Cunt,' Dean shouted after her as he got out of the car.

Dean went into the reception area. Danielle appeared from the side door, Pat with her.

'I'm here for Cheryl,' Dean said.

'She's been given the day off,' Danielle said.

'No fucking way. Get her back here now. She's coming away with me.'

'No, she needs rest.'

'What's this? A fanny union? I want Cheryl and I want her now.'

'Pick someone else,' Danielle said.

'Don't want no one else.' He glared at Linda. 'I told you to keep her for me.'

Linda looked at Danielle and shrugged.

'Bookings are made through me now,' Danielle said.

'That's a load of bollocks. I'm not some scummy punter. You hear this shit, Pat?'

'Ged's orders, Dean. Danielle's in charge now,' Pat said.

'Well, I'm next in charge after Da, and I can overrule his orders.'

Danielle picked up the phone and handed him the receiver. 'Call him. You can discuss it with him yourself. And don't forget to tell him you wanted to take one of the girls off. That's one less to earn us a profit tonight.'

Dean slammed down the receiver.

'Piss off. Who else is around?'

Danielle read out the list of available girls. None of them were Cheryl. Cheryl was the one he wanted.

'What happened to her anyway, Cheryl? Why is she not here?'

Pat glanced at Danielle.

'Don't mind yer looks to one another and saying nothing.' Dean said. 'Why *is* Cheryl not here?'

Pat cleared his throat. 'Bit of an incident.'

'Go on.'

'Punter slapped her about a bit.'

'Who?' Dean charged around the desk and started to press random keys on the keyboard. 'Come on, what's the password?'

'It's fine,' Linda said. 'Danielle handled the situation.'

'Did she now?'

'Yes. Sorted. End of,' Pat said.

'It's not *end of* anything when she's not here to work and we're losing money,' Dean said.

'No money was lost,' Pat said.

Dean shrugged. 'Fine. Who looks the most like Cheryl, so?'

Linda pointed at a couple of the names.

He picked one at random. 'Here, Aimee. I'll take her. Get her ready. I'm taking her out — well, not out, but away from here anyway.'

After ten minutes, Aimee appeared. Black hair falling to her shoulders, smoky-eyed and deep red lips, she was wearing platform heels and a tight satin dress in purple. She slipped into a grey felt jacket and tied the belt.

'What time will you have her back to me?' Danielle asked.

'Count her out for the night. I'll be showing her a right good time of it,' Dean said.

Dean held out his elbow and Aimee hooked her arm into it. He led her outside to the waiting car.

'My flat, Mark. Straight there, and step on it.'

Aimee smiled at him. She wasn't Cheryl, but she wasn't a bad compromise. She'd do for what he needed.

CHAPTER 22

The hospital receptionist directed Danielle to the recently delivered mothers. Ged had asked her to collect Hazel from the maternity hospital and take her and the baby to their new home. It wasn't her job, but doing as Ged asked might loosen his lips. It would also give her more time alone with Pat.

The lift was full, so she took the stairs. Doctors rushed here and there, while zoned-out significant others floated by, no doubt weighing up their new responsibilities. On her way up, she caught sight of the doors to the chapel. Needing some comfort, she went inside.

Thankfully, the chapel was empty. She sat on a pew near the back and took a deep breath. She gazed at the altar and was suddenly overwhelmed by grief. The sadness she had been holding deep within her began to rise to the surface, like bubbles in a pool of water. Finally, after so long, she allowed her tears to flow.

When it was over, she fixed her gaze on the wooden cross and the figure of Christ. Revenge is wrong, he had said, wrath a deadly sin. Yet it was wrath that had given her the strength to carry on, given her tenacity and focus. *They had no fixed plan, only intentions, no day, date and time had yet been chosen. It was too soon to make contact with Saoirse. This was the research-gathering phase, with much to discover before they knew how to act.* She lowered her head, not in a bow to Christ, but an affirmation of her intention.

She took out her compact, repaired her make-up and headed for Hazel's room.

She found Hazel dressed in leggings and an oversize top, a scarf draped around her neck. The baby was lying in her cot.

'Congratulations, Hazel, she is gorgeous. Can I have a cuddle from her?'

'You can have what you like. Take her away if you want,' Hazel said and slumped back on the bed.

'Aw, you can't be serious, she's so adorable.'

Danielle picked her up and breathed in the milky smell of baby. Her heart went out to this innocent little being. For a long time, Danielle couldn't bring herself to even admire someone else's newborn child, let alone pick one up. But counselling and time had done their work. The baby gurgled and smacked her lips, began to fuss and whinge in her arms.

'She's probably hungry,' Hazel said, and with a sigh began to unbutton her top.

Danielle handed her over and watched Hazel feed her. 'What are you going to call her?'

'Nothing yet. I was waiting for her dad to make a few suggestions. But as he's not even here to collect me, what's the point?'

'The house is ready for you. Ged has it set up,' Danielle said.

Hazel grunted. 'That's good of him.'

Hazel was in a right mood, but Danielle was not feeding into it. 'Look at the two of you. She loves you.'

'Loves me? She's three days old. I'm a glorified feeding station.'

'Come on, Hazel, this is your hormones talking. Look at you two bonding.'

'No, this is me talking. And this.' She gestured towards the baby. 'At least I'll get my figure back with this yoke sucking the calories out of me.'

Danielle wanted to grab Hazel and shake her. Shout at her. *How can you say such a thing? Don't you realize how lucky you are?*

But all she said was, 'Well, Ged seems to think a lot of you both, setting you up like he has.'

'He has to.'

'What do you mean?'

'It's the least he could do, look after his own flesh and blood.' She stared at Danielle. 'Did you not know? This is his daughter.'

'Oh, right, I see.'

'And I'll be back to work the business as soon as I can persuade him to let me. Whenever that is. He's obviously avoiding me.'

'I doubt that.' Danielle lied.

'Yes, he is.' Hazel looked down at the infant and frowned. 'What good is she to me if Ged just shoves me into some fancy house and never visits?'

'But she's your daughter too, regardless of how he acts,' Danielle said.

'Why the fuck do you think I had her? I was sure he'd leave that witch. Anyway, what the hell am I talking to you for? You'll only run back and tell her. I'll lose everything then.'

'Of course I won't. What do you take me for?' Danielle said. 'Like I said, it's your hormones talking. You need time to bond with her—'

Hazel pulled the child from her nipple and it immediately started to wail. 'Here, feed her yourself, see if you can fucking well bond with her.'

She landed the baby on Danielle's lap.

'I'm going for a walk. Be back in a few minutes.'

Danielle held the baby up over her shoulder to try and wind her. Eventually the infant burped, rubbed her face in Danielle's cotton top and, to her surprise, nodded off. Danielle smiled.

A smell announced that baby needed her nappy changing. With no sign of Hazel, Danielle decided to tackle the task herself. Two nappies later, Baby Girl Brady — not Lewis, Danielle noticed from her name tag — was ready for the off.

Danielle's phone vibrated with a message from Pat, still waiting in the car.

Where the fuck are ye???

Yes, where the fuck had Hazel got to? *Shit, who is going to mind the little one if Hazel has done a runner?*

It was another twenty minutes before she strolled in, holding a takeaway cup of coffee in one hand and a half-eaten KitKat in the other.

'Still quiet? Good. May she stay that way.'

Hazel ignored the proffered baby seat and headed for the door.

'Hey, aren't you forgetting something?'

Hazel glanced over her shoulder. 'You can lug the baby shit,' she said and stalked out of the room, leaving Danielle to manage bags and baby.

The man occupying the lift said 'Congratulations' as she stepped in.

'Thank you.'

Back at the car, Pat jumped out to open the door for her. He helped her with the baby seat and hefted the bags, while Hazel sat examining her nails. Pat and Danielle exchanged looks.

They drove in silence to Hazel and baby Brady's new home.

116

CHAPTER 23

Bird had long given up getting his hands dirty. Even in the yard, he stuck to the office and left Bosco and Sal to do the messy jobs. But today, he meant to handle things himself, so he donned overalls and gloves. A thief and a rat had lost them €200,000 worth of heroin, which had been seized by the guards. Only a handful of people knew the details of the delivery. He'd engaged an outside enforcer, Anto Doyle, to handle the shipment, with one of his own men inside Anto's crew to oversee it. It was his own man who'd betrayed them. Jason had found proof, and Anto had been invited to witness the consequences of crossing one of the Flynns.

Bird had intended to break a few fingers, a knee, but frustration overwhelmed him like a tidal wave. Danielle being back and him not getting within a mile of her. Marion doing God knows what behind his back. Brenno taking it upon himself to act the hitman and fucking up the job, leaving him not knowing where he stood with the Lewis crew. And now, being down this amount of money. It was all too much.

Swing after swing, impact after impact and bang after bang, Bird went at the rat with the steel baseball bat. Finally, Jason caught his arm just as he landed another blow.

Bird straightened up, panting, bat loose in his hand, pieces of flesh dripping from it. Anto looked at him wide-eyed, then down at the mess at his feet.

Jason rubbed his face. 'Christ almighty, Bird. He's gone.'

Anto looked at Bird. 'I thought this was a punishment, not an extermination.'

'It's the only thing to do with rats, Anto.'

Anto spread his hands. 'No worries with me, Bird.'

'Good.'

'But what now?' Anto asked.

'Yeah, Bird, he had a lot of contacts,' Jason added.

He looked from Anto to Jason. 'You're both wondering who's going to pay the €200,000 debt now?'

Anto shrugged.

'Well, yeah,' Jason said.

Bird pointed the bat at Anto. 'You.'

'Bollocks to that, Bird. It's not mine to pay.'

'I'm out of pocket, you led the deal, the debt passes to you. End of.' He tightened his grip on the bat and squared up.

'Where the hell am I supposed to get that kind of money?' Anto said.

'You can do a job for me to the value of it and we'll be even.'

Anto didn't look happy. 'Go on, so, Bird. What's the plan?'

'I'll let you know when I'm ready. Might be today or it might be next week. Be ready, is all I'll say for now.'

'But what am I agreeing to?' Anto said.

Bird raised the bat. Shook it a little.

'Fine, fine. Let me know, yeah,' Anto said. 'I don't like waiting around.'

'Right, get a shovel, will you?'

'Huh?' Anto glanced down at the broken body. 'Where the hell do I start with this?'

'Jesus Christ, step the fuck away from it and I'll get someone who knows what they're doing. Sal?'

'Yes, Bird?'

'Make a call. This needs to be spotless. And Anto?'

'Yes, Bird.'

'Piss off for now. You'll know when I need you.'

'Fine,' Anto said.

Bird went to the office at the back of the factory, where there was a toilet and a shower. He scrubbed himself clean, dressed himself in a new suit that had been hanging in the office and got into his car. Sal was waiting at the wheel.

'I need a walk after all that,' Bird said, when they reached the gates.

Sal parked up while Bird headed for the shops and snapped up the red-top in the local newsagent's. The headline read, *Top Cop Leads The Drugs, Gangs Fight*, followed by smaller print: *Detective Superintendent Terry Cashman steps up following the near-fatal shooting of Dean Lewis nearly two weeks ago*.

'Cops and reporters, all fuckers,' Bird muttered, tossing some coins on to the counter for the newspaper.

He left the shop, tapping his hand with the rolled-up newspaper.

Back in the yard, he found Sal greasing the pivots on one of the JCB excavators.

'You see this?'

He showed Sal the headline.

'Yep,' Sal said, wiping his hands on a grimy rag.

Bird shrugged. 'No more rats. Only people I can trust one hundred per cent. Speaking of people we can trust, how about the hospital? Any idea what Marion was doing there?'

Sal let out a sigh. 'I tried my best, but no amount of charm, wit or banter would persuade the brunette at the desk to open her mouth.'

'Did you put on enough pressure?'

'The security guard was behind me, so I had to be wise with my words.' Sal said. 'Look, the granddaughter works on the cleaning crew, my eldest's young one. But fuck it, she's clueless. She's no access to the records or anything, but if she'd any brains she'd find a way. Fuck's sake. But I'll keep at her. There must be a way to find out.'

119

'Find one,' Bird said.

Sal leaned against the machine. 'What are you thinking, Bird?'

'Not sure. I mean, why not say something to me?'

'Maybe it was a job interview?' Sal said.

'And ruin those nails of hers? Christ no. Her shift'd be done by the time she'd got herself ready.'

'Would she tell you straight if you asked?'

'She'd better. Although we don't do too much talking when I'm there. I try not to hang around too long after, no point her getting her hopes up. I think I'll do a bit more sussing before asking.'

'Good idea. Oh, the granddaughter did say she saw a Lewis in there.'

'What? Who?'

'She said the one with the long dark hair. She didn't get the name, but it has to be Danielle.'

'In the maternity? Really?'

'Yep, saw her leaving one of the rooms, carrying a new-born in a car seat.'

'What the fuck?'

'She did say she'd to clean the room after whoever it was. I'll ask her who it was in there.'

'You do that, Sal.'

'Yes, Bird.'

'Right.' Bird disappeared into his office.

CHAPTER 24

After dropping off Hazel and the baby at their new home, Pat left Danielle at the apartment in Clonliffe. At last, she was alone. But sleep evaded her, the memories kept flooding back. She had sprinkled her baby son's ashes on her mother's grave, and she needed to go back there, back to the place where it all went to shit. It was taking a risk, but she had to do it.

The following morning, dressed as inconspicuously as possible while wearing a bulletproof vest, she headed off to the cemetery, tired from lack of sleep and full of dread.

A pair of stone pillars marked the entrance to Glasnevin graveyard. In the background, the O'Connell Tower reached up through the trees. Her throat tight and her mouth dry, she eyed the other visitors warily. None looked threatening, but how could she tell? Her legs felt weak.

There it was. The grey headstone with its white lettering. If she looked closely, would she still see splashes of blood on the pebbles covering the grave? No blood, but she at once made out the notch where the bullet had chipped the headstone. Lucky it hadn't ricocheted and injured anyone else. The second bullet had knocked her on to the pebbles. She recalled her hands instinctively going to her belly, the blood seeping between her fingers. The officer who'd saved her from death that day couldn't prevent his own. He was buried here too, somewhere.

She scanned the names on the neighbouring headstones until she found it, a few rows behind her mother's grave. People on both sides of the law shared the same ground here, their families treading the same worn paths to pay their respects. Gavin Kelly, the name etched in gold on black granite. Someone had laid fresh flowers. Danielle wondered who. Not *her*, surely? They had agreed not to come. Yet here was Danielle, in defiance of the agreement.

The morning's rain had cleared, the clouds giving way to a clear sky and a light breeze. She stood before his grave, reading his name, the dates —his life had lasted a mere twenty-eight years, ending here, his future come to nothing. Like hers, shattered and destroyed in a moment.

For a few years, tributes were paid to him on the anniversary of his death. The guards swore never to give up the hunt for his killers. The criminals would be brought to justice, they said. Gradually, the memory had faded. Now, a decade later, few were left to recall a colleague's brutal slaying.

Whether Danielle or his family wanted it or not, she and Gavin Kelly would be linked for ever. In the aftermath, that link became unbreakable — on the day she met Saoirse Kelly.

She pressed her palm to the cold black granite, in silent commemoration of his strength, his heroism.

She drew her hand away. It suddenly felt invasive. Who was she, the cause of his death, to be standing here? She had no right. But for her Gavin Kelly would still be alive, happy, a proud father.

He wasn't even supposed to be there that day, he just happened to be near the cemetery when the shots were fired, on a covert operation. Rushing to save her life had resulted in his cover being blown, and in his murder.

If only.

There was no note with the flowers, nothing to indicate who had left them. A family member? A former colleague? She straightened up and went to catch the bus home.

She was horrified at the upsurge in violence since her departure. Maybe she'd have been better off staying in London. But then she'd have spent the rest of her days never knowing who was behind it all. No, she needed the answer. Without that, she would never move on.

CHAPTER 25

The day after her visit to the graveyard, Danielle was back at Berkley Street and two girls down. Aimee still hadn't returned after heading off with Dean. Cheryl was also off, waiting for her cuts and bruises to heal following her encounter with the punter. She checked the bookings on the computer. The remaining girls were in for a busy Saturday night.

At the sound of the buzzer, Danielle released the door and to her relief, Aimee staggered in. She looked tired, but at least she was intact, so Danielle sent her to one of the bedrooms upstairs to sleep it off.

A few of the girls were reserved by regulars, and two clients had already enquired about Cheryl's availability. Danielle tried to call her — surely her bruises had healed by now — but there was no answer.

Concerned, she found Cheryl's address and set off to see how she was. Outside in the street, Danielle stopped. When had she become a mother figure? Cheryl was a prostitute, an employee on the payroll, nothing more. And why was she having to look after her uncle's girlfriend, too? Instead of worrying about either of those women, who in any case she didn't give a shit about, she should be focusing on herself, her position within the family and the gang. But, most of all, on the reason why she had come back here — to find out who was behind the hit on her all those years ago. Fuck Cheryl, and fuck Hazel too.

Danielle turned around and began to make her way back to Berkley Street. As she waited to cross the road, her phone rang. It was Linda, and she wasn't making a lot of sense.

'Slow down. I'm not getting what you're saying.'

'Where are you?' Linda whispered.

'On my way back. Why?'

'Hurry. You must get here quick.'

'What's going on?' Danielle asked.

'Not over the phone. Are you far away?'

'No, just around the corner.'

'The cops are here.' Linda's voice was now muffled.

'What d'you mean?'

'They're here — in Berkley Street.'

Danielle thought fast. 'Did they knock, or kick the door in?'

'Um, knocked.'

'Warrant?'

'No.'

'Nosing?'

'Not sure. They're looking to speak to the boss. It's a detective.'

Shit. Shit. Shit. There was no way she wanted to answer questions about her business. She just hoped Aimee had the sense to stay in her room, out of sight.

'Did you get his name?'

'Richards or Richardson or something. Detective Sergeant, he said.'

Double shit. 'You're the boss when I'm not there, Linda.'

'Yes, but—'

'But nothing. Deal with it, and let me know what it's all about. Only answer what's asked, don't volunteer any information and wait to see what they have first. It's too early for customers, so we should be okay.'

Danielle had set up a nail bar just behind the reception, stocked with shellac, nail gel and a full colour palette. There

125

were posters advertising bronzer and waxing, and the two front rooms were kitted out with tanning beds and spray booths, with a massage table and various oils and lotions, adverts for chemical peels and Botox injections. The tanning beds were a popular extra with some clients. A few days ago, she'd ordered the girls new outfits — navy skirts and pink or blue crossover buttoned tops, in line with what you'd find at a regular beauty salon. Just like her business in London. There were brochures offering various aesthetic services to both men and women. All bondage gear was tucked away before they closed for the day. Unless the police had a search warrant, nothing untoward would be found.

Danielle stopped off in a nearby coffee shop, ordered a latte and sat facing the building.

After about ten minutes, she saw a man descend the steps and get into a dark car parked illegally across the cycle lane. She waited for Linda to call.

When she did, Danielle made her way back, keeping her head down, pretending to be absorbed in her phone. She glanced at the car as it drove away. The detective didn't appear to look in her direction, though that didn't mean he hadn't seen her.

She walked beyond the building for a few yards and looked back to see if the detective had returned or if anyone was watching the building. Satisfied no one was there, Danielle went back inside.

The front office was empty.

'Linda! Linda, where are you?' Danielle called out. No response.

Danielle opened the door to the kitchen. Linda was sitting at the table, sobbing, her face streaked with mascara, while Aimee stood rubbing her back. At least Aimee had removed her make-up. She now wore a dressing gown and her hair was pulled back in a ponytail.

'What's going on?' Danielle asked, dropping her handbag on the table.

Linda blew her nose. 'It's Cheryl.'

'What d'you mean, it's Cheryl? What's happened?'

'She's dead. Cheryl is dead,' Linda wailed.

'Dead? How?' Danielle asked.

Linda lifted her head and gazed at her. 'Murdered. Someone fucking murdered her.'

'What?'

'The detective came here after he found our card in her pocket.'

'What did you tell them about this place?' Danielle demanded.

'Is that all the fuck you're worried about?' Aimee said.

'No, of course not. Did they say what happened to her?'

'Only that she was found beaten to death in an alley.' Linda said. 'Dumped at the kerbside like a pile of rubbish. I told them she helped out here doing nails and the tans. Cheryl was a good girl, she didn't do drugs or anything. She was saving up to go to college.'

'Shit,' Danielle said.

Poor Cheryl. Not a junkie, not a dropout, just a girl needing extra cash to build a better future for herself. But why had someone beaten her to death? Shit, this was nasty. And it had happened on her watch. Someone would pay for this, and it wouldn't be some pissy little fine either.

CHAPTER 26

A handful of people stood outside the entrance to the garage, smoking. Inside, wearing a blue suit jacket, shirt and jeans, stood Darren Holton, with not a care in the world. Danielle picked up the first thing that came to hand, a golfing iron. Pat, who had driven her there, grabbed her arms, holding her back.

She wrestled free and swung the iron, bringing it smashing down on the windscreen of a new BMW parked outside the garage doors. The glass cracked but didn't shatter. She raised it above her head to strike again but Pat grabbed her arm.

Holton ran out, screaming. 'You mad bitch! Jesus Christ, what have you done to my car?'

The group of smokers melted away into the building. Danielle made to swing her weapon at Holton, but Pat kept his hold. 'Calm the fuck down,' he said through gritted teeth.

Holton charged towards them. Pat pulled up his shirt, giving him a brief glimpse of the firearm tucked into the waist of his pants. Holton raised his hands and backed off, while Pat wrestled Danielle into the car and drove off at speed, in the direction of O'Connell Street.

Fuck. She hadn't meant to draw attention to herself like this, but she'd needed to expunge the rage burning inside her. Things were getting very fucked up, very fast.

Something clattered in the boot as they rounded a corner.

'What the fuck was that?'

'The nine iron you tried to demolish his car with. I wasn't leaving it at the scene, was I?'

'He deserved it.'

'Did he, though? He was right to call you a mad bitch.'

The adrenaline began to drain from her body and her muscles relaxed, though she was still too angry to speak.

'Oh, now you've nothing to say,' Pat said.

Silence.

'You'll be paying him for the damage,' he said.

'The fuck I will.'

'How did you know where he'd be, anyway?'

'I rang his office.'

'Well, I'm pleased you haven't left your voice in the lane along with all that destruction.'

'Piss off.'

'No. I won't.' He tapped at his bottom lip. 'When?'

'When what?'

'When did you ring his office?'

'After Linda explained why the detective sergeant was there.'

'And they told you where he'd be, just like that? Some strange woman who rings out of the blue?'

'No. I told her there was a deposit for a house burning a hole in my pocket, and I only had thirty minutes to get it to Darren. I said I needed to give it to him in person as my offer was chain-free, so she mentioned that he was getting his car looked at.' Danielle stared ahead, smiling faintly.

'But a fucking golf club?'

'It was the first thing I saw as I went in. There were worse things I could have used.'

Pat shook his head. 'Fuck's sake, Dani, that's not the kind of attention we want drawing to ourselves.'

'Oh, you mean besides the murder of one of our girls?'

'At least it didn't happen on the premises.'

'That makes it so much better, does it?'

'It may not even be connected to her work with us.'

'My gut says it is.'

'Well, your gut should have stopped you acting out back there. What if he calls the guards?' Pat said.

'Then he'd have to explain how he is associated with us,' she said.

'And how would that look bad for him? Pat asked.

'It's obvious, isn't it?'

'If he reveals our business dealings, it'll reflect worse on us than him. Do you not think?' he said.

'He was seen with Cheryl, his DNA is probably still all over her. Let him explain that.'

'Wait,' Pat glanced at Danielle, 'you think he had something to do with her death?'

'Makes sense. He sees her as his, to do as he pleases with. He gets his ass handed to him by me, costs him a whole wad of cash, and now she's dead. Jigsaw puzzle pieces fitting into place, no?'

Pat pursed his lips. 'I don't know, Dani, I just don't know. He could still report you for damaging his car. He could say you are a rejected lover, or a pissed-off customer. Something, anything, to get you done. He's got a good reputation. His word would stand against yours.'

'Sure, but I still can't see him reporting that smashed windscreen. He'll pay for it himself, you see if he doesn't.'

Pat frowned. 'That's just one aspect of the matter.'

'What do you mean?'

'Did you not think that if he's capable of offing Cheryl, he may just do the same to you?'

'Would he?'

'It's a possibility you need to look at. Just be wary, Danielle. That's all I'm saying.'

'I'm used to that. And by the way, I wish you hadn't dragged me out of there before I had a chance to look at his knuckles.'

'His knuckles? Why?'

'Cheryl was beaten to death. Maybe there were marks on them.'

'Well then, it was you who fucked that up by going about it the way you did,' Pat said.

'No, I didn't. He was mad enough at me to raise them at me, and you or I could have looked at them.'

Pat shook his head. 'I could have if I'd known that was the plan.'

'I didn't exactly have a plan that I could have shared. But you could have gone with it and backed me up, not grabbed me like you did.'

Pat muttered something under his breath.

'What, Pat? Don't you like a woman taking control of a situation? Come on, what have you to say?'

'Nothing.'

'No, you obviously do have something to say.'

He brought the car to a halt. Staring ahead through the windscreen, he said, 'Why the fuck did you have to come back? Things were fine, you were safe, and now here you are, going around doing stupid things as if you're untouchable.'

Danielle opened her mouth to speak, but he didn't give her the opportunity.

'We've been trying to stay under the radar for years and we were just getting there. New recruits, different faces, have helped us become invisible. We've crawled out from under the constant stop and searches, the random checkpoints set up just for our crew — with a few exceptions, of course.'

'Don't tell me you're trying to appear legit? Give me a break. Do you really think the cops don't have their eyes on you?'

'Us, you mean. You are part of it too, don't forget. And why *not* try to appear legit? The businesses are ticking along.

More than that, they are a huge success, the profits are flying in. Just do what the fuck you are supposed to do.'

'I am doing what I'm supposed to do — what a *Lewis* does, which is not take shit from the likes of him. If he had anything to do with the death of one of my girls, I want him to get the message that it's not to be tolerated. It's not as if I buried the golf club in his head — which I could have done, by the way — is it? No, I gave him a warning.'

'She was not one of *your* girls, she belonged to the company. Any retaliation should have been approved by Ged, or Dean, and not without some proof of his involvement.'

'Well, Ged's not here. And Dean? Give me a break.'

'And even if he did turn out to have a hand in it, the family would have to decide on the course of action. That is how we work now. I suppose you don't know that.'

'I'm learning,'

'Not quick enough.' Pat pulled the car out into the flow of traffic.

With his elbow on the window, his finger tapping, he half turned to face her. 'Just don't fuck up what you've had no part in building, because there will be consequences if you do.'

Her shoulders felt rigid with tension. 'I have no intention of fucking it up. But I will not take shit from a punter. The light's green, by the way.'

He accelerated away, throwing her back into her seat.

'Like I said, you have no idea if he was involved or not.'

'Since when did this gang need irrefutable evidence before they decide to act?'

'Fuck's sake, Dani. We are not a gang, and don't let Ged hear you saying that out loud. We do things differently now.'

'Ooh, listen to the expert. How long have you been working for Ged, a wet week?'

'Longer than you think,' he said.

'Really? Well, I don't remember seeing you around before I left for London.'

'Maybe you didn't look hard enough.'

'You've all the answers, haven't you?'

Pat sighed. 'You're avoiding the point. Just because Holton is pissed off at not being allowed to slap her about a bit doesn't automatically lead to him murdering her.'

'Slapping her about? He could have broken her nose. He'd have put her out of business for a while, losing us money,' Danielle said.

'And he paid for it. Besides, we're providing a community service.'

'What?'

'Well, if he gets to slap around someone he pays for, his missus at home might be spared a few digs.'

Danielle stared at him. 'You are all that is wrong with this business.'

He shrugged. 'No, I'm just honest.'

'Well, I don't regret busting the stupid fucker's windscreen.'

'I thought so.'

He whipped the car around and headed back along the way they'd come, throwing Danielle forward.

'Ow. Jesus, Pat, take it easy. Where are we going? Berkley Street is the other way.'

'Back to the apartment. If you won't follow the rules, you can stay the hell there until you do.'

'Who do you think you are? You're an employee. Do not tell me what to do.'

Pat pulled up a block from the apartment complex.

'Get out.'

'Excuse me?'

'Get the hell out of the car now. I'm done with this.'

'No.'

He got out of the car. Coming around to the passenger side, he released her seat belt and dragged her out.

She swung her handbag, which connected with his shoulder. He tightened his grip on her arm and walked her to the footpath, holding her upright when she stumbled.

'Jesus, woman. You're as stubborn as a mule.'

'Let me go or I will punch you so hard you'll be smiling at the back of your skull. And don't think I won't.'

He stopped, held her by the shoulders and brought her face close to his.

'Oh, I know you will. I know what you're capable of.' His breath smelled faintly of menthol chewing gum and coffee.

He fixed his eyes on hers. His hands moved to her back, pulling her close. Suddenly, they were kissing. Her fingers caressed the back of his neck and they clung together as if they were already naked.

But they weren't naked, they were out on the street, people passing them by. It was stupid, ridiculous, reckless, but she didn't want it to stop.

CHAPTER 27

Danielle sat on the penthouse balcony surveying the early morning sky and listening to the mounting traffic as the city came to life. It had been one hell of a night at Berkley Street. Once news filtered through that one of them had been murdered, a number of the girls were too upset to work. She hadn't intended to go in at all, but her phone, and Pat's, kept ringing, demanding her presence there. The skeleton crew just got on with the job but, still, they were fearful.

Linda refused to do anything more than greet the punters. Despite Danielle's insistence, she stood firm, saying she was exempt from working the rooms. Aimee offered to stay on. Considering the hours she'd already put in, Danielle was impressed.

She tried to avoid thinking of Pat and what that unexpected kiss might mean, but the memory of it lingered, the sensation of his warm lips on hers. Shaking it off, she ran her fingers through her hair. Some of it came away in her hand.

'Fucking extensions.' A visit to the hairdresser was long overdue.

Her phone rang, startling her out of her reverie.

To her surprise, the caller was Hazel, announcing that she wanted to attend her nephew's funeral.

'Right, okay. Do you need a lift then?' Danielle still felt bad about Jake Brady. She had been there when he was killed and had done nothing to save him, so the least she could do was give his aunt a chance to say her goodbyes.

'No, I want you to mind the baby. That nanny Ged hired for me hasn't a clue, and you settled her so well that day in the hospital. I won't be long. I was at the wake last night and I'm tired.'

Fucking hell. Minding a new baby? It was a huge responsibility.

'What about Linda?' Danielle said, crossing her fingers. 'Didn't you two work well together?'

'Linda? As in that dope at Berkley Street?'

'Yes, her.'

'She couldn't mind a bag of chips. Fine. I'll drag the kid along with me then.'

Remembering Hazel's behaviour at the hospital, dragging her was probably just what she'd do. 'Don't do that, she's too little. Have you anyone else?'

'Would I be ringing you if I had?'

'Okay, Hazel, I'll watch her. Just this time. When do you need me for?'

'Well, there's the removal this evening, a few drinks after. The funeral is tomorrow.'

'Should be all right,' Danielle said, her heart sinking. 'I'll get Pat or Mark to drop me over. Is later this morning okay?'

'Yeah, sure.'

'Did you pick a name yet?'

'What? No, not yet. Call her what you want. See you later.' Hazel ended the call.

Christ, that poor child. She was a week old now, and Hazel still hadn't bothered to give her a name.

Danielle's thumb hovered over Pat's number. Did she really want to see him again, so soon after last night? The sound of the front door buzzer came as a welcome relief. It was Ged, back early from Belfast.

136

She released the door to let him in and legged it to the bathroom to wash her haggard sleep-deprived face.

She heard his shoes squeak on the kitchen tiles.

'Uncle Ged.'

'Danielle.'

He had used her full name. Not a good sign. 'Yes?'

'I'm not happy.'

'Why? Did the trip to Belfast not go well?'

'All right, I suppose, but I've to head back there again. I'm going with Ritchie later.'

'Then what is it?'

'You, yesterday. Not on.'

She guessed burying a golf club in a suspected murderer's car wasn't something she ought to be doing. He probably thought that sort of thing was best left to the men.

Huh. Well, Pat is some bollocks to have told him. She'd have to rethink the whole—

'Why did you leave Linda to deal with that detective on her own? You should have been there.'

'What? Sorry. I was too far away. I couldn't make it back in time.'

'That's not what she told me.'

The sly bitch. 'What exactly did Linda say?'

'That you told her to deal with it. That you arrived not long after he left.'

'I don't remember it that way,' Danielle said.

'The cameras do. They have you passing the door, walking further on and then going in.'

Shit. 'I don't remember that. Besides, should she not have been able to deal with him?'

'You were close enough to help. And what if they *did* have a warrant, and something had been found?'

'They had no warrant. Besides, there was nothing to be found. Linda always makes sure of that.'

'Don't leave her in the lurch like that again.'

'I thought I was in charge there. I issued an instruction to her that she should be able to follow,' Danielle said.

'It's not good to leave the girls without support. Once you knew they were enquiring about Cheryl's death, you should have gone back there at once.'

'But I didn't know that. Linda only told me after I returned.'

'Is that so?'

'Yes, I swear.'

'Linda is reliable and trustworthy. Whether you knew or not, it was a visit from a detective. These "enquiries" are never about what they appear to be, there's always more to it. You should have been there to manage the situation.'

'And let the cops know I'm back in the country?'

'What's your problem with that? Announce it from the rooftops.' He spread his arms wide.

'I thought it better that I keep my return discreet, especially after—'

'After what? That's ancient history. Get over it, Danielle, and get on with the job you've been given.'

So what happened to her was nothing, was it? 'Well, I trusted my instincts, so, and they said not to run into that detective sergeant that day.'

'What day? The day of the shootings?' Ged rubbed his forehead.

'The day the detective sergeant called. The thing we were just discussing.' She frowned, puzzled.

'What?'

'Are you okay, Uncle Ged?'

'Yeah, yeah, fine. Just need to sit for a minute. Get me a whiskey, will you?'

'Sure.'

The leather creaked as he sank into the couch, his fingers still on his forehead. He began kneading his temples. 'What were we saying about warrants?'

Danielle poured him a generous measure, the ice dancing through the liquid as the level rose. 'That the detective sergeant didn't have one, and me not wanting to be in the line of fire. As I'm the boss there, I instructed Linda to deal with him.'

'Yes, yes, Linda. She's a good girl, definitely a good girl. I trust her.'

'Here,' she said, and held the glass towards him. 'I was there most of last night anyway.'

The lie came out without thinking. He didn't need to know she'd spent the evening smashing up someone's car.

'Good. Good.' His hand shook as he took the glass.

A door banged behind her. Danielle jumped.

Then she heard Ann's rasping voice. 'Why didn't you wait for me?'

Either he didn't secure the doors, or Ann had all the access codes, too.

'Get that into you and come on,' Ann said, and looked at Danielle. 'He was in a mad rush over here for something.'

'Sit down, woman, give me a minute, will you?' Ged said weakly.

Ann perched on the arm of the couch. 'You may as well get me one too, Dani, love, seeing as I'm here and waiting. It's drink o'clock somewhere in the world.' Her cackle ended in a choking cough.

Ann waved away the glass of water Danielle offered but took the whiskey. 'Cheers.'

'So. What are we toasting then?' Danielle asked.

'Pour yourself a strong one and I'll tell you,' Ann said.

Mindful of her babysitting duties, Danielle turned away from them and poured herself a ginger ale.

Ann raised her glass. 'To the Lewis family. May we always have the strength to fuck others over.'

'Cheers,' Ged added.

Danielle took a sip of her ginger ale.

Ann, meanwhile, had finished her whiskey in two gulps. 'Did you get through to Pat yet?'

Danielle froze. 'Pat? Why would I—'

'I'm not talking to you. It's Ged I'm asking.'

'Oh, right, of course.'

'Ged?' Ann tutted. 'He's not a bit tuned in. Ged?'

'Um, no, I'll try him again.'

As Ged fumbled for his phone, the door buzzer sounded. Danielle checked the video feed. 'Cancel the call. It's Pat.'

He breezed in, gave the three of them a nod. As if last night had never happened.

Ged struggled to stand. 'Are you okay?' Ann asked him.

'Yep, stiff hip, that's all. Don't worry.'

'Okay, I won't.' Ann took a drag of her cigarette.

Pat rested his hand for a moment on Danielle's back. Her skin tingled.

'I'll look after these two,' Pat said to Ann. 'Mark will take you on your errands.'

'What are you doing today then, Danielle?' she asked. 'Linda's looking after the beautician's, and I need someone to go shopping with.'

Danielle desperately tried to think of an excuse for not going but her mind was a blank. Ged stared.

Ann tapped the table. 'Don't you want to go with me then? What's wrong? You used to fall over yourself at the chance to spend your uncle's money.'

'She's doing a collection run with Mark, then she's back here,' Pat said.

Grateful as she was to Pat for helping her out, Danielle was disappointed that they wouldn't get a chance to discuss what had happened between them.

'Oh, right. Looks like I'm on my own, so. Credit card?' Ann held out her hand and clicked her fingers.

Ged took a card from his wallet and handed it over.

'Right, we'll head.' They trooped towards the door.

Danielle stood alone in the kitchen.

Apart from his hand on her back, Pat had acted towards her as he always did. Well, what did she expect? She wasn't sure. What did she want from him? Nothing. What she *did* want was to know just who had been behind those shots fired at her all those years ago, so she, and Saoirse too, would finally have closure. That kiss was an unexpected complication, and definitely not part of the plan. She needed to bring the shutters down around her heart. She must not allow herself to forget the reason for her return.

She shook herself. Time to see if she could get a last-minute hair appointment before collecting the baby from Hazel's. Then she could do what she needed to and get the hell back on track with her search for answers.

CHAPTER 28

Teenage Gangland Victim's Burial — A Mother's Heartbreak.
Danielle found the newspaper lying on the back seat of Mark's car. A week ago, Jake's murder had been all over the front pages accompanied by pictures of the scene taken from a distance. Inside the crime scene tape lay an abandoned white dirt bike. Today, the story was relegated to page eight, a brief paragraph giving the details of his removal and funeral. It made much of the fact that the white coffin was to be decorated with the Liverpool colours and borne to its final resting place to the sound of 'You'll Never Walk Alone'.

When Mark pulled up at her house, Hazel was already standing, jacket on, at the door. The moment Danielle stepped out, she flung instructions at her. 'She's inside in the cot. You'll find bottles of expressed milk in the door of the fridge. If she's still hungry, formula will do her.'

'Sorry for your loss,' Mark said.

Danielle spun around to face him. How could he—?

But of course he was speaking to Hazel.

'Thanks,' she said. 'Is Ged coming?'

'No. He's been called away,' Mark said.

Hazel folded her arms. 'Bastard. So I'm supposed to get a cab to my own nephew's removal, am I?'

'Hop in, I'll take you,' Mark said.

Inside the house, the baby set up a wail.

'You'd better see to that,' Hazel said, dropping her handbag on the seat and climbing in.

Beads of sweat formed at the back of Danielle's neck. Her ears pounded. The cry intensified. She glanced towards the house and back to Hazel. 'No.'

Hazel stopped, one foot in the car, and stared at her.

'Get the fuck in and settle your own baby.'

Hazel got slowly out of the car. 'Excuse me?'

'You heard me. You're her mother, you see to her.'

'But I . . . I need to get to the removal.'

'Mark's not going anywhere until I say, so. Come on, you have plenty of time. Act like a mother for once. And don't you ever speak to me like that again.'

Mark raised his eyebrows.

Hazel hesitated for a second or two and then went back into the house. When the sound of crying had died away, Danielle went in. She found Hazel rocking her daughter in her arms.

'Give that child a name too, for Christ's sake.'

Hazel began to cry.

'What now?'

'I don't want to give her a name because I'm not keeping her.'

'What? I don't understand,' Danielle said.

'All I want is to get back to running the business and have everything the way it was before — before I got saddled with her.'

'Hazel, no one can ever go back. Life moves on. How do you think Ged would take you just giving his baby away?'

'He might come round. In time. He'd hardly miss her. He hasn't visited since she was born. And then sending you to collect me . . . the bastard.'

'He was busy. Anyway, how can you just erase her from your life? You think you can just forget giving birth, holding her, feeding her? No way. However much you try, she will be there. No matter where you are, you'll always hear her cry.'

'How the hell do you know?' Hazel retorted. 'How many kids have you given birth to? Talk to me when you are a mother.'

Hazel's words cut deep, sent Danielle literally staggering back against the wall. The bitch had no idea of the treasure she possessed.

'I may not be in your position, but that doesn't matter. You wanted to trap him and got caught yourself. Tough shit. Deal with it. And I'll tell Ged exactly what you said. You're an ungrateful cow, and don't deserve for the Lewis money to be spent on you like this. I'll tell you what else you don't deserve too — this little one.' She pointed at the baby who'd began to fuss. 'You'll drag her up to be a slut just like you. So, yes, do, give her away. It will save her from a miserable childhood, years of being made to feel like an inconvenience. All because your plan didn't work.'

'He'll never believe you.'

'You don't think he'll believe his own blood over a cheap ride, do you? Oh yes he will.'

'He'll never see his daughter then.' The baby started to cry again.

'He didn't see much of his son either. He was too busy building up the business. Did you think your little family would be any different? Look at today, Hazel, he can't even make time for your nephew's funeral.'

'Well, she's going to another family if I don't see him soon.'

'Do you really think he deals in ultimatums when a child is involved?' Danielle said.

'I don't fucking know. He might.'

'So, you think giving her away will sort everything?'

'Yes, I just want things to be the way they were, and if she wasn't around, they would be.'

'You wouldn't harm her though, would you?'

Hazel's hesitation made Danielle's skin prickle.

'I just don't know what to do with her, she's baggage I don't need. I'd be better off—'

'Really? Right. Let's see.'

Danielle snatched the baby from Hazel's arms. The car seat was in the hall and she settled the baby gently into it, ran to the fridge and took out the bottles, which she tucked in beside the baby. That done, she headed for the door. Hazel stood in the doorway, blocking her exit. Danielle pushed past her, elbowing Hazel in the chest and sending her slamming back against the wall.

Danielle ran out to the car, calling to Mark to open the door.

He stood beside it, wide-eyed, his mouth open.

'Just open the fucking door!' she shouted.

He ran around and held it open as she set the baby carrier down on the seat. The baby wailed while Danielle, her hands shaking, fumbled with the seat belt. Mark shoved her aside and, in a beat, had it secured. They got in.

'Where to?'

'Back to the penthouse.'

The car pulled away, Hazel running after them.

They drove on in silence, while Danielle allowed her galloping heart to settle and the baby continued to cry. After a while, Danielle said, 'Pull over, would you?'

Mark brought the car to a halt and Danielle got out and went round to the back seat beside the howling baby. She took out one of the bottles and held it to the baby's lips. The baby would not drink. 'Shit, of course, it's cold.' She sighed. 'It'll have to do her.' She shook some on to her finger and into the baby's mouth. The baby began to suck. Danielle switched finger for bottle and the baby began to suck. 'That's it. Good girl.'

'Will I carry on?' Mark asked.

'Do, please.'

Back in the apartment, the baby settled, Danielle looked helplessly at Mark.

'What the fuck am I going to do with her?'

'Did you not have a plan when you took her away?'

'What the fuck do you think?'

'I don't blame you. She was being a cunt to you. I don't know why we had to be there anyway, though I'd hoped you'd tell her to fuck off, not leave with the baby.'

'I'd offered to help while she went to the removal.'

'Why?'

She shrugged. 'I guess I felt responsible.'

'We didn't shoot Jake Brady.'

'I know, but—'

'Did Ged tell you to get involved?'

'He asked me to collect her from the hospital.'

'And beyond that?' he said.

'Just to keep an eye on her, and if she needed anything, to try to help as best I can,' Danielle said.

'And this was what he meant by keeping an eye and helping, was it?'

'No.'

'Then you'll have to come up with an explanation.' He gestured to the sleeping baby.

'Hazel was talking shit. Ranting about getting rid of her. What if she'd harmed her? I got the feeling she would.'

'That's not your problem,' Mark said.

'Well, fuck me. I seem to have made it my problem now. I can't exactly drive back there now. No, I have to save face and keep going.'

'You can't return, not straight away. Is Ged aware that you know she's his kid?'

'No idea. Hazel told me in the hospital,' Danielle said.

'He probably does, then. You'd better hope Ann doesn't call.'

'Shit, yeah.' She began to pace. 'Oh God, does she know?'

'Ann won't be long working it out, if she hasn't already. Ann has more of an idea of what's happening than she lets on. All the shit about her suffering with her nerves and having to take herself off to Limerick for a break is a load of bollocks. She's just strengthening ties. Making sure her extended family is kept informed of what's going on, in case she needs to call on them for backup.'

'Really?'

'Don't be so naive as to underestimate her.'

'Right. Okay.' Danielle chewed on her cheek and stared at the baby. She could see a resemblance to Ged.

'She might not even be Ged's,' Mark said.

'He must be sure she is, if he splashed all that cash on her.'

Mark shrugged. 'Hazel is very persuasive.'

'Whose could it be then?' Danielle asked. Mark seemed to know a lot about Hazel. Maybe he fancied her himself.

'Hazel was one of Ged's favourites,' he said. 'Who knows, she probably only got promoted to run Berkley Street because he didn't want some punter getting a bit of what was his.'

'Fuck.'

'Exactly.'

'God, what have I done? Apart from having to explain it all to Ged, I've no clothes, no cot, nappies, formula, nothing. I don't even know how much a baby that age drinks.'

'Well, let's drop her on the steps of a Garda station, so,' Mark said.

'Jesus Christ, no.'

'The hospital then?' he said. 'Let some family who wants a baby have her.'

'And what if we're seen?'

'Pick one with no cameras. Leave her outside the gate or something.'

'No.'

'See, you do give a shit. That's what will cost you. Once you start to care, you're wide open. Next thing you know, you'll be on your knees for the Flynns.'

'What shit are you spouting, Mark?'

'Don't do as Ged asks. He's not thinking straight. Stay away from Jason and Bird. They're too dangerous. You even talk to them, you'll be feeding their egos. Use your brain. You did not get to where you are today by being anyone's fool. No need to start now.'

'Be careful there, Mark, you're starting to sound like you give a shit.'

He shrugged. 'Take my advice or stick it where the sun don't shine.'

'You've hardly spoken to me since I got here. Now all at once you're the fountain of wisdom,' Danielle said.

'Like I said, take it or leave it.'

'Is one of the Flynns behind the hit on me?'

Mark sucked on his bottom lip. 'No one knows.'

'But could they be?' she asked.

'Anything is possible. Take your blinkers off.'

'What do you mean?'

'Look, I heard about the golf club and Holton's car, and now this. You'll get yourself killed. My advice is not to.'

'Thanks.'

'Rein it in. You're one extreme or the other. When you boil over, you've no control over who gets burned, including yourself.'

'So, Pat told you about Holton?' she said.

'You were lucky the guards weren't called. I mean it, curb your temper, Dani.'

She sighed.

'Now. That's the end of my lecture,' Mark said. 'Do with it what you will.'

Danielle looked at the sleeping baby. 'What are we to do about her?'

'Leave it with me,' Mark said. He scooped up the baby carrier and headed for the door.

'Mark! Jesus Christ, where are you going?'

'What do you take me for? I'm taking her back to her mother. It's the best place for her.'

'But she'll be wanting to go to the removal.'

'Surely not after that confrontation with you. If she has any heart she'll be worried sick and waiting for us to bring her back. You'll be lucky if she hasn't called Ged about what happened.'

'Shit, yeah.'

'Now, go on with your evening and forget about the baby.'

Danielle opened her mouth, but no words came. It would have been nice to have the baby for a little while, just to see what kind of mother she might have been. Ah well.

She feared getting sucked back into the mayhem, the violence erupting everywhere she turned. There was no going back to this life. Coming home was meant to be a hit-and-run, but as more time passed, events kept drawing her into it all again. Things kept coming at her and blowing her away from her purpose. The risks to her safety became greater as her freedom slipped further away. Scared, she needed support, someone she could trust.

CHAPTER 29

Having ordered the wine — the most expensive one on the list — Bird was keen to eat. He already knew what he wanted to order, but Marion was taking her time perusing the menu. She glanced up at him and beamed.

'Look at you, being all romantic. You'd remembered how much I love Italian food. And here was I thinking you'd forgotten my birthday. First the perfume and now this.'

Balls, he had forgotten it, and he was fucked if he could remember the exact day. 'See, I never let you down, do I?'

'No, you don't.'

She'd dressed up for the occasion, in sparkles and heels, the Louis Vuitton handbag on the floor at her feet, the Chanel Mademoiselle vying with the tagliatelle. Tonight was the first time he'd seen Marion in a week, and he was still no closer to knowing why she had gone into the maternity that day. The only piece of information that had eventually come his way was that Sal's granddaughter had seen Danielle collecting an unknown woman and a baby and taking them away. Well, either Marion would give him answers tonight, or she was getting the elbow. He had brought her to the res-taurant because if he did dump her, it would be harder for her to make a scene.

The maître d' had seated them at a corner table a decent distance from its neighbour. Secluded behind a large pot plant, it was perfect for Bird's purpose.

A waitress came to the table to ask if they were ready to order. Marion, unable to pronounce her choice of dish, pointed to the item on the menu. Bird had no such difficulty.

Orders dispensed with, Bird reached across the table and held Marion's hand. 'But I don't want you letting me down either.'

'What do you mean?' Marion said. 'I've asked Brendan to move out. That's what you wanted, isn't it? But I never had a chance to tell you, not having heard from you in days.'

'But he's still there.'

'It gets lonely.'

Bird sighed and pulled his hand away.

'Bird? What did you mean?'

He drummed his fingers on the table. 'I just hope you're being completely honest with me.'

'Why wouldn't I be?'

'Then tell me why you were at the maternity hospital.'

She adjusted the serviette in her lap, drew a breath. Avoiding his eyes, she took a gulp of wine.

He slapped his knees. 'Fine. If that's the way you want it, this'll be our last supper, then.'

'No, that's not how I want it.' Her lip quivered.

'It's going to be a silent one, so, unless I get an answer.'

Marion set her glass down with a sigh. 'I was visiting someone.'

'Oh? Who?'

'You really want to know?'

'Would I be asking you if I didn't?'

'Hazel Brady. She had a baby girl.'

'What's her connection with Danielle Lewis?'

'How do you—'

'There's very little I don't know.'

'But you don't know why I was there,' she said.

'Maybe I do, maybe I don't.'

'Which is it, Bird?'

'That's what I'm waiting for you to tell me.'

'I wanted to see the baby.'

'How come you know Hazel Brady so well?'

'She replaced me in the business on Berkley Street. Remember, when we got serious, and you wanted us to have a future. Promised me the earth—'

'But you never worked together.'

'We did for a bit, while she learned the ropes. Anyway, we just clicked.'

'And Danielle?'

'I don't know. Maybe she was visiting her, too.'

'No. Danielle collected her and the baby.'

Marion shifted in her seat. 'Oh, right. How do you—'

Bird took a sip of his wine, watching her. He'd guessed right, then. 'Go on.'

'Ged must have told her to.'

'Ged Lewis?'

'Of course. Who else?'

'The baby is Ged's?' Bird sat forward.

'Well, that's what Hazel told him.'

'But you think otherwise?' he said.

'Yes, I believe I do.'

The waitress arrived with their starters. Bird waited until she'd gone.

'Go on. Tell me more.'

'She no longer wants the baby, now that he hasn't come running to her. He never had a notion of leaving Ann for her. I told her that, but off she went, telling him he was going to be a daddy in the hope he'd change. Men like Ged Lewis never change. They make promises they've no intention of keeping.' She stared hard at Bird, while he busied himself with his bruschetta.

'He set her up in a house but hasn't been there since, and now she's rethinking the whole thing. She's asked me to take her — the baby, that is.'

Bird was overtaken with a fit of coughing. 'You?'

'Yes.'

'Why you?'

'Why not? She knows I'll look after the kid. It would give her back her freedom. She suggested it when I went to visit her. At the time, I dismissed it as a bit of postnatal depression, but she's called me a couple of times since and asked if I'd made my mind up yet.'

'You're not seriously thinking about doing this, are you?'

'I am.'

'How will that work and us seeing one another? I'm not getting saddled with someone else's brat, Marion.'

'There are babysitters, you know. And it gets really lonely. I thought we'd have—' she shrugged — 'a different kind of relationship by now. You know, that we'd at least be living together. I've spent years of my life with you, Bird. You seem to forget that.'

Bird's jaw stiffened. 'I already told you it's complicated. There's no point you getting caught up in my business.'

'Yes, you did tell me. But I can be whatever you want me to be.'

'I need you to be there when I call, ready for me, not be in the middle of changing shitty nappies. A baby is a handful, you should know that.'

'But if we set ourselves up in a nice house, even your place, I'd be busy with the baby when you're not there. My figure wouldn't be ruined with giving birth, and we'd be a proper little family.'

Bird's jaw tightened. She wasn't listening to him. He stood up.

'Where are you going?'

'For a piss.'

The toilet was locked. He paced up and down outside the door, wondering how to get through to her. *Wants some brat now, does she?* Wait, it wasn't just anyone's brat. It was a Lewis brat, a connection to Danielle. The man occupying the toilet emerged, fixing his trousers. Bird headed in. This could work out to his advantage. Nevertheless, he wasn't letting Marion off too lightly.

When he returned to the table, Marion was staring at her phone.

'Look.' He reached across the table and took her hand. 'I asked you to get Brenno — I mean, Brendan — to move out to give us more time together, and now you want to saddle us with a child that's nothing to do with either of us?'

'Well, that's not strictly true.' She pulled her hand away and downed the remainder of her wine.

Bird stared at her. Now what? The sound of an Italian love song blared out across the restaurant. Someone should turn that shit down.

'Hazel is saying that the baby isn't Ged's. She isn't a Lewis at all. She's a Flynn.'

'Wait a minute. What are you trying to say? I've never slept with Hazel.'

'Not you. The baby is Jason's. Hazel thinks Jason could be the father. Which means she's possibly your niece, your blood.'

'Does Jason know?' Bird said.

'Apparently not.'

'No idea whatsoever?'

'Nope.'

'Sounds odd to me. Hazel will have been claiming all along that Ged is the father, and now suddenly she's saying Jason is?'

'Yes.'

'And you believe her? Hazel hasn't exactly got a good track record for honesty, has she?'

'I agree, but let's imagine that Hazel is telling the truth or, at least, insists that Jason is the dad — it means the baby is a Flynn, and one of yours. If she is, do you want that Lewis crowd raising her?'

'Fuck, no way.' Bird's mind raced. 'But if you take the baby while there's no official proof of who the father is, what's to stop her changing her mind again? She could just turn up one day and take her back.'

Marion shrugged. 'I suppose so.'

His brain sparked. 'What name has she put on the birth certificate?'

'I don't know. I'm not sure she's registered the birth yet. She hasn't even given her a first name. Why?'

He smiled, an idea forming. 'What if she puts him, Jason, on the birth certificate as the father? She can't turn up and take her back then.'

'Right.'

'And if she doesn't tell Ged he's not on the certificate, and he is still under the impression that it's his, the idea of his blood living with me would drive him insane. It might be enough to do him in. Now, that *would* work in our favour.'

'Would Ged care that much?' Marion asked.

'If he thinks she is a Lewis, yes, he would.'

'What if he tried to take her?'

'How would he explain it to Ann?'

'But what if he got hold of a copy of the birth certificate?'

'We'd do an alternative one. Keep it handy. We'd threaten to send it to his wife if he ever caused us trouble.'

'Hazel will want a fee,' Marion said.

'I'll pay, and pass the cost to Ged.'

'Would Jason go for it?' she asked.

'If we kept her, yes, he would. If he raises any objections, I'll talk him round.'

Marion's phone rang. She glanced down at it and said, 'But what if Jason takes it out on Hazel?'

'You give a shit about her? My supposed niece would be away from them and getting proper care.'

'You mean we'd give her proper care?'

'Yes, yes, that.'

'I think Hazel could be back on the gear, too. And if she isn't already, she soon will be. She's not right,' Marion said.

'Was she taking drugs while she was pregnant?' Bird asked.

'No, apart from some weed. She managed to keep off anything harder.'

155

'Jesus, what a saint to have just taken weed. Fuck's sake, no wonder society is screwed. If she goes back on anything harder, she can't care for a baby, can she? All the more reason to move quick on this.'

'So, we can move in together? Be like a proper family?' Marion's eyes lit up.

'Um, let's get hold of the baby first and see. You're talking about a new addition, and possibly a house move to accommodate all your stuff and whatever a baby needs. That's a lot of stress, Marion.'

Her phone rang again. 'Who the fuck is that?' Bird asked.

'It's her. Hazel. I've missed seven calls.'

'Jesus Christ. Ring her. See what's up.'

Marion got up and walked away with her phone to her ear. It wasn't long before she returned. 'It's the baby. Danielle was to babysit tonight but they ended up having a row. She told Hazel she wasn't a fit mother, loaded the child into the car and left. Hazel is frantic.'

'What was Danielle doing looking after the child?' Bird said.

'It's that boy's removal tonight. Hazel wanted to go, as he was her nephew. The funeral's tomorrow.'

It sounded like Danielle had built a rapport with the new baby. That could work in his favour, especially if Danielle believed Jason to be the father. She'd have more reason not to go back to him, leaving the field open to him, Bird. 'Oh, yeah? Well, what are we waiting here for, so?'

'Really? You want to come too? Maybe you should let me deal with it, you know, so we're not being too obvious about the child.'

'Of course I'll come. I'll be supporting you. I won't give anything away.'

She smiled fondly at him. 'You are so good.'

'I am, aren't I?'

Bird called the waitress and paid the bill. This was working out better than he could have imagined. One way or another, he'd get to see Danielle tonight.

156

CHAPTER 30

The sudden buzz of the intercom made Danielle jump. She looked at the video feed and saw Bird Flynn standing at the door with a strange woman. *Shit.* How did they know where she was? Where the hell was her bag? She looked around and saw it next to the door. Tossing lipsticks, foundation and tissues aside, she found the Beretta.

She closed her fingers around the cold metal and took a breath. Did she even need this?

They leaned on the buzzer again. Danielle stuck the gun into the pocket of her jeans and pulled down her top. No way was she letting them in.

She slipped on her boots and jacket and went down to open the door. How far away was Mark? He hadn't said whether he was coming straight back. The gates, which had closed behind them, felt more like a trap than protection.

'Oh, you just caught me. I was heading out.' She looked from Bird to the woman, who was drawing on a cigarette.

'Where is she?' the woman demanded.

'Who are you looking for?' Danielle said.

The woman brought her face close to Danielle's. Her breath smelled of alcohol. 'You know who I'm talking about.'

'I've no idea.'

'Yes, you do. You know exactly who I'm talking about.' She crossed her arms. 'Bird, get her to tell you.'

Turning to Bird, Danielle jerked her thumb back at the woman. 'What the fuck is this?'

Bird looked past her. 'Calm down, Marion. We'll get our answers, just—'

Marion launched herself at Danielle, screaming. Danielle spun her around, threw her against the wall and held her there while she pulled out the gun. Bird took a step towards them. She aimed the gun at his face while the other hand kept a tight grip on Marion.

'Woah.' Bird stepped back, his hands up. 'Come on, Danielle, you know me. We're not looking for trouble.'

'Oh, really?'

'You're hurting me, bitch,' Marion cried out.

Danielle tightened her grip. Bird stood frozen to the spot.

'You turn up on my doorstep demanding to see someone I don't know, then you come at me. What do you expect me to do?'

'It's a baby. A little girl,' Bird said.

'Oh, right. I see. And why the fuck would you think I have a baby girl?' She fixed Bird with a hard stare.

'Look, can you put down the gun so we can talk like adults?' Bird said.

'I didn't notice this cow talking like an adult.'

'Marion is . . . passionate.'

'Is that what you call it?'

Bird lowered his hands. 'Please, put that away, Danielle. Marion meant no harm.'

'You need to learn to control your bitch,' Danielle said.

'Fuck you,' Marion said.

Beyond Bird's shoulder, Danielle saw Mark's car come into view. At least she had back up now. She released her hold on Marion, took a step away, but kept the gun pointed in their direction. Marion pulled at her dress and patted down her hair.

'Are you going to let her do this to me?' Marion demanded of Bird.

He didn't answer, his eyes fixed on Danielle.

Mark drove towards them, leaped out of the car and ran up the steps. Danielle lowered the weapon.

'What the hell's going on here?' Mark's gaze darted from Danielle and the gun to Bird and Marion.

'Just a conversation,' Bird said.

'Are you sure?' Mark asked.

There was a muffled cry from the car. Marion darted over to the car and began rattling the door handle. 'Open this door!'

Danielle looked enquiringly at Mark.

'I knew she was here!' Marion screamed. 'Get her out.'

Danielle crossed her arms. 'What? Hand over a baby to a woman who can't seem to control her anger?'

Marion looked back at Bird. 'Do something, Bird, she's crying.'

'What's the baby doing here?' Bird asked.

Mark stepped closer to him. 'Why do you want to know?'

But Bird continued to gaze at Danielle. Uneasy beneath that fixed stare, she said, 'You heard him. Why do you want to know?'

Bird walked over to Marion and whispered in her ear. She huffed a little, but nodded.

'We're sorry we interrupted you,' Bird said. 'We thought there was an issue here, but I see you have it all in hand.' He put his hands on Marion's shoulders and turned her around. They both left via the side gate.

'What the fuck are you doing back with the baby, Mark?' Danielle demanded.

'There was no sign of Hazel. The door was wide open, her handbag still on the table, but she wasn't there.'

'Did you look? Maybe she was in the toilet.'

'What do you take me for, Danielle? Of course I checked, even the back yard.'

'Well, she'd probably gone to the removal, then, like I thought.'

'Without her handbag?' Mark asked.

'Maybe she took another one, I don't know. Anyway, we're stuck with the child for now, especially if Hazel goes to the pub with the rest of them after.'

'Being stuck with the child didn't bother you earlier, Danielle,' Mark said.

'It did, actually. But when she spoke to me like that, I saw red.' That was her trouble, wasn't it, always seeing red? 'What am I going to do? I haven't a thing for this baby.'

'I stopped at my sister's. There's nappies, outfits and formula in the boot,' he said.

'Thank you, Mark. Does this mean you're helping me out here?'

'Uh-uh. I didn't like to see the child suffering because you couldn't control your temper, that's all.'

Well, she could hardly argue with that, could she?

'Anyway, what did those two want, and what the fuck were you doing with the piece in their faces?'

'Bird's muppet girlfriend went for me. I just reacted out of instinct.'

'And you were going to shoot Bird Flynn in the face? Here?'

Imagine the fallout from that, she thought. 'Christ no, Mark. Do you think I'm an idiot?'

He raised an eyebrow. 'Then you shouldn't have pulled it. He won't forget a thing like that.'

'They arrived here out of the blue, demanding the baby. I didn't know what the hell it was all about.'

'Well, whatever it was, you need to watch yourself, Danielle. All this flipping out will get you into trouble,' he said.

'Thanks for your advice.'

'Hazel must have rung Bird after we left,' he said, 'especially after your encounter with her.'

'But I thought Hazel worked in our business. What's her connection with Bird?'

'That woman is Marion Ahearne. She was doing Hazel's job up to about five years ago. She worked the reception and wasn't on the menu. Bird persuaded her out of it. Promised her the world.'

'And did he deliver?' Danielle asked.

'Well, they're not living together. Bird has her son running errands for him, doing drug runs and whatever other shit he throws at him.'

'I see. You mean Brenno, the one who's behind Dean's shooting?'

'Yet to be proved. Dean won't confirm it, so we can't take action. You were there when Bird denied being involved. So, unless we want to start a war . . .'

'I get you. Hazel is pissed that Ged hasn't dropped everything for her. She could be stirring, trying to get Bird and Marion on her side to get revenge on Ged.'

'More than likely,' Mark said, 'but why would Bird risk taking Ged's daughter away?'

'Hmm. While we have her, maybe we should get a DNA test done on Baby Girl Brady.'

'Maybe we should. Then get her back to her mother. But for now, you are her only option, so we'd better get her inside.' Mark got the child out of the car and handed her over, along with the equipment he'd obtained from his sister.

The baby gurgled, tiny lips at the soother. Danielle gave her a wry smile. 'Well, kid, looks like you're stuck with me for now, God love you.'

What a complication. Danielle did not need to get attached to anyone here. Least of all a baby.

CHAPTER 31

Despite all his efforts to fall asleep, Dean's brain kept racing round in circles. After several phone calls, he was no wiser as to where the equipment had ended up, or the cash. No one knew a thing about it, or so they claimed, anyway. How would he explain this to Bird? He'd surely want compensation. With his money tied up in upcoming jobs, Dean would have no recourse but to go cap in hand to his da. *Shit.* He'd insisted that Ged could trust him with this, and now it was fucked up, big time.

Dean still had the van with the Louth registration plates, so he took it on a spin to Ritchie's house. Danielle was no help. When he'd asked her about Ritchie's whereabouts, she had clammed up. Something was going on behind his back. Was she trying to muscle him out? It felt like it. Well, he was fucked if he was going to let her get away with that.

The early morning sun sent shafts of light on to the dilapidated houses. Apart from the crows picking at discarded takeaway cartons, there were few signs of life on the estate. Blinds were drawn, curtains closed across windows barred with steel.

There were five newly built properties just down from Ritchie's. Dean parked two houses up on the other side of the street, outside a house boarded up after a recent fire. Next door, two dogs — a pit bull and some sort of terrier — charged out and ran after the crows, barking. A woman in a dressing gown and slippers emerged and dragged them back inside.

Ritchie's house was in darkness. After a few minutes, a light came on behind the glass panel in the door, illuminating the steps. Dean sat forward, his arms hugging the steering wheel. The silhouette of a person passed behind the door, moving across the hall.

Dean hopped out of the van and headed for the house. He knocked. Listened. No sound came from within. He knocked again, and a shape loomed up behind the frosted glass. 'Who's there?'

'Ritchie, it's Dean. Open the door, will you? I'm freezing my balls off out here.'

Dean heard the rattle of three bolts unlocking, and the door swung open. 'Cold? It's the middle of summer. It's a line or two of something is what you need.'

Dean giggled. 'Look at the state of you, in the dressing gown.'

A creak sounded above them. Ritchie glanced up at the stairs. 'Yes, 'cause it's stupid o'clock. What do you want?'

'Let me in and I'll tell you.'

Ritchie sighed and stood back to allow him in. He stuck his head out and peered up and down the street before closing the door again. 'Go on in there.' He pointed towards a door off the hallway.

'Why are you whispering like that?' Dean asked.

'I don't want to wake the whole house, do I?'

'You got company then, have you?'

'Maybe. Come on.' He ushered Dean into the kitchen. 'Now, Dean. What do you need at this ridiculous—'

'Answers, that's what I need. The equipment and cash weren't at the location. The coordinates led me to a place in Fermanagh with nothing to see there but a great big steel shed. Empty.'

'Well, I don't know. I've been on the Belfast job with Ged. I only just got back. I thought you were dealing with the equipment.'

'But I thought you were to stay and look after Danielle, not head up north.'

'Nah. Someone's filling you with crap.'

Dean began to pace. 'Fuck.'

'Are you okay?' Ritchie asked, watching him.

'I am. This latest shit is melting my brain. I overdid it after the arson attack. It didn't affect me at the time, but now I keep getting these mad fucking images — visions, flash-backs, whatever.'

'Stay away from it while you're on a job,' Ritchie said.

'I know, I know. Easier said than done.'

'Who'd you get to look after everything for you? Who gave you the coordinates?'

Dean pulled out a chair and sat down at the kitchen table, head in his hands. 'Anto Doyle. He drove the low-loader away. Said he knew a place to hide the stuff.'

'Then get over to his place and find out what the story is.'

'I couldn't get hold of him yesterday.'

'Can you trust him?'

'I've known him for years. He wants in with our crew. Knows a thing or two about the Flynn brothers that'll help me oust them. Brenno has time for him, too.'

'Brenno? I'm not sure if I'd put too much trust in him. Didn't you think he pulled the trigger on you?'

'No, I don't think it was him.'

'Really?'

'Yeah. I can trust Brenno. He has my back. He'd like to work full-time for me, but he can't because Bird is screwing his ma.'

'Gross. Don't make me even picture that at this time in the morning.'

'Anyway, Brenno hates Bird.'

'So there's no way it was Brenno?'

164

'If he was involved, he was only doing it because he had to.'

'Just make sure you know who is on your side and who is not,' Ritchie said. 'You need to get your hands on that equipment, get it back to Bird, along with any money he is owed. And another thing. You are *not* starting a war with that family. Do you hear me?'

'Yeah, yeah. Do you not think it's already begun, though, Ritchie?'

'Sounds like you *do* know who put the hit out on you. Well, come on. Tell me,' Ritchie said.

'Who do you think put the hit out on me, Ritchie?'

'How do I know? Jason? Bird? Maybe the other brother, Dwayne, sunning his knob in the Caribbean. One of them? Or all three? Maybe it's one of their men — Bosco? Sal? Come on, spit it out.'

Dean shrugged. 'Bird is all I know for sure.'

'Fuck. How sure are you? Are you certain this isn't all in your head?' Ritchie tapped his own temple.

'Very sure.'

Ritchie grunted, paced for a moment. Stopped. 'Does Ged know?'

'I told him, but I didn't mean to, so then I said I wasn't totally sure. He went and met with Bird, who denied the whole thing. Danielle was there too, to soften the threat, just in case. Everyone knows he has the horn for her. Always has.'

'Yeah, but why would Bird call a hit on you?'

Dean shrugged. 'Dunno. Not happy with his cut on the ATM robberies maybe, and the delay in getting back the low-loader and trailer. Still pissed about his gear gone to the cops? All of the above?'

'Wouldn't he be getting fifty per cent for supplying the equipment to you?' Ritchie said.

'Exactly. But the haul wasn't huge, so. Look, I've hung on to it longer than he's happy with. I was doing it to build it up further, by adding more hauls, but it didn't work out for me.'

'So, he just goes and orders a hit? That makes no sense, Dean.'

Dean shrugged. 'Seems like he did.'

'Jesus. How are you not over at his place with a nine mil pressed to his temple?'

'Well, Bird is out of pocket quite a bit more than he'd anticipated.'

'Now that's a different story.'

'Anyway, I don't want to go over there with a gun, not until I'm ready to pull the trigger. I thought a tit for tat would draw heat, and I'm playing a longer game with this.'

'If Bird is out of pocket, he'd be right to be really pissed at you. Dean, this is really important. You need to discuss it with your da and get his advice.'

'Well, he had enough to worry about. I wanted to prove I could handle this myself.'

'What kind of a dickhead are you? Nothing is done without his say-so.'

Another creak came from above them.

'Who have you up there? One of the girls from Dani's place? Which one? It'd better not be Cheryl. I wouldn't be too impressed with that now.'

'Cheryl? Why would you say that? I thought you heard.'

'Heard what? It's not her, is it?' Dean said.

'She's dead. She was found murdered. Beaten to death.'

Dean felt as if he'd been punched in the guts. He ran his hands through his hair, then slapped his forehead. 'I went for her only the other night. She wasn't around. Trouble with a punter, they said. And now you're telling me she's dead? Anyone pulled into the cop shop for it?'

'I've heard nothing since,' Ritchie said.

'Jesus Christ. Is there attention on Berkley Street because of it?'

'A little. Nothing more than an enquiry. All we know is that a detective sergeant called around asking Linda if she knew Cheryl.'

'Right. Linda covered it, though?'

'I heard she did.'

'Where was Dani?'

'On the way there, but didn't make it on time to meet the detective.'

'Why?'

'Don't know. Ged wasn't impressed that she'd left it to Linda.'

More noises filtered through the ceiling, and the stairs creaked.

'What are you doing, Ritchie? Are you coming back up?'

Dean glared at Ritchie. He stood up, sending his chair crashing backwards. Ritchie blocked his path.

'It's not what you think,' Ritchie said.

Dean shouldered him out of the way and charged out. Halfway down the stairs, clad in a pink dressing gown and drawing on a cigarette, stood his mother.

'What are you doing here, Dean?'

Dean turned and ran towards Ritchie, driving him back against the counter. He put his hands around Ritchie's neck and squeezed, while Ritchie clawed at his fingers, trying to prise them loose. Pummelling his back with her fists, Ann yelled at him to get off. After a few minutes of this, Ritchie began to go limp.

A blow to the side of his head drove Dean sideways. He crouched, shielding his head with his hands, his ear hot and ringing. He risked a glance up. Ann was standing over him, arms raised, ready to bring the frying pan down on him again.

'All right, all right. Cool it, Ma.' Dean took hold of a chair and hauled himself up.

Ritchie was folded over, coughing. Ann looked from Dean to Ritchie, swinging the pan. 'Do I need keep hold of this, or are you both going to stay in your corners?'

'I'll stay put, Ma.'

Ritchie nodded, still holding his throat.

Ann slammed the pan on to the table, making Dean jump. She reached into one of the cabinets and retrieved three glasses and a bottle of vodka. She filled the glasses, downed hers neat, refilled it and handed one each to Dean and Ritchie. Dean swallowed his in one, wincing. It tasted like nail polish remover.

She poured herself and Ritchie another measure, but Dean shook his head.

Her eyes narrowed. 'If it came from a tit, you'd drink it, wouldn't you?' Ann poured some more into his glass. 'Don't be a pussy and swallow.'

The taste was no better the second time around.

'That's more like it. You've had a shock, Dean, the alcohol will help.'

'It'd give anyone a shock finding his mother—'

She slapped his cheek, hard.

'I broke the news to him about Cheryl. He hadn't heard,' Ritchie rasped.

'Ah, no wonder you reacted like you did,' Ann said.

'I reacted like I did because of seeing you . . . And him.'

Ann reached for the frying pan. 'I'll do real damage if you repeat that.'

'Fine, fine.'

She let it go. 'Now, let's get this straight. You saw nothing, did you? Did you?'

Dean shook his head.

'Your da has his stuff going on and I have mine. Neither of which is your business. You have enough problems of your own without worrying about me. Ritchie keeps me safe when your da is off and about. If I kip here now and again, that's my concern, not yours. It's better than being alone and vulnerable in that big house in Clontarf, wondering about every noise. Worried if it's him stumbling around or maybe someone breaking in to get at me. Since the arson attack and your—' she pointed to his shoulder — 'my nerves have been all shot.'

'Okay, Ma, I get it. I thought you'd have gone to stay in Limerick.'

'I'll do what I like, and now I'm making sure you don't go running to your da after getting some wrong impression.'

'I didn't, I promise. I'm upset, that's all. I've equipment and cash gone missing, and I just found out Cheryl's been murdered.'

'And you wanted to add to all that shit by strangling him.' She jabbed her thumb towards Ritchie.

Dean glanced at him, trying not to picture Ritchie and his ma together. He wanted to punch something, or someone, hard.

'It's all her fault,' Dean said.

'Whose?' Ann asked.

'Danielle.'

'What about Danielle?' Ann asked.

'She's brought nothing but bad luck since she landed back. I mean, the day she arrives I get two bullets. After that, the new pub is nearly burned to the ground, and I'm down a fortune because Da said I'd be running it, then changed his mind.'

'Danielle had no hand in any of that,' Ritchie said.

'Maybe not. But she's bad for business. Ever since she gave Jason the elbow, everything's been shit. Bird's had a thing for her for years, and now all this. Could be him messing with us.'

'Why?' Ritchie asked. 'Bird Flynn denied being involved in your attack. He met with your da, and I thought it was sorted. Do you have any proof of what you're saying?'

'No.'

'Well, stop spouting theories you can't back. You'll get yourself — or one of us — killed.'

Dean stood up. 'Don't you tell me what to do.'

Ritchie squared his shoulders.

Ann stepped between them. 'Go, Dean. Get out of here and cool down before one of you ends up dead. And the minute you leave, you're to scrub your brain of anything you think you saw here.'

Dean kept his eyes on Ritchie. 'That won't be a problem.'

'Good,' she said. 'And leave Danielle out of it. She is tough, and we needed her back. Now that she is, I don't want your delusions messing things up. Ease off on the stuff, if it's wrecking your head. We need to concentrate our anger on those trying to take us over, not one of ourselves.'

'Okay, Ma.'

'Good. Now, off with you.'

She followed him towards the door. 'Aren't you forgetting something?'

Dean turned. She pointed to her cheek. He leaned in and kissed it. 'Sorry, Ma.'

She put her hands on either side of his face and held his gaze. 'That's better. Now, calm it. You're only giving others the opportunity to fuck with us. Don't let that happen.'

'Of course, Ma. You're right.'

Slowly, Dean walked back to the van. He'd noticed his ma and Ritchie exchange looks, but never thought they'd cross that line. From what he'd heard, Ged and Ritchie had fallen out years ago. Had it been going on that long?

It was one thing for Da to play away; men had the right. But Ma . . . Jesus Christ. The family would be nothing without her. She deserved his trust. So did Danielle, if Ma was supporting her. Shit, he'd have to pull back on the blow. It was fucking with his head.

CHAPTER 32

Hazel had not been among the throng of people lining the streets and piling into the church for the removal of Jake Brady. Bird and Marion had driven to Hazel's new house, but there was no sign of her there either. Marion was talking about reporting her missing if she didn't turn up for the funeral today. Bird couldn't make up his mind — was the baby really Ged's, or was it Jason's?

After trying Hazel's number again and again, Marion eventually gave up and nodded off in his bed. Unable to sleep, Bird got up and poured himself a brandy, running through all the places Hazel might have got to, and what their next move might be. He needed to talk to Jason. Then there was Danielle. He'd never seen her pull a gun before. What had got her so jumpy? She'd moved swiftly enough on Marion, yet she also seemed to be holding back. He wondered why.

He was headed back upstairs when someone pounded on his door. He checked the time — just gone eight. Normally he'd be on his way to the yard by now, but today he'd left Sal and Bosco to handle things.

Another thump.

'Christ, go easy, I'm coming.' He landed the glass on the locker to the sound of more loud knocking.

'Fuck's sake,' he muttered. He drew the curtain aside. A man in a suit stood at the door, along with a woman with a ponytail, who stepped back and looked up at the windows. She was carrying a manilla folder. Fucking guards. What the hell did they want at this hour? He stomped downstairs and threw open the door.

'Bruce Flynn?' the woman asked.

'Who wants to know?'

'Detective Garda Sinead Teegan, and this is Detective Sergeant Dave Richards.'

They held up their badges. Bird inspected them minutely. 'I know the detective sergeant, thank you very much. How are you, Detective Sergeant?'

'Good, Bird. We haven't had to call on you in a while.'

'Nope. That's the way I like it. Are you showing this one the ropes?'

'This one, as you put it, does not need anyone showing her the ropes. She has something to discuss with you.'

'Have you got a warrant?' Bird folded his arms across his chest.

'No need. We're only here to talk.'

He settled his gaze on Dave. 'Fine, I'll talk to you, Detective Sergeant. I don't know you well enough, love, sorry. What did you say your name was?'

'Detective Teegan.' She didn't seem the least bit fazed.

'Right, Detective, love. Not today.'

'No can do, Bird. My colleague here is the lead on this case, so she is in charge,' Dave said.

'Ah, it's like that, so, is it?' He winked at Dave.

'It's not like anything,' Teegan said.

'Right. The lead on what case?' He looked from one to the other, annoyed at having to entertain a rookie.

'The suspicious death of Sarah Cooper,' Teegan said.

'Who the hell is that?' Marion appeared beside him, wiping the sleep from her eyes.

The detective looked at her, then back to Bird. 'She worked as a beautician at a premises on Berkley Street.'

Bird shrugged.

'You might know her by another name — she also called herself Cheryl,' Teegan added.

'I'm still not sure I know who you're talking about,' Bird said.

Marion moved closer. She had lost all trace of sleepiness.

'A phone number registered to your plant-hire company was found to have called her number four times on the night before she died.'

'I have plenty on my payroll who have phone numbers registered to the company.'

'So, can you provide us with a list?' Teegan asked, pulling a notebook from her pocket.

'Depends what they are being accused of. How is that relevant anyway? I didn't think it was an offence to call someone.'

'We're investigating her murder, Mr Flynn. Everything is relevant.'

'Right, I'll get that list for you. Is that all?'

'How long will it take?'

Bird stared at her for a moment, as if she had set him a difficult problem. 'I'll have to call to the office and check the records.'

'I hope you are not driving, with breath like that,' she said. 'Is it last night's drink or this morning's?'

'Don't worry about me,' Bird said. 'I have drivers.'

'Good,' the detective said. 'Can you not do it online while we wait?'

'Sorry, I'm changing broadband providers at the minute.'

She took a card from the back of her notebook and thrust it at him.

'As soon as you can, please, Mr Flynn.'

'Soon as I can,' he echoed mockingly.

Bird was about to close the door when the detective sergeant said, 'Your brother?'

'What about him?'

'Is he here?'

'No, why would he be? He doesn't live here.'

'Right. We've called to his apartment several times, but we're having no luck getting hold of him.'

'I'm not his fucking keeper,' Bird snapped. He had had enough of this officious dickhead.

'You surely know if he'll be coming round to see you at some stage,' Teegan said.

'What do you want with him?'

'Same as we want with you — we'd like him to help us with our enquiries.'

'I'll tell him when I see him.'

'You do that, please. In the meantime, may I have your contact numbers — both of you, if you don't mind.'

'I can never remember my number,' Marion said.

'We'll wait while you get it,' Dave said.

Marion disappeared, while Bird gave them his number.

'I can't figure this thing out,' Marion was saying, returning with the phone in her hand, tapping and flicking.

'You do know how to make a call?' Detective Teegan asked.

'Of course I do. I'm not stupid—'

'Yes, she can,' Bird interjected, before Marion lost it and called the detective something she wouldn't forget.

'Then dial the number on the card and we'll have it.'

Marion tapped out the number slowly.

The detective showed her colleague the number. He wrote it down, then flicked through his notebook and held it up to show her something.

'How long have you had that number?' Teegan asked.

'About four months. Why?'

'One of the last numbers Sarah Cooper called also received several calls from this number — yours.'

'I don't know Cheryl. Why would I ring her?'

'That's not what we're saying,' Dave said. 'There's another number, you see, one that you rang, but which was also called by Sarah, er, Cheryl.'

'Does she know you're checking her phone?' Marion said.

'Does who know?' Dave said.

Bird elbowed Marion aside. 'All right. That's enough.'

'This may be relevant to the investigation,' Dave said.

'Fine. It's early, she's only just awake and I'll get you that list the first chance I get. Now, if you don't mind, I've breakfast to cook.' Bird put his hand on the door, but Dave put out his foot to stop him closing it.

'There's something else, Bird,' he said.

'What now?'

Dave leafed through his notebook. 'You recently reported a seven-tonne excavator, tractor and loader missing.'

'Yeah, yeah. I hired it out to someone who didn't return it.'

'Are they due to be returned, or were they stolen?' Dave asked.

'Well, I need to get them to hurry up and get them back to me. I'm losing money while they're unavailable.'

'So, which is it?'

'Due to be returned, I guess. The guard on the desk said it was a civil case.'

'Who did you hire it out to?' Dave asked.

'I'll have to check my paperwork, but it looks to be a dodgy sort. Could have given me false details.'

'You hired them nearly a hundred grand's worth of machinery and you didn't do a check on them?'

'Yeah, one of the lads in the yard thought he knew them.'

'Well, if they're dodgy, we could be looking at a theft, or a fraud,' Dave said.

'Grand. I'll report them stolen, so,' Bird said.

'For insurance purposes,' Dave added.

'Yeah, yeah, something like that. Then I can get some reference number or something, so.' Marion had been banging on about doing that.

'I can take the report from you, then we might have to examine the yard,' Dave said.

'Look, I'm not saying someone broke in to take them. They were hired out and not returned. I can get you the paperwork, but I reckon they are long gone. Probably on a ferry by now.'

'No bother. Give me the details, and I can get you a PULSE ID number so you can claim.' Dave took out a sheet of paper.

It took a few minutes, but that was fine with Bird. If it gave him a way to claim the money back, he'd be sorted, and the detectives would be busy chasing fuck all.

Dave thrust the sheet at Bird and pointed out where to sign.

'Are you sure about this, Bird?' Marion asked.

His jaw tightened. How fucking dare she question him in front of a pair of scumbag cops? He took the sheet and the pen from Dave and hesitated. Maybe Marion had a point.

'Why the fuck would you care if I get compensated?' How come the cops were making it this easy for him? There had to be a catch.

'I don't give a fuck if you're compensated,' Dave said. 'What I do give a fuck about is crime. There are way too many thefts occurring and businesses are suffering.'

'You can get me the number now?' Bird asked, pen still hovering over the sheet of paper.

'Yes.'

Bird put pen to paper.

Teegan turned away, took out her phone and made the call.

'Right, have you a bit of paper?'

'Haven't you plenty of it?'

With a sigh, she took a blank page from her folder and scribbled it down. She held it out towards Bird, who snatched it from her hand. 'Sign here.'

Finally, the two detectives left. Bird closed the door behind them. 'Don't ever question me in front of the likes of them, ever. You hear me?'

'I just wanted to know if you were sure,' Marion said.

'Not in front of the scumbags. Who do you think you are? Anyway, you want to be sure what you say yourself.'

'What?'

'Whoever they're talking about. You nearly handed them information.'

'In the past couple of weeks, I have called three numbers — yours, Brendan's and Hazel's. It had to be her they were talking about. Cheryl kept ringing Hazel, saying she was holding back money from her.'

'But how do you know either of those detectives had a name?'

Marion's mouth opened and closed.

'See? How do I know you'll keep quiet about our plan for Hazel's daughter?'

'Of course I will. That's different. The guards'll hardly be asking about her, now, will they?'

'If Hazel reports her missing, they will. Don't ring her again. In fact, I'll get you a new phone.'

'Okay . . .' Marion bit on her thumbnail.

'What?'

'Nothing,' she said.

'You'd better tell me.'

'What if they were listening to our conversations, Bird?'

'You tell me. Why would you be worried about that? What didn't you want them to hear?'

Marion made a face. 'Nothing . . . nothing important. Only to arrange a meeting, that's all.'

'You sure, Marion?'

'One hundred per cent.'

'Right, now get back up to bed and give me some space to think.'

Outside the house, the rumble of a motorbike engine dwindled to a purr. Bird opened the door to see Jason pulling off his helmet.

Bird glanced up and down the street. 'Did the detectives see you?'

'No. I waited till they were out of sight. What did they want?'

'They were asking about one of the girls at Ged's knocking shop on Berkley Street — Cheryl. They called her Sally Cooper or something. They've been looking for you, too.'

'Why me, Bird?'

'They didn't say. What brings you here at this hour of the morning?'

'Hazel is spreading some bullshit story about her new baby being mine and not Ged's.'

'What? Where did you hear that?' Bird said.

'Hazel rang me, told me herself.'

'And is it?' Bird asked.

'Fuck no. I've never even slept with the bitch. She's Ged's. Why would I even think about going there?'

'So, what if Hazel is saying it's yours? You'll be getting one over on Ged Lewis, won't you? It'll be helpful, make him take his eye off the ball and give us a chance to muscle in on his businesses.'

'I keep telling you, we're better off working with Ged than against him. I said Dean would be bad for business, and I was proved right.'

'You know it all now, don't you, Jason? Maybe I should give you a medal for it.'

'No need for smartness, Bird. I know enough, and one thing I do know is that what Hazel is claiming is bullshit. If Dani gets wind of it, she could end up fucking off back to the UK and I'll never see her again.'

Bird laughed. 'What? You think you've a chance with Danielle after what you did to her? You abandoned her at the worst time of her life. And you didn't just leave her, either. You know you did the dirt on her, Jason. That was cruel. That's what sent her packing.'

'It was my baby too, Bird. I was grieving as well, you know.'

'Oh, really?'

'I was off my head. I hardly knew what I was doing. I was stupid.'

'Stupid to get caught, you mean,' Bird said.

There was a noise from upstairs. 'I thought you were alone,' Jason said, and sniffed the air.

'I'd know that perfume anywhere,' he said. 'It's the one Danielle wears.'

Bird opened his mouth, but Jason was already bounding up the stairs.

He flung open the bedroom door.

Marion, half undressed, screamed and snatched at her dressing gown.

'What the fuck are you doing, Jason?' Bird came up behind him. Marion must have used the whole bottle; the room was filled with the scent of citrus and vanilla.

Jason stood in the doorway. 'Oh. I thought . . . That's the perfume Danielle wears.'

Marion stopped struggling with her dressing gown. 'What the fuck? Bird? You want me to smell like her?'

'No, Marion. Just shut up a second.'

'Don't you speak to me like that, Bruce Flynn.'

'Marion, will you just shut the fuck up while I deal with Jason.'

Marion sat on the bed and glared at him.

'Look at the trouble you've caused, Jason. Get the fuck out of my house.'

'I'm not getting out of your house. I came here to talk to you,' Jason said.

'No. Get down those stairs and keep going out that fucking door.'

'I'm looking for something important, and I'm not going until you tell me where it is.'

'What are you going on about?' Bird said.

'Dwayne got his hands on some evidence about Danielle's shooting. And I want it.'

'What kind of evidence? And why would you think I know where it is?' When he thought about it, Bird vaguely recalled something about a memory card that Dwayne had said was important and had to be kept safe. But that was a couple of years ago. Their oldest brother had never been much of a talker. Like last month. He mentioned he was heading to the US to build business links and that was it, he just left, telling Bird to mind the yard and keep an eye on his office. Shit, Dwayne's office. Bird had been using it on and off since.

'Because I've looked everywhere,' Jason was saying. 'And the only place left is the offices at the yard.'

'So, let me get this straight, Jason. You've been rummaging in everyone's business, looking for something you think might be evidence about Danielle's shooting, and you've never said anything to me before now?'

'I didn't know how much you knew. I thought you might be keeping something from me.'

'Do you think our Dwyane tells me everything?'

'Well, you've always been closer to him than me.'

'Poor fucking Jason. Well, I've got news for you. He tells me fuck all, but always manages to know everything that's going on.'

'You haven't answered me, Bird. Do you know where it is or not?'

'No, I fucking don't. Ask Dwayne yourself when he's back.'

'I asked him a few months ago and he pretended to know nothing about it.'

'Well, maybe it's all in your head,' Bird said.

'I overheard him talking about it.'

'I think you heard wrong. You fucked up with Danielle and now you're trying anything you can to win her back. Well, that is not going to happen.'

'Why?' Jason asked and glanced at Marion. 'Because you want her for yourself?'

Bird lunged at Jason. Both of them ended up on the floor beside the bed, Bird on top of Jason. Jason kneed his brother in the balls, pushed him off and stood up.

Bird unwound himself from a foetal position and hauled himself up on to the bed. When he looked up, Marion was standing there with a gun in her hand. She had it pointed at Jason, who had his arms raised.

'Get the fuck out of this house, Jason,' she said.

'Yeah, Jason, get out,' Bird croaked.

'And you, Bruce Flynn,' Marion said. 'Sit there and shut the fuck up. I'm not done with you. I am sick of you talking to me like you do, buying me perfume that Danielle fucking Lewis wears. I've had enough of your shit.' She gestured with the gun. 'Now, Jason Flynn, you'll get the hell out of this house if you know what's good for you.'

Jason thundered down the stairs. The sound of the door slamming reverberated through the house.

'Put the gun away, Marion,' Bird said.

Slowly, Marion placed the weapon on the dresser. 'Start explaining to me, so — and I'll know if you are lying.'

He doubted that, but he had to say something to fix this. She'd seen too much to make an enemy of. 'You've got it all wrong, Marion. I had no idea that was Danielle's perfume. I wanted to treat you, and the saleswoman recommended this one. Look, I was trying to be nice.' He held out his hand to Marion. 'Come here, love.'

'Yes, but there's the way you speak to me. You dismiss me all the time. How do I know that what Jason said isn't the truth?'

'It's not, I promise. I don't want anyone else, only you. How can I make this up to you?' Meanwhile, Bird's mind was ticking over. Jason had way too much power in the family now. If word got out that he and Bird had fallen out again, the vultures would circle.

'You can let me move in here,' Marion said. 'Let's make a right go of it. That way, I'll know that it's me you want and no one else.'

'Done, Marion. Move in this minute. There. Are you happy now?'

'I'd be happier with a big rock on my finger.'

'Leave it with me, Marion. I won't let you down.'

Fuck it. He was stuck with her now. Well, there was nothing else to be done. She knew way too much. It was safer to keep her close — for now, anyway.

CHAPTER 33

Dean drove aimlessly around, trying to get his head around what his mother had said. The image of her at Ritchie Delaney's house had kept him awake for the last two nights. Who the fuck did she mean? Who was worming their way in and trying to take over? She hadn't mentioned names. His head still smarted where she'd hit him with the frying pan. *Think, think.* She had to have a plan, but just wasn't sharing it yet. There must be another reason she'd stayed at Ritchie's, other than the obvious one — that they were screwing.

The hairs on his arms stood up. Ma had to know about Hazel, about the baby being Da's. That was the only thing that made sense. Was Hazel trying to take her place? Fuck that. He needed to find Hazel and slap the truth out of her mouth. It was enough that Danielle was back thinking she could take over, let alone having another brat added to the Lewis clan. It had to be stopped. Too much was happening at once.

Dean found himself driving along the Old Airport Road. Through the fence, he could see the planes lined up at the end of the runway. He slowed to look at them. It'd be nice to go somewhere sunny, escape all this madness.

While he dreamed of beaches and palm trees, a car sped past, a car he knew well. He followed it at a reasonable distance until it pulled into a lay-by. Dean parked on the opposite side of the road, a little further back, with his engine running. Anto Doyle got out of the driver's door, walked to the front of the car and bent down to examine the tyre. Pulling his hood up over his head, Dean floored the pedal and drove straight at him. Anto saw him coming and ran for the fence, while the passenger door opened and Brenno headed off in the opposite direction. Dean braked hard, swinging the van around to block Anto's exit. By the time Dean got out of the van, Brenno had vanished, while Anto struggled to get over the fence.

Dean grabbed Anto and pinned him with his face against the wire mesh. He patted him down and removed a gun and a phone from his pocket. He pressed the gun to Anto's neck, putting the phone into his own pocket.

Something hard pressed against the back of his head. He released Anto and dropped the gun.

'It's me, you pair of assholes.' The pressure on his head eased.

Brenno tucked the gun into his jacket. 'You prick. I could have put one in you.'

'Jesus Christ, Dean, what were you trying to do?' Anto asked, picking up his gun.

'Keeping you both on your toes. You were well able to move.'

'Fuck off,' Brenno said.

'Fuck off yourself. You're the one that put a hole in my arse and fucked up my shoulder,' Dean said.

'Yeah, well . . .'

'Well what?'

'I had to make it look convincing,' Brenno said. 'We talked about all that, didn't we, Anto? You were there, too.'

Anto nodded.

'Convincing? You could have shot me in the head.' He turned to Anto. 'And you, dickhead. You nearly ran over me that day, I only just managed to roll into the gutter. I thought you were meant to be a good driver.'

'I avoided you though, didn't I?' Anto said.

'It came too close for comfort, though.'

'And what about those two lads, the ones playing at being heroes?' Anto asked.

'They're sorted,' Dean said, with a smirk.

'What do you mean, sorted?' Brenno asked.

'One of them's already rotting in the ground,' Dean said, still smirking.

'What? Who? The lad the paper reported was buried earlier this week?'

'Yeah.'

'You?'

'Not directly.'

'Why?' Brenno asked.

'They knew too much,' Dean said. 'And they couldn't even tell the time.'

'Huh?' Anto said.

'Yep. Midnight, that's when they were told to torch the pub, after everyone left, not while we were all in there having a singsong. Danielle and Ma would have got the brunt of it if they hadn't gone outside for a smoke. The petrol bombs landed right where they'd been sitting.'

'Why torch your own pub?' Anto asked.

'Because Da promised that place to me. Next thing I know, Danielle is back and he announces that she's to run it. Fuck that.'

'Jesus Christ, Dean,' Anto said.

'Well, if I can't have it, she can't either.'

'No, I meant taking those boys out. They're only kids,' Anto said.

'They were given a chance to work for me and they fucked up. You do that and you get taught a lesson. The lad that didn't get shot will never get the time wrong again, will he?'

'Harsh, Dean,' Anto said.

'Nope. Necessary. It would have been worse if one of my family was hurt. Anyway, we've a bigger problem.'

'What? Bigger than murder?' Anto said.

'What's this problem, anyway?' Brenno asked.

'The machinery, the money, the gear gone. Bird won't even waste his cash paying for a hit; he'll shoot me himself if I don't get it back to him.'

'You do have a problem, so, Dean,' Anto said. 'You should have seen what Bird did to the rat.'

'I can only imagine.'

'But wait a second. Bird didn't put the hit on you,' Anto continued.

'What?' Dean said, and glared at Brenno. 'You mean you shot me for the hell of it? What the fuck?'

'No, of course not, Dean. I got it straight from Bird, I swear. What shit are you talking, Anto?'

'Don't worry about it. I shouldn't have said anything,' Anto said.

Dean took hold of Brenno and planted him against the bonnet. 'So, what's the truth, Brenno?'

'I didn't do it off my own bat, I swear. Let me go.'

'One of you better start filling me in. Anto?' Dean asked. 'What do you know?'

'Get your hands off Brenno and I'll tell you what I heard.'

Dean released him.

'Back at the factory, the day Bird put the debt on me — the two-hundred-grand fine for the missing gear . . .'

'Yeah, go on.'

'I overheard Jason and Bird talking. It was Jason who suggested having you offed,' Anto said. 'He said you were losing Bird too much money and you needed getting rid of. Bird told him he had gotten Brenno to do it, but that you got away. Then they discussed whether it was worth another try.'

'So, you're telling me two out of three of the Flynn brothers wanted me killed?'

'Sounds like it, yeah,' Anto said.

'But at least you can believe me now, Dean, it wasn't off my own bat,' Brenno said.

185

'That's little consolation, Brenno.'

'Yeah, true, I suppose.'

'But how do I know I can trust either of you?' Dean asked.

'I left that little memory card for you — well, I gave it to Cheryl. There has to be something good on it if one of the Flynns wanted it hidden away,' Brenno said.

'I'll bet you it's some random porno or something,' Anto said.

'No way,' Brenno said. 'This was hidden in Dwayne's office.'

'Dwayne? Oh shit, he's no joke,' Anto said.

'None of them are,' Brenno said.

'Now I'll have the third Flynn brother after me,' Dean said. 'Jesus Christ.'

'Let's figure out what is on it first. Did you get a chance to have a look, Dean?' Brenno asked.

Dean's brain was clouded from the week's drugs binge. 'I didn't get no little memory card,' he said. 'So, when did you give it to Cheryl?'

'A good while ago,' Brenno said.

'Where did you meet her?'

'She was on her way to work. It was the bank holiday Monday. She said you'd headed off up north. You should have told me you were going. There was something I need to tell you about—'

'Wait. Why did you give it to Cheryl?' Dean said.

'I couldn't chance Bird seeing me with you so soon after the hit. And I knew you had a regular thing with her and you've always said you trust her, so I thought, why not?'

'Did you see her after that, Brenno?'

'No. But wait, listen, the equipment. Bird's stuff—'

'Cheryl was murdered a few days ago. Beaten to death.'

Brenno looked like he'd been struck with something heavy. 'Fuck.'

'Yeah. Fuck,' Anto said. 'You do realize what this means, don't you?'

'No,' Brenno said.

'You're probably the last person to have seen her alive.'

'How could I have been? She was on her way into work. Anyway, Dean must have seen her. Didn't you, Dean?'

Dean hadn't seen Cheryl since before he got shot. Now he wasn't ever going to see her again. 'No, she wasn't available. I took Aimee instead. Danielle said that Cheryl was off. What day did you say you saw her?'

'The bank holiday Monday.'

'Beaten to death. Shit. Nasty way to go. Was it a sex game gone wrong, I wonder?' Anto asked.

'Show a bit of respect for the dead.'

'Jesus. Sorry, Dean.'

'You will be if I hear you talking shit about her.'

Dean turned back to Brenno. 'Tell me more about this memory card.'

'Bird beat the shit out of me for not finishing you off. I was trying to clean myself up in the toilet off Dwayne's office and I found it in the cistern. It was in a cash box. All wrapped in plastic. I opened it up, and the only thing inside was this memory card — SD card or whatever you call it. It was small enough to stick behind one of the loops on my jeans. I gave it to Cheryl to pass on to you.'

'We need to find it,' Anto said.

'But we've no idea where it is,' Brenno added.

'Her flat?' Anto asked.

'It's probably crawling with detectives. Was her body found there?' Brenno asked.

'No, in an alley,' Dean said.

'She could still have had it on her,' Dean said. 'Which means the cops have got it. If they haven't, it could be anywhere.'

'A tiny SD card. We'll never find it,' Anto said.

'We'll find a way,' Brenno said.

'If it's that important to the Flynns, and one of them realizes it's you who took it, Brenno, and that we knew about it too, we are all dead,' Anto said.

'But if Jason ordered the hit on me in the first place, he won't be happy till I'm dead anyway.' Dean stared at Brenno.

'Bird was the one that gave me the order. Are you sure about what you heard, Anto?' Brenno said.

'On my daughter's life.'

'Fuck,' Brenno said.

'Yeah, fuck,' Dean said. 'Jason is a whole other level. Christ, remember the damage he did to that young fella who shorted him on a deal that time?'

'Yeah, not a joint left in his body, he bounced the hammer off him so hard,' Brenno said.

'Hammer Flynn. Would you ever be brave enough to call him that to his face, Brenno?'

'No fucking way, Dean. Call him that and they'd be the last words you'd spit.'

'At least Dwyane is out of the picture for the moment. He's gone abroad. No one knows when he'll be back,' Anto said.

'I hope he's in no hurry back to Dublin, because he's like a heat-seeking missile if he's out to get someone. He doesn't give up for anything,' Dean said.

'There's talk of him and Bird expanding his haulage business,' Brenno said. 'He's meant to be sorting it at the moment — in the Caribbean, New Orleans, or some such place. Even Romania, for all I know. Listen, Dean, they'll wipe the floor with you business-wise if they succeed. You, Ged and now Dani are the only things standing in their way. They're talking drugs, people trafficking, the lot. We need to get on top of this.'

'Fuck you, Brenno. There'll be no wiping the floor with any Lewis, and don't you ever let me hear you say different. We are coming out on top. They'll be licking our boots, you wait and see. That is why you two are collaborating with me. The Flynn family have done nothing but fuck you both over, so from now on, you'll be my chief enforcers. I need to find this machinery, though. And the funds. Da is working on other things that should net us a few million, but in the meantime, my own stuff needs to be sorted.'

Anto whistled. 'Wow, a few million.'

'Listen, Dean, I've been trying to tell you. It was me moved the equipment,' Brenno said.

'What? Why?'

'Because I was afraid that Bird was on to the location. Your lads did the right thing bringing it there, but I got it diverted.'

'Where to?'

'Um, Bird's empty warehouse at the Eastpoint Business Park.'

'Are you off your head?' Dean said.

'Nope.'

'You've given Bird the low-loader, digger and the fucking money?'

'Not exactly. He doesn't use that place much.'

'And you're only telling me this now?'

'I was just about to when you told us about Cheryl. God rest her soul.' Brenno made a sign of the cross. 'I figured that if Bird got it back, he'd be happier and wouldn't have any more reason to have you killed.'

'Are you really that thick?' Anto asked.

'What? No. My ma says there's always a peaceful solution and sometimes you've to dig deep to find it.'

'You mean you moved it to the place where he met my da and Danielle to tell them he wasn't behind the hit on me?'

'First off, I didn't know they'd be meeting there. Anyway, it was after that, obviously. And he won't go there again unless he needs to. So I can tell him it's there when the time is right.'

'You're talking about a seven-tonne Hitachi excavator, tractor and trailer, not a fucking handbag for your spare fucking underpants. You can't just move them on a whim. What the fuck, Brenno? Not to mention my wasted journey to the North. I could have been stopped at any time. In fact, some dope did drive into the back of me, and I'd to persuade him not to call the cops.' Dean dragged his hands through his hair.

'Shit, Dean, you said strict phone silence. We weren't due to meet until tomorrow as it is. I couldn't run anything by you, so I used my initiative.'

'I'll take your initiative and shove it up your hole.'

'Please, Dean, wait. There's logic to what he's saying,' Anto said. 'Hear him out.'

'This logic better be good, that's all I can say.'

Brenno took a deep breath. 'Bird says I owe him a hundred and forty-five grand for the missing machinery. It's my punishment for not putting you in the ground.'

'Where are you going to get that kind of money?'

'This is what I'm telling you. I was thinking I'd tell him I recovered the equipment, get him to agree to clear the debt and keep it hidden and he'd make an insurance claim. Then he'll be quids in and not mad with you. No money owed and I'm back in his trust.'

Dean took in a sharp breath. 'I'm the one who has to give this the nod. Not you.'

'Of course, Dean, you're the boss. I did think it was a clever plan, though. You'd have thought of it yourself, told me to go ahead — if we'd been able to talk. Better than him finding the place in Fermanagh and taking it back himself, and the money.'

'Hmm, right, I get you,' Dean said.

'You're okay with that, so?' Brenno asked.

'I wouldn't say that. I can see the advantage of getting him off your back to keep looking for it, but I can't risk him still claiming it's missing and blaming me. What if he cancels your debt, but orders another hit?'

'That's where I thought I'd tell him you agreed. That way, he'll still believe you don't know who shot you. Gives him the impression that I have an in with you, and it's to his advantage.'

'Have you spoken to him already?' Dean asked.

'I had to say something to get his brain into gear. He has no idea that I'm the one who stashed it. I suggested he claim off the insurance.'

'Without talking to me first?'

'I knew you'd have come up with it yourself, given the time,' Brenno said.

'Right, yeah,' Dean said. 'Wait. You're not playing me, are you?'

'No way, Dean. I swear on my ma's life. Would I have given you the SD card if I was?'

'You didn't give it to me, you gave it to Cheryl, and now we have no clue where it is.'

'Well, I didn't expect her to be killed now, did I?' Brenno said.

Dean gave him an evil look.

'Sorry.'

'Back to the money. Where is it?'

'I have it secured,' Brenno said.

'It better be secured at my place in the next two hours.'

'Yes, of course. I was always going to get it to you.'

'Right. Anything else?'

'What should I do about the cash he says I owe him for the loss of the drugs?' Anto asked. 'It had nothing to do with me. But that doesn't worry Bird. He seems to be able to tax anyone he wants.'

'What exactly has he said about it?' Dean asked. 'That you've to pay up or else you're for the mincer? What?'

'No. Just that I'm the one who now owes it.'

'Why?'

'Despite the rat being one of his men, he said I should have known — and that he was talking to the cops under my watch. He did say he'd let me off the debt if I do a job for him instead. But fuck knows what that will be. What kind of a job pays two hundred grand? Another hit?'

'Bollocks to that. Bird needs to be taken out,' Dean said.

'Jesus Christ, that is a huge move, Dean. But it would solve a lot,' Anto said.

'But then we're left with Jason and Dwayne,' Brenno said. 'They're not going to lie down and do nothing if their brother is killed.'

'We just have to be cleverer than them, then,' Dean said.

'With all our brainpower combined,' Anto said, 'we should be sorted.'

'Let's get out of here, in case we're seen together. We'll meet again in two hours — my place — and work out a solid plan.' Dean turned and headed for the van. 'And don't forget the cash.'

'No worries, Dean,' said Brenno. 'You can rely on me.'

CHAPTER 34

Five days after Jake Brady's funeral, there was still no sign of Hazel. In the meantime, Danielle had to get back to running the business. *This is what mothers must feel like*, she thought, *trying to combine everything*. She smiled down at the baby in the buggy Mark had found for her. The girls in the Berkley Street business were charmed by her cute dimples and tiny fingers, but whenever her nappy needed changing, they were suddenly busy elsewhere. Danielle's options on who to get to mind the baby were limited.

'I'll change her,' Aimee offered.

'You sure?'

'Yeah, I don't mind a crappy nappy. I've baby sisters. I can feed her too, if she's due one.'

Danielle rooted into the bag for a bottle, which she handed to Aimee. 'Thanks for doing that.'

Baby Girl Brady started to grumble and wriggle. She opened her mouth to let out a yell and her soother tumbled to the floor, bouncing out of sight.

'Shit.' Danielle got down on to her hands and knees and felt around on the floor, while the baby began to scream. She peered under the counter and saw the soother, lodged in the panel beneath. 'I have it.' She lay flat, hooked her finger round it and tugged. She held up the soother to Aimee. 'Here. Give it a rinse.'

'I know.' Aimee glanced down at the prone Danielle. 'You've held your figure well for just after giving birth. You didn't even look pregnant.'

'She's not mine.'

'Oh, I see. You got caught to babysit. Well, if you're ever stuck, I can help. I love babies.'

'Thanks, Aimee.'

Aimee headed off, carrying the squawking tiny person, wipes and a nappy.

The panel beneath the counter had come loose, so while she was down there, Danielle thought she might as well slot it back in place. It immediately popped out. She tried again, and then realized there was something behind it — a blue leather handbag. Why would anyone stick that in there?

Danielle pulled it out. It was a Tom Ford, designer and expensive. She opened it up and looked inside. It was empty but for a pochette containing a passport-size photo of Cheryl. Danielle turned it over. Written on the back was the name Sarah Cooper. Her throat tightened. She hadn't been able to find the details of Cheryl's funeral in the press. Now she had her real name.

Meanwhile, what should she do with the handbag? Give it to someone — a sister or mother? But how to explain where she'd found it, who she was and how she knew Cheryl — or rather, Sarah? Could she leave it in the church with her picture in it? No, someone else might take it. She couldn't leave it here, either.

As she slid the photo back in, her fingers touched something small and flat. She took it out and held it in her palm. It was a micro SD card.

Danielle got to her feet and rooted around in one of the drawers for an adapter so she could view it on the computer. No luck. She'd buy one on the way home. She'd be better off looking at it away from Berkley Street anyway. If it was stuffed behind the panel like that, it was bound to be dodgy.

She pushed it back into the pochette and idly pulled open the front zip. Jesus Christ. There were rolls of fifties in there, it looked like a few grand. Was this what Cheryl was killed for? Hastily, she thrust the bag inside hers.

Using the torch on her phone, she checked to see if anything else had been hidden behind the panel, and found a set of keys attached to a grimy-looking pink fur pom-pom. While she was fitting the panel back into place, the buzzer went. She scrambled to her feet, knocking her head on the edge of the desk.

It was Pat.

'What are you doing with them?'

He was pointing to the keys still dangling from her little finger.

'Oh these? I found them lying on the floor. Why? Have you seen them before?'

He held her gaze for a moment. 'They're for a place only a few of us know about.'

She looked from the keys back to him. 'Go on.'

He glanced around. There was no one nearby.

'It's where Ged brings the Eastern European girls. That's what he was doing in Belfast. There are eight girls due down the day after tomorrow.'

'I thought it was another kind of delivery.'

'Yes, that's covered, but then he returned to Belfast to sort out the girls.'

'No wonder he's not rushing back.'

They smiled at each other.

'Yeah. When they arrive, they stay in the house you've the keys for. They entertain a few high-profile clients, then some of them move on to Limerick and Cork.'

'Would any of the girls be brought here to work?'

'Hmm, not usually. Dean uses the place. I think he took Cheryl there a few times, maybe Aimee too. It's inconspicuous and secure.'

'Oh, so why not bring those girls here to work for me?'

'They're for a specific set of people who prefer a little more discretion.'

'Right. I wouldn't mind hosting one of those events.' Someone there might have the answers she needed.

He raised an eyebrow. 'Not unless you want to get stuck in yourself.'

'Ah, I see. No thank you.'

'I'm glad to hear it.'

'Really?'

'Yes. Hey, do you want to see what this house looks like? It's something else.'

'Yes. Oh, wait. I have the baby.'

'What baby?'

'Did Mark not tell you? I had a run-in with Hazel when I got there — she was completely off her head. It wasn't safe to leave the baby with her, she might have done her some harm, so I took her away. I wasn't intending to keep the baby, just until Hazel got a bit of help to look after her, but now she's gone missing and no one can get hold of her.'

'Jesus Christ.'

'That's one way of putting it.'

'Right, um.' He checked his watch. 'Linda is due on. Let her look after it.'

'She is not an "it",' Danielle said. 'I'm not sure. According to Hazel, Linda "couldn't mind a bag of chips", let alone a baby.'

'Wait a second.' Aimee, holding a now perfectly content bundle of pink, was staring at Danielle. 'You never said this was Hazel's kid. What the fuck are you doing with her?'

Danielle's jaw tightened. 'Who do you think you're talking to?'

Aimee's mouth opened. 'Er . . .'

'Well? Don't you dare speak to me like that again.'

'I . . . Sorry.' Aimee blushed.

'Give her here.' Danielle held out her arms.

Pat watched her take the sleeping infant. 'You're a natural, Danielle.'

She bit her lip, recalling that first scan and the heart-beat intertwined with her own, Jason holding her hand and squeezing. Both of them with glowing smiles, awash with joy and love. Then the heartrending loss. She swallowed.

'This is a temporary arrangement,' Danielle said to them both. 'As soon as we can locate Hazel, she is going back.'

'Why? Where is Hazel?' Aimee said.

'We don't know,' Pat said.

Aimee took out her phone and made a call. 'It's going straight to voicemail.'

'We keep checking the house, but there's no sign of her,' Danielle said.

'I know she was struggling a bit,' Aimee said. 'And her nephew dying and all.'

'Do you have any idea where she might have gone?' Danielle asked her.

'Have you tried her family?'

'Yes. Well, Mark has,' Danielle said. 'They say they haven't seen her, and they don't want to, either. They cut her off when she got with Ged. Let me know if you do hear anything, or she rings you. Tell her the baby is safe.'

'I will.'

'Aimee?' Pat said. 'Can you look after her for a while?'

'What about my earnings?' Aimee said.

'She has three punters booked in for today,' Danielle added.

The buzzer sounded and Linda appeared on the screen. Danielle let her in.

Pat regarded the baby for a moment. 'Look, bring her. If we get stopped by the guards, we'll look like a regular couple with a child.'

'Why would we get stopped by the guards?' Danielle said.

'You never know where they'll be lurking. She'll be fine — so long as she doesn't start bawling.'

'Nah, she's quiet, aren't you, Baby Girl Brady?'

Danielle loaded her into the car, along with her handbag, forgetting that it held a little more weight than usual.

She wondered what sort of place this was going to be. Somewhere discreet, for sex, and plenty of it. Was that his intention in taking her there? The penthouse wasn't ideal, what with people arriving at all hours of the day and night. She glanced at Pat. Maybe he wasn't thinking along those lines at all, especially now they had a baby on board. Anyway, why leave it to him to make the next move? It was up to her to decide which way she wanted things to go. A kiss, that's all it was, something that happened in the heat of an argument. Stupid and ridiculous. Plus, it risked totally derailing her plan.

'Here we are.'

A high wall. Large timber gates, which swung open at their approach. It took Danielle by surprise. She had been expecting a secluded little flat tucked away in a mews somewhere, not a mansion in Foxrock with a garden the size of a field. She gazed up at the expansive red-tiled roof, the timber gables.

'Wow.'

The property, surrounded as it was by trees and tall hedges, could have been out in the countryside rather than the outskirts of a busy city.

He parked to the side of the house and walked around the back. She followed him, carrying the baby.

'Go on. You have the keys.'

An alarm beeped as she opened the door. The baby didn't stir. Pat entered a code on a panel by the door and the noise stopped. Picking up the baby carrier, he led Danielle through to the kitchen, a vast expanse of stainless steel like that of a restaurant.

'Here.' He set the baby down on a wide bench. 'Lock the door. No one will come in, but just to be safe. She'll be fine here while we take a tour.'

Danielle sniffed. 'Do you smell that?'

'I do.'

'Not changed the bins lately?' she asked. 'It's pretty ripe.'

'The cleaner comes every Friday,' Pat said. 'I'll just check the roster to see if she's due. Meanwhile, feel free to have a nose around, and if the baby wakes up, I'll ring you.'

'Ring me?'

He grinned. 'Yeah. Don't get lost because the rooms are soundproofed, and I won't hear you scream if you get into trouble.'

Trouble? Surely they were alone here? Was she safe with him? But she remembered the way he'd kissed her, how gentle he was being with the baby.

She climbed the stairs, went into the first room on the right and saw spots. She blinked. Leopard print on the walls, leopard print on the ceiling, leopard print on the rumpled covers of the unmade bed, even on the furniture. One of the dresser drawers had a key hanging from it. Unable to resist the temptation, she turned the key and opened it. Inside was a cash box, its lid open, nothing in it but a bunch of elastic bands and some empty money bags.

So there had been cash in this cash box. She glanced at her handbag slung over her shoulder, Cheryl's bag still inside. Pat had said Dean used to bring Cheryl here. Did the money in her bag come from here? Even if it was Dean's money and he was keeping it safe here, it wasn't worth killing her for. Pat needed to see this. She pulled out the cash box and locked the drawer.

The next room was all glitter and glam, totally over the top. Even the floorboards had sparkles in the varnish. For fuck's sake. Who the hell did the decor? The next room was more tastefully decorated and the bed was made with clean, fresh-smelling sheets.

Someone came up behind her and took hold of her arms. The cash box clattered to the floor. Warm breath on her neck, lips just tickling her skin. Danielle relaxed, melted. She turned and kissed Pat, hard, on the lips. Suddenly, he pushed her aside.

She staggered backwards. When she regained her balance, he was on his knees, staring at something in his palm.

He held it out towards her — a gold chain with the letter 'H' inscribed on it. Pat lay flat on his belly and reached under the bed.

'Recognize this?' He was holding a brown silk scarf.

'It looks like Hazel's,' she said. 'I think she was wearing it the day I collected her from the maternity hospital.'

'What was that you dropped when I came in?' he asked.

'A cash box,' Danielle said and picked it up.

Pat took it from her. 'Dean uses elastic bands and money bags for rolls of fifties. He keeps thousands at a time in here.'

'Why keep it here?' she asked. 'Why not a safe or something, if he didn't want to bank it?'

'Dean calls this his play money, like petty cash. There's always a large amount of money in here.'

'You seem to know a lot about it,' Danielle said.

'He treats that cash box like a wallet, dips into it whenever he feels like it. We all know it's here.'

'Could one of the girls have taken it?' she said.

'It'd be taking a huge risk. Who knows what he'd do if he found them.'

'Could he beat them to death?'

'You mean Cheryl? Nah. He was looking for her, but to screw, not to murder.'

'Yes, but maybe he was saying that to cover himself if suspicion fell on him.'

'That's risky talk there, Danielle.'

'Why? What's he going to do to his own blood, beat me to death too?'

Needing to clear her head, Danielle left the room. Opposite was a closed door. Inside, she found a bathroom with a jacuzzi and an enormous shower. She withdrew and turned to a door at the other end of the hall. It was locked. She pressed her ear to it.

'You wouldn't hear anything.' Coming up beside her, Pat took the keys from her and opened it.

The foul smell knocked her backwards. Her hand to her mouth, she peered inside, trying to locate the source of the smell.

She saw clothes strewn across the bed, a pair of shoes and a handbag on the floor. The bag was definitely Hazel's, Danielle remembered seeing it hanging on the banister. But hadn't Mark said it was on the table when he'd checked the house? Maybe that was another one.

The door to the en suite stood ajar, a foot protruding, blotched, purple, toenails painted silver. The smell was intolerable.

Danielle knew who they would find. Almost black against the white tiles of the floor, lay Hazel's rotting corpse.

CHAPTER 35

The stench followed them downstairs and into the kitchen. Danielle pulled her phone from her pocket.

Pat snatched it from her hand. 'What the fuck are you doing?'

'Calling the police, of course.'

'Why?'

'*Why*? Are we just going to leave her?'

'She killed herself with too much gear. Did you not see the state of her?'

The state of her was burned into Danielle's brain. 'Hazel deserves answers, a decent burial. Anyway, I don't believe she was suicidal.'

'How the fuck do you know?'

'I don't think she was alone here. You don't come here to find solitude. This is a place to party. Her chain, the scarf on the floor in a different room. The chain is broken. It could have been pulled off. She could have been strangled with the scarf, then dragged into the bathroom to make it look like an overdose. The door was locked, Pat.'

'Jesus, Dani, slow down. Your imagination is gone a little wild there.'

'Let's hear your theories then, genius.'

'There was a key inside. I managed to shove it out of the lock when I opened it. It was on the floor when we entered the room.'

She didn't remember seeing any key. Though that didn't mean it wasn't there.

'Look, Dani, we can't call the cops to a house used by the family for entertaining high-profile clients with sex workers. Have you thought about the outcome? You say she deserves a decent burial — well, why? She couldn't even be bothered to fucking name her baby.'

'Fuck this, Pat.'

'You're not thinking, Dani. The Lewis family has worked hard to take the spotlight off themselves. There have been no killings, no shootings, no assaults, in years.'

'What about Dean's shooting? The arson attack on the pub?' Danielle said.

'Dean is not pressing charges and the arson attack was an insurance job.'

'But the petrol bomb landed right where I was sitting,' she said.

'That was unlucky. It wasn't meant to happen until much later.'

'Wasn't meant to? Jesus. What else are you not telling me?'

Pat sighed. 'Dean was jealous because Ged decided to have you run the pub instead of him. He got those young fellas on the dirt bike — the cousins, Jake and Sean Brady — to lob a couple of petrol bombs into it to do some damage and delay handing over to you while Dean tried to persuade his da to change his mind. The boys weren't meant to do it until later, after everyone had left. They fucked up.'

'Did Dean . . . ?'

'What? Kill them? I'm not sure. They could have pissed off other people besides Dean. It could have been anyone.'

'How do you know so much about the arson attack?' Danielle asked.

Pat shook his head. 'I've said too much already.'

'You spoke to Sean Brady again, didn't you?'

Pat said nothing.

'Come on. You can't stop there.'

'Yes, I spoke to Sean Brady.'

'He told you they were working for Dean?'

'Yes, but Dean was furious about what had happened. He was ranting.'

'And yet you were with us at Clonliffe View and saw how stressed we were. We were all wondering who was attacking us, and you just sat there saying nothing. You didn't even tell Ged?'

'Do you remember when we had to rush away — me, Mark and Ged?'

She thought back to that night. She'd been left in the apartment with Ann and Ritchie. 'I do.'

'We were called to the maternity hospital. Hazel had just given birth. So I wasn't about to bring it up then, was I? Besides, it was Dean's place to tell his father, not mine. If I told Ged and then Dean denied he had anything to do with it, what do you think would have happened to me?'

'But Ged trusted you, surely he'd take your word for it.'

'Over Dean's word? I doubt it.'

'And you spoke to Sean after Jake was shot?'

'Yes, and he confirmed that Dean had gotten them to carry out the arson attack.'

'Jesus. Jake was only a child. To have had him killed for that? That's low.'

'They wanted into the business. There are consequences. But like I said, we have no idea who was behind Jake's shooting.'

'Come on.'

'It could be anyone, Dani, and that is that. Drop it now.'

'Fine. But back to Dean's shooting. The guards are still investigating it, aren't they?'

'I told you Dean didn't make a statement.'

'It was still the discharge of a firearm. Under the Offences Against the State Act, the guards can't just ignore it.'

'You seem to know an awful lot about the law,' Pat said.

She knew much more than that, thanks to her own case.

'Don't they need proof that a firearm had been discharged?' Pat asked.

'Did they not seal the scene when they arrived? Were the bullet casings collected? Since Dean was trying to save his own arse — literally — at the time, I doubt he thought of picking them up. What about witnesses? Neighbours, taxi drivers, anyone with a dashcam?'

'Jesus Christ, Dani. We should plant you in the cop shop. You can warn us if they're sniffing too close.'

'That's not even remotely funny. Look, Pat, if you want to keep a step ahead of them, you've to think like them.'

Danielle looked around.

'What are you looking for?' he asked.

'A toilet that doesn't contain a body.'

'Behind you. There's one just off the utility room.'

Away from Pat's presence, she was able to think more clearly about the situation. Pat had a point. The guards would want to know who the house belonged to, leading them to the extended Lewis family — to her. But if she helped to cover up Hazel's death, what about her daughter? How could she tell her that her mother was found on a bathroom floor, a spoon and a lighter beside her, a needle protruding from her arm.

Danielle had always known that returning to Dublin and back to the family would be risky. But how far was she willing to go to find her answers? Getting involved in the undignified disposal of a body would serve her purpose, but was it right? Oh God, the plan was going south. She needed to get out.

'Have you fallen in?'

'I'm fine.' She returned to the kitchen. 'Okay. Do what you need to do.'

'There's no danger of you getting back up on your moral high horse?'

'No. She chose to take drugs. There's no point her taking all of us down with her. She's not worth it.' The baby stirred.

Her tiny fingers clenched and released. Danielle looked at her for a moment, tenderly. Then she turned away. 'Do you need to make calls, Pat?'

'Yes. Do you want to leave? What you don't hear, you can't tell.'

'Yeah, she'll be hungry when she wakes. I'll get a bottle while you do your thing.'

'Okay. Leave it with me. And here . . .' He handed her Hazel's scarf and chain.

Danielle shoved them in her bag, which now contained mementos from two dead women. She took the baby out to the car, fed and changed her and returned to check on Pat, leaving the baby asleep in the car seat.

'I'm still thinking we should report Hazel missing,' she said.

'Why?'

'She worked for us. I have her daughter. They could wonder why she hasn't been to collect her. And what about her relatives? They'll wonder why she didn't go to the funeral.'

'None of that is our problem. From what I hear, her family aren't too fussed about her since she got with Ged.'

'Bird or Marion might tell the guards or the social workers that I have the baby.'

'Let them. The child is fine, she's being well looked after.'

'What do I say if someone calls to check, a social worker or someone? Won't they wonder why Hazel didn't attend any follow-up medical appointments?'

'Tell them the truth. Hazel left her in your care and she hasn't turned up to collect her, nor is she answering her phone. I presume you did call her?'

'Mark did.'

'Right, someone did. Fuck it after that. Come on, Danielle, think like a Lewis. What's one thing you're all good at?'

'Making money.'

'That and diverting attention to others. Covering up. Just focus on what you need to, don't overthink this. You came back for a reason. Don't go getting yourself embroiled in something that's easily sorted.'

'What do you mean, I came back for a reason? I wanted to be reunited with my family,' Danielle said.

'Exactly. What did you think I meant?'

Shit. 'Nothing. I'm upset, that's all. That smell is stuck at the back of my throat. I need a drink, something strong. These clothes need to go, too. Don't worry. I'll get myself right.'

'Do. Sooner rather than later.'

She opened her mouth to give him a smart retort, but nothing came out.

'Right, come on,' Pat said.

'Where to?'

He pointed through the kitchen window, towards a shed, tucked away underneath the hedge.

Danielle went out. The baby was still asleep.

'Shit. The cash box.' Danielle rushed back upstairs to retrieve it.

When she got to the shed, she found Pat in a tracksuit, the clothes he had been wearing lying in a barrel.

'Right, strip,' he said.

She changed into the clothes Pat tossed over to her. It was the first time she'd been naked in front of him, but he wasn't looking. Instead, he was busy pouring petrol on to their discarded clothing. He set it alight.

'Now, let's get the fuck out of here and leave the experts to clear up.'

'And Hazel's body?'

'They'll deal with that.'

'How do you get in touch with the likes of them, then?' she asked.

'Too many questions, Dani.'

'Is that what you meant when you said the Lewis family are good at covering up?'

'When did I say that?'

'Just now. When we were still in the house.'

He sighed. 'Dani, this is a stressful situation. Take no notice of what I say. Now, are you hungry?'

'Jesus, how can you even think of eating? I don't think I'll be hungry for the next week.'

'Fine. I'm grabbing something once we're finished here.'

What kind of a human being was he? Cold, businesslike, ticking jobs off a to-do list . . .

A. Organize the disposal of a dead body.

B. Get takeaway.

Shit. She told herself that this family — her family — needed to be cold in order to survive in the criminal world. She was being naive; it was stupid of her to let a kiss obliterate the truth of what Pat was — her uncle's lackey, and nobody's romantic hero.

Suddenly, they heard a vehicle roar up to the gate and scream to a halt. A van door opened and slammed shut.

'Is that the cleanup guys?' Danielle asked.

'Can't be. I just rang them. They said they'd be here in twenty minutes.'

'Pat, the baby's in the car.'

'Well, what do you expect me to do about it?' he said.

'Get her.'

'Jesus Christ. I didn't sign up for this shit.'

He took his gun from his belt and crept towards the car, Danielle following, her pistol in her hand. Pat crouched down behind the car, while she risked a peek at the still-sleeping baby.

The gate opened and Dean raced in, his eyes on the car. They stood up and Pat called to him, just as he reached for his gun. When he saw who it was, he put it back in his jacket and slowed to a walk. 'Christ, Pat. I could have shot you.'

'What are you doing here?' Pat said, putting his own gun away.

'Me? What the hell are you two doing here?'

'Checking that everything's clean and ready for the girls tomorrow,' Pat said.

'Oh, right, the girls. Me too,' Dean said.

'Oh really?' Danielle couldn't picture Dean giving a crap about whether the place was clean or not.

'Yeah, and, ah, the last time I was here I left something after me. Upstairs. Good job I met you two. I left my keys after me, too.'

'Here.' Pat tossed them over. They fell at his feet.

Dean looked down, then up at Pat again.

'We found them inside,' Pat said.

Danielle raised an eyebrow. This was news to her.

Dean picked the keys up and started to move towards the house. Pat stood in front of him, blocking his path. 'You can't go in there.'

'Get the fuck out of my way,' Dean said.

'Fine.' Pat stepped aside.

'Wait. What's going on?' Dean asked.

'Go and see for yourself,' Pat said.

Dean turned to Danielle. 'What's going on?'

'There's a body upstairs,' Pat said.

'Who?' He looked at each of them in turn. 'One of you better tell me. Now.'

'Hazel. And from the looks of it, she's been there a couple of days,' Pat said.

Dean kicked out at a small rock, which bounced against the car. The baby began to cry. 'Jesus Christ. Was the child here too, around her dead body?'

'Um, yeah,' Pat lied. 'She's fine, though, don't worry.'

'Sick bitch. Back on the gear, after she's only just fired out the sprog. Whore.' He spat on the ground. Meanwhile, a cloud of black smoke drifted into the air. Dean looked up at it and then back to Pat. 'I get it. That's why you're slumming it in the trackie.'

'Exactly. The cleaners are due any minute, so we'd better get the fuck out of here,' Pat said.

'Wait, no, I need to get something from inside.'

'I hope you haven't had your lunch,' Danielle said.

'That bad?'

'That bad,' she said.

'Nah, have to do it.' Dean continued into the house, Danielle following.

He took the stairs two at a time, stopping halfway up to retch.

As Danielle expected, he headed straight for the leopard-print room and began pulling open various drawers. He stopped at the dresser and fumbled through the keys.

'Here, Dean. Let me help.' Danielle took them from him and found the correct one. 'Are you by any chance looking for a cash box?'

Before she knew what was happening, he'd shoved her back against the wall, his hand at her throat. 'What the fuck do you know about that?'

She struggled until black spots rose up in front of her eyes. In a last determined effort, she dug her fingernails into the back of his hand and, with her other hand, felt in her pocket for the gun. She lost her grip and it fell to the floor with a thump. The noise distracted him and caused him to loosen his grip slightly. Her knee connected hard with his balls. He folded, whimpering. Snatching up the weapon, she pointed it at his head.

'What the hell's going on?' Pat was standing in the doorway.

Danielle shook her head, unable to speak. Pat eased the gun from her fingers, and she staggered over to the window to get some air. Looking down, she saw a car drive in and park outside the front door.

'It's the cleaners,' Pat said. 'Come on. Out. Now. We don't want them thinking our vehicles are part of the job.'

Pat helped the groaning Dean down the stairs and outside. He retrieved Danielle's bag, keys and the cash box and handed them to her.

Dean's eyes opened wide. 'Here. That's the fucking box I was looking for. Where's the cash that was in it?'

'It was empty when I found it,' Danielle croaked.

'Was it now?'

'Fuck off, Dean.'

'Come on, we need to get out of here,' Pat said. 'Can you drive, Dean?'

'Yeah, Look, sorry, Dani — a red mist came over me. The money in that box is what I live on between jobs. No one touches it but me.'

'It really was empty,' she said, eyeing the thing with loathing. A stupid box that had nearly caused her death. 'Here. Have it back.'

Pat was in the car with the engine running. Dean hobbled towards his van. As they passed the cleaners' vehicle, she craned her neck to catch sight of the people inside.

'Don't even look,' Pat said.

The van and the car powered out through the open gates, passing a hearse on its way in. Pat pulled up alongside it and the driver handed a piece of paper to him.

'What's that?' Danielle asked.

'The number of the plot she'll be buried in. In time, her daughter might like to have a grave to visit.'

'Oh.'

'What did you think we were going to do? Dissolve her in a vat of acid?'

'Well, I . . .'

'What do you think this is, *Breaking Bad*? Jesus, Danielle.'

'Nothing would surprise me, after what's been going on.'

Danielle had agreed with Saoirse that there would be no contact unless things were going very wrong. Well, right now a lot was going wrong. It was getting too deep and too dirty. Danielle couldn't risk using her phone, so she decided on a written note. A few words, that was all, just enough to convey the seriousness of the situation and tell Saoirse to get back to Ireland as soon as she could.

CHAPTER 36

Dean, still in pain from where Danielle had kneed him in the balls, had a sudden urge to infuse something into his bloodstream, to zone out for a while and forget all this shit. Maybe Anto would have something handy, if not, he knew where to go. Brenno had dropped the money as planned and was due to call later for it to be divvied out.

He was going over all this in his mind, along with getting himself a decent car, when he heard the siren behind him. 'Fuck.' He indicated and pulled off on to the hard shoulder. In the side mirror, a guard loomed up from behind the van. He didn't need this shit today. He buzzed down the window, staring straight ahead, rhythmically squeezing the steering wheel.

'You drove through a red light back there,' the guard said.

'I don't think I did, Officer.'

'Oh yes you did. We were right behind you.'

'You must have driven through it too, then,' Dean said.

'It was a pedestrian crossing,' the guard said, ignoring Dean's comment.

'There wasn't anyone on it.'

'You were lucky then. Driver's licence, please, certificate of insurance too, if you have it on you. If not, it will do in ten days at your nearest Garda station.'

Dean retrieved the documents from the glove box. The card case with the details of the rear-ender tumbled to the floor in the process. Leaving the card holder where it was, he handed license and insurance certificate to the guard, who made a note of the details.

'Turn off your engine, please,' the guard said.

Dean switched off and watched the guard walk round to the front of the van and write down the registration number. Then he did the same with the discs on the windscreen. Tax and insurance were all up to date and displayed correctly. No prick in blue was going to catch him on a poxy road traffic offence.

Dean was seized with the impulse to turn the ignition back on and floor the accelerator. Instead, he snatched back the documents the guard held out to him between thumb and index finger. *Prick*. He turned on the ignition and put the van into first.

'Before you go . . .'

Dean glared at him. 'What now?'

'Get around, don't you?'

'What are you talking about?' Dean said.

'Monaghan.'

Now what? He could hardly deny it. The guy who'd rear-ended him must've reported the incident after all.

'I go lots of places. It's a free country.'

'Did you head north?'

'What if I did? Not against the law, is it?'

'Did you meet anyone along your route, say, not long after crossing Finn Bridge?'

'I couldn't tell you.'

'A guy popped into the station the other day, looking for a replacement driver's licence. Reported his lost, along with a few bank cards. He happened to mention an encounter with a man matching your description, down to the clothes you've on now, driving a Louth-registered van.'

Shit. Why hadn't he disposed of the van as soon as he got back? 'And what about it?'

'He says he couldn't find his card holder after your little, er, chat.'

The card holder on the floor at his feet seemed to pulse and glow. Dean kept his eyes forward. 'Then maybe he should look a bit harder for it, shouldn't he?'

'Maybe,' the guard said.

'They'll probably turn up when the replacement arrives. Usually happens.'

'Yeah, probably.'

'Anything else, Officer?'

'No. You can head off on your way now.'

'Thanks, Officer.' Dean rolled up the window and pulled away, muttering 'Wanker.'

Dean waited until the patrol car had disappeared before pulling in again and bending to retrieve the card holder. He took all the cards out, had a read of them and stuffed them back into the glove box.

He drove along Enniskerry Road, past tall trees and hedgerows, and took a left at the roundabout into Belarmine Avenue. Here, the hedges were neatly trimmed, and behind them blocks of apartments signalled the outskirts of the city. Finally, he came to an estate of detached houses. He turned in and drove around until he came to the house he was looking for. A black Audi stood in the driveway, the damage to the front grill still evident. Lazy bollocks hadn't even got it fixed.

He drove past the house, turned and went by again. He did one more drive past in the hope that the sight of him would be enough to put the shits up the fella who'd rear-ended him.

His mobile at his ear, the bearded guy emerged and headed for the rear of the car. Dean slowed to a crawl and buzzed the window down. Bearded guy glanced up. They looked at one another. Dean grinned and put his finger to his temple in imitation of a gun. Bearded guy scowled and shook his head.

His attention on the man, Dean didn't see the woman run out into the road. Dean couldn't stop in time. All he saw were the handles of a buggy and something flying in the air. There was a thud and bump as he floored the pedal and drove hard towards the roundabout. He was halfway around it when a patrol car came into view, approaching at speed. Lights flashing, it pulled across in front of him. He contemplated driving at it when another, unmarked car, pulled in behind him.

Before he even knew what was happening, his door was flung open. Strong hands grabbed him, dragged him out. As his hands and knees planted on the tarmac, he knew he was screwed. If the child he'd hit survived, it would surely have horrendous injuries.

One of the guards dragged him upright and cuffed his hands behind his back. '. . . *not obliged to say anything* . . .' He'd heard the caution before. It was the guy who'd stopped him.

'Watch the shoulder. It's damaged.'

'Explain this.' Another guard came over and thrust something in his face.

'I told you, watch the shoulder. Police brutality.' He looked around. 'Is anyone recording this intimidation?' he shouted to the empty road.

'We found it in the glove box of the van you were driving. It was reported lost, so since it's in your possession, we could be looking at theft.'

'Kiss my arse.'

The guard who'd cuffed him pulled Dean towards the marked cars, shoved him into the back seat and slammed the door.

The passenger door opened. 'Well, you weren't first in the queue when they gave out the brains,' the woman detective said.

'Fuck you and your red head,' muttered Dean.

She laughed and flicked her ginger ponytail. 'It's Detective Teegan to you, Dean Lewis. We're seizing the van, too.'

'What am I being arrested for?'

'Apart from dangerous driving, try theft.' She waved the card holder, now wrapped in a clear plastic bag.

'Yeah. So what? I found it.'

'Where did you find it?'

'On the road. A few days ago.'

'Where?'

'Past Finn Bridge in Monaghan.'

'And you were driving so slowly that you saw this little thing on the road, and, ever so helpfully, you stopped to pick it up.'

'Yeah, yeah. It only had cards in it, no money. Nothing is missing. The address is on the licence, and I was dropping it back to the man. That's not a crime.'

'Dangerous driving and leaving the scene of a traffic accident is,' Detective Teegan said.

'What dangerous driving? He ran into the back of me. He was wrong. Everyone knows that's the law. Like the ad on the telly one time said, always expect the unexpected. The driver behind should be able to stop and he didn't. I offered to let him off, 'cause the van's a piece of crap anyway. So how's that an offence on my part, Detective?'

'You are very sure of yourself, aren't you, Dean?'

'Yeah, so what? He's wrong, not me. I've done nothing except return the man's property.'

'When? Where?'

'Where what?'

'Did the man run into the back of you?'

'In Monaghan.'

'And you didn't report it?'

'Nah. If anyone left the scene of the accident, he did, especially since he was in the wrong. Arrest him for not reporting it.'

'Thanks for the information.'

'You're welcome. Wait. What information?'

'The information you just gave me about the RTC in Monaghan.'

'But you said about leaving the scene of an accident.'

'Yes, I was talking about the accident that just happened here at Belarmine, not Monaghan. I didn't know about that one until you told me.'

Shit, he was losing his edge. And now she was talking in Garda-speak. 'What's RTC?'

'Road traffic collision.'

'Right.'

'What business had you in Monaghan?' she asked.

'Mind your own fucking business, you smart bitch. Anyway, were you following me? You were. That's police intimidation. That's what caused the accident here; you distracted me.'

'No, we weren't following you. We were on our way to a funeral on the other side of the city when we had a call come in about a suspicious van driving around, the driver behaving in an intimidating manner. This was followed immediately by another call about an accident. We were passing and came across you. I understand those guards had already pulled you over once and spoken to you. They too happened to be nearby.'

'Yeah. Like a rash. Well, I'm delighted I made it easy for you all. Maybe I wanted you to catch me.'

'Why would you want that?'

'So I can sue the holes off ye for wrongful arrest. Bet you can't wait to get me in an interview room. You and me, Ginger, bring it on. Bet you'd love a bit of this.' He thrust his hips upwards. Pain shot down his leg.

She raised an eyebrow. Looked him up and down. 'Hah, I'd laugh at your best. No, I won't have the pleasure of interviewing you for this. As I said, we have a funeral to go to. We'll leave it to the member who arrested you. Good luck.'

She opened the car door.

'Wait.'

'What is it?' She sat back in her seat.

'Is the child all right?'

'Do you really give a shit?'

'Why do you think I'm asking?' Dean said.

'There was a child, but her mother grabbed her in time and managed to avoid the impact. It was a toy buggy and a baby doll on the road. It had rolled away from the little girl.'

'So I didn't hit a child or the woman?'

'No, you didn't.'

He let out a long breath. Lesser charges, so. Thanks be to fuck. And these scumbag cops just got lucky, were in the right place at the right time. There was no way that bearded fuck was making a complaint against him for theft or intimidation. No complaint, no charge. However, if he decided to open his trap again, he'd be a very sorry boy.

CHAPTER 37

It took Danielle several showers and half a bottle of whiskey to rid herself of the smell, though she still couldn't sleep. At least she and the child, still nameless, had settled well together. And Linda, far from not being able to mind a bag of chips, turned out to be a brilliant babysitter. She was here now, for Danielle had something important to do.

'I won't be too long,' Danielle said.

'No problem. Take your time paying your respects. Cheryl deserves that,' Linda said.

Danielle opened the door and collided with Ann, her fist raised to knock.

'Jesus Christ. I never saw you on the camera.'

'How was I to know that?' Ann said. 'Do you think I was sneaking in or something?'

'No, not at all.'

Ann regarded her for a moment. 'You should know better. Not paying attention will cost you.' She pushed in past her. Danielle closed the door and followed. Linda, the baby in her arms, was walking to and fro, humming quietly.

'What the fuck is that?'

Ann whipped around to face Danielle, who widened her eyes at Linda, hoping she understood what was wanted of her.

'My niece,' Linda said smoothly.

'What are you doing here then?' Ann asked.

'My sister and her fella had a row. They asked me to take the baby for a bit, give them a break.'

'That still doesn't explain why you're here.'

'They'd done more than row,' Danielle said. 'Her brother-in-law thumped her. It was safer here for the baby. He knows where Linda lives. He's pissed drunk and he threatened to take her.'

'I fail to see how that's our problem. Why must we get involved in someone else's domestic shit?'

'Because Linda runs the beautician's, and she does an excellent job.' Danielle cleared her throat. 'I told her she could spend some time here while he calmed down. It was safer for everyone, whereas it would affect us if he decided to turn up at the business and create a ruckus.'

'He's not sure exactly where I work,' Linda said, 'but I couldn't risk him following me.'

'And I think it's a good thing that our best employees know we have their backs,' Danielle added.

Somewhat mollified, Ann plonked her handbag on one of the stools at the breakfast counter. 'Fine. I get your point.'

'Everything I do is for the good of the family and the business,' Danielle said, rather sententiously.

'That's the only way it should be. Pour me a whiskey, Danielle, my nerves are shot. And that yoke had better not start squawking while I'm here.'

'She's actually a very quiet baby,' Danielle said.

'How would you know?'

'Linda told me.' Danielle scanned the room. She'd tidied away the evidence — no nappies, bottles or formula littered the room. But did she close the bedroom door? *Oh shit.* If Ann needed to go to the toilet or something, she'd wonder what the hell a cot was doing in Danielle's bedroom. Danielle poured a measure into a glass and shoved it towards Ann.

'Are you not having one with me?'

'No. It's not even midday yet. Anyway, I was just heading out.'

'Where? And why, when you have a visitor, even if it is just Linda?'

Linda sat demurely on the couch. The baby was in a Moses basket.

'Oh, I thought of going to get some wine and chocolates — you know, a little sweetener for Linda's family. It might help.'

Linda nodded and smiled.

'Is there not something in the pantry?' Ann asked.

'I fancied some Lily O'Brien's chocolates. Something a bit special.'

'Oh, excuse me. Posh chocolates, is it now? Fine, I shall drink on my own.' She took a gulp of her whiskey. 'By the way, your voice sounds fucked. You got a cold or something?'

'No, I'm fine.' *What is this, an interrogation?*

'You better be. Don't go passing anything to me.'

'No danger.'

'And what's with the scarf?'

'I just said, Ann, I was heading out.'

Ann snatched at the silk scarf and dragged it away.

Danielle's hand shot to her neck in a vain attempt to cover the finger marks.

'Actually, Linda—' Ann swivelled on the seat — 'why don't you fuck off to the shops and let me and Danielle have a chat.'

Linda stood up and reached for the baby.

'It's okay, leave her here. She'll be fine,' Danielle said, and mouthed *thank you*.

Ann waited until Linda had gone. 'Rough sex, or did someone have a go?'

'You don't want to know.'

'Fine.' Ann tossed the scarf at her. 'Have you seen Dean lately?'

Danielle gulped. 'Dean? Er, why?'

Ann chewed the inside of her cheek. 'It's the nose candy, it's softened his brain. I was just wondering if he has said anything strange to anyone. You, for example.'

Danielle's hand went to her throat. 'No.'

Ann scanned her face. 'Let me know if you do hear him rambling. Take whatever he says with a pinch of salt.'

'Sure.'

'Can you persuade him to pull back on the blow?'

'Me? Are you joking?' Danielle said. 'He doesn't seem to think much of me.'

'If the business is at risk — wait. Did he do that?' She jabbed her finger at Danielle.

Danielle looked down, trying desperately to think what to say.

'He did, didn't he?' Ann put a hand to her head. 'Jesus Christ. This is ridiculous. What happened?'

Danielle sighed. 'He turned up at the house on Brennanstown Road, looking for something he thought I had taken. I tried to tell him I hadn't, but he went ballistic and attacked me.'

'I hope you socked him in the jaw,' Ann said grimly.

'Kneed him in the balls, actually.'

'His dad would want to get back to Dublin quicksmart, and not to mind bollocking around in Belfast again. Dean has gone off his head, and he needs pulling back. He's a liability, the way he carries on.'

'When is Ged due down?'

'Yesterday, but he got delayed, of course. Typical.' She downed the last of the drink. 'Right, I'm off.'

'To look for Dean?'

'No. Well, not immediately. I've an appointment with an eye doctor. Fucking cataracts. Pat is waiting for me in the car.'

Pat and Danielle hadn't spoken since they'd found Hazel's body two days ago. 'Did he not want to come up?'

'Nah, he'd a few phone calls to make.' Ann picked up her bag and headed out.

Danielle stared at the door for a few minutes, wondering what this sudden visit from Ann was all about. Dean? Checking what she was up to? Or just after a sip of good Irish whiskey? Ann never popped in for just a chat. She might have heard what happened and wanted another side of the story. Maybe Pat had told her. Danielle shook her head. It was hard to trust this family, or anyone connected to it.

CHAPTER 38

Linda reappeared within minutes of Ann's departure. 'That was close,' Danielle said. 'Thank you for playing along.'

'That's okay. Are you going to say anything to Cheryl's family?' Linda said.

'No, I'll stay in the background.'

Linda nodded. 'I've told the girls not to go to her funeral. I wouldn't trust some of them to dress appropriately, and there's no point Cheryl's family knowing what she did to fund her studies.'

'Are you sure you didn't want to go yourself?' Danielle asked.

'Me? No. I don't do funerals.'

'Well, I'll only be a few hours. If anyone comes to see me, we'll stick to the story that she's your niece.'

'Okay.'

'And I'll pay you extra for helping to cover up with Ann. You did some quick thinking there.'

'Cheers.'

* * *

Danielle, in dark glasses and nondescript clothing, listened with only half her attention to the priest reciting the Rosary over the freshly dug grave. Among the small crowd of mourners, she noticed the two plain-clothes detectives. They stuck out like a sore thumb.

Having paid her respects, Danielle wandered away, intending to go straight home. Instead, she found herself staring at the name on the black granite headstone, back in that terrible moment — hearing the bang, the wail of sirens, seeing the blood. Things had never gone right for her since.

'Shouldn't you be visiting your mother and our baby, rather than some scumbag detective?'

Jason Flynn stood behind her. She spoke without turning around. 'I'd be dead but for this man.'

Jason stepped forward to stand beside her. His hand brushed hers.

'This man saved my life, and he died an awful death because of it. His wife lost their child, too,' Danielle said, her eyes still on the grave.

'How do you know that?' Jason said.

'I just do. None of it was right.'

'Depends on how you look at it.'

'Do you know who did it, Jason?'

'What? Killed him? As far as I'm concerned, his death means one less scumbag detective for us to deal with.'

'What about the shooter?' she said.

'You asked me that so often I got sick of it. The answer's the same. I have no idea who it was,' Jason said.

'It wasn't an excuse for you to go and fuck someone else. And to let me catch you in the act. What a slap in the face.'

'You were hard to live with,' he said. 'All that crying, day and night.'

'What did you expect? I was heartbroken. I still am.'

He turned to look at her, his eyes soft, searching her face. She slipped off the sunglasses. He frowned and stepped away.

'What's wrong, Jason?'

'Is there a way back for us?' He held her gaze, the harsh caw of a crow in a nearby tree the only answer.

'Too much time has passed,' she said.

'Can't we at least try?'

Danielle ignored his question. 'How did you know I'd be here?'

He indicated the little group of mourners. 'Cheryl. I guessed you'd go to her funeral. Her murder can't have been good for business at Berkley Street.'

'She wasn't murdered there, Jason.'

'I heard she was beaten to death,' he said.

'You seem to know an awful lot about it. Wait, is that why she's here, in the ground? Did you—'

'Don't ask questions you don't want to hear the answer to.'

'I want to know. Tell me.' Here he was, playing games with her again.

'No, I didn't kill Cheryl,' he said.

'How do I know that's the truth?'

'You suppose I give a fuck about what you think?'

'At one time you did.'

'As you've just said, too much time has passed.'

'What's this? Sour grapes now? Just because I won't jump back into your arms at the drop of a hat?'

'That's not it, Danielle. I'm sorry.'

'Sorry, is it? I've lost count of the number of times I've heard you say that.'

'I was sorry long before you kicked me out.'

'You were sorry you got caught,' she said.

'I'm not going there again, Danielle.'

She sighed. 'Let's get back to Cheryl, shall we? Do you know who killed her?'

'I don't for certain, but I have heard talk.'

'And are you going to share it with me?' she said.

'Not until I'm sure I'm right,' Jason said.

'Fine.' Danielle turned to go.

'Wait, Danielle,' he said. 'There's something else I wanted to talk to you about.'

'I think we've said all we needed to say.'

He blocked her path. Put a hand inside his jacket. Now what? Was he going to shoot her? Here? Where she'd been shot before? The exit was too far for her to make a run for it. He pulled something out. A phone.

'Hazel has been spreading false rumours and I want to set the record straight,' he said.

'Rumours like what?'

'That your uncle Ged is not the father of her baby.'

'Who is she saying it is, then? You? And you wanted to know if there was a way back for us. Jesus.'

'It's not true. I've never slept with Hazel.'

'Then why would she be saying that you're the father?' Danielle said.

'Because Ged wouldn't leave Ann for her.'

'Are you serious, Jason? You expect me to believe you?'

'Yes. I want to see the baby.'

Her stomach churned. 'Then why talk to me? Talk to her — Hazel.'

'I can't get hold of her. And you have the baby.'

'How do you know that?' Danielle asked.

'Bird told me.'

Danielle spread her hands. 'You see any baby on me?'

'Then who has her?' he asked.

Danielle shrugged. 'Maybe her mother collected her.'

'I don't think so,' he said. 'And kidnapping a child is a crime.'

'What? You think I'd steal someone else's child? I didn't kidnap her. Hazel needed some space away from her. She was overwhelmed by it all, and I stepped in.'

'Should her family not have stepped in?' Jason said.

'I've been trying to get in touch with them.'

'Right. I didn't realize that, Danielle.'

'I have been. Why do you want to see the baby anyway, Jason?'

'To take a photo of her, show them she looks nothing like me and is the image of Ged. Hazel told Marion, Bird's woman, so now the whole town will think it's mine. I don't want to piss Ged off just because his girlfriend is unhappy with the way he is treating her.'

'You won't prove anything with a photo, Jason.'

'Well, you shouldn't be looking after a baby that isn't yours, Danielle.'

'I'm well aware that she's not mine. But she is Ged's, and now I'm caught between doing the right thing by the baby and making sure Ann doesn't find out. Ged is away on business, and I aim to talk to him as soon as he gets back. What do you expect me to do, leave the child on the doorstep of the nearest Garda station?'

'No.'

'Or I could hand her straight over to the first guard I meet. I think I saw two detectives at the funeral. If I hurry, they might still be around. I can give them my address and tell them to call for her.'

He sighed. 'Don't be so dramatic, Danielle. I just want to see her. And I was hoping I could persuade you to help me.'

'How?'

'I might report that you took her,' Jason said.

'That's not persuading me, that's threatening me,' Danielle said.

'Take your chances, so. Let's see how it would play out, shall we? There you are, still grieving, years after losing your own baby, so you steal one belonging to another woman. It wouldn't look very good, would it?' Jason said.

'I told you, I can't get hold of Hazel,' Danielle said.

'Well, try harder,' he said. 'Get Hazel to change her story, and don't you dare come to me with your accusations. How do I know you really aren't still grieving? Or that you don't really intend to get your hands on what's not yours?'

He stared into the distance, his expression unreadable.

'I spoke to someone and got counselling after it happened,' she said. 'You punched walls, slept with other women, became angry and sad. It was pathetic.'

He took hold of both her arms, shook her. 'Pathetic, you say?'

'Is everything okay here?' A woman stood beside her. Danielle did not take her eyes from Jason's.

It took a beat, but he loosened his hold. 'Keep walking, darling. It's nothing to do with you.'

'I asked her if everything is okay, and I'm staying here until I get an answer.'

'What the fuck business is it of yours?' Jason growled.

'This lady looks like she's being held under duress. This concerns me, especially if it's a Flynn doing the holding.'

Danielle glanced at the speaker. Thank fuck, it was one of the detectives who'd attended the funeral. Before she could speak, Jason took a step back. Danielle's legs nearly buckled under her.

'And who the fuck are you?' Jason turned his ire upon the woman.

'Detective Garda Teegan. If you take a look behind you, you'll see Detective Sergeant Richards.'

Jason held his hands up.

'Have you anything on you that you shouldn't?' Detective Teegan asked.

'The fuck I do. What are you going to do, search me in a graveyard?'

'That's right — unless you want to come back to the station to be searched there,' she said.

'She's making no complaint.' Jason and the detective glared at each other.

The gun in Danielle's handbag felt huge. If they found it on her, she was fucked. At the very least, she'd be charged with possession. Could she say it wasn't hers, and that she had found the snazzy handbag in the graveyard? Maybe, if it didn't match her fucking shoes.

Jason held his arms out. 'Work away, so, darling,' he said, smiling.

The detective sergeant patted him down.

The search concluded, Detective Teegan turned to Danielle. 'Are you okay?'

'Yes, fine. It's . . . we . . . we were just talking.'

'Right. And why this particular grave?' Detective Teegan asked.

'I'm paying my respects,' Danielle said.

'Hmm. I suppose you do have a connection,' Detective Sergeant Richards said, his eyes on the headstone.

Danielle stared at him.

'Did he not save your life?' Richards said.

'Yes, he did, that's right. How do you know who I am? I doubt you were even in the job a decade ago.'

'I found out who you were when I spotted you at the hospital after your cousin's shooting,' Detective Teegan said.

Shit. They never missed a thing.

'He's still not cooperating, refusing to give a statement,' the detective added. She glanced at the handbag. 'Chanel. Nice.'

Danielle looked at it as if seeing it for the first time. 'What? Oh. Yeah.' Terrified the detective would ask to look at it, Danielle adjusted the gold chain on her shoulder.

'Here.' Detective Teegan pulled a card from her pocket and held it out to Danielle.

She looked down at it. 'No thank you.'

Her bag vibrated. She'd shoved the phone to the bottom. Not wanting to open it in front of the detective, she ignored it. No sooner had it stopped than it rang again.

'You'd better get that,' DS Richards said.

Holding the bag towards her, she eased out the phone from beneath the gun. The caller was Ann.

'Hello?'

She heard a series of screams and cries. Danielle was trying to get some sense out of her when Mark came racing towards them. 'It's Ged,' he said, panting. 'He's—'

At the same time, Ann was saying, 'He's had a stroke.'

CHAPTER 39

As soon as she heard the news, Danielle ran for the exit.

Just as she got to the car, Mark was beside her, shaking the keys. 'Where are you going?'

Her hand was on the driver's door, ready to open it. 'Any chance I can drive myself?'

'Are you as good a driver as me?'

'I can handle a car,' she said.

'Leave it to me today,' Mark said.

'Fine.' She went around to the other side and got in.

Coming out of the churchyard he took a left, narrowly missing a bus.

'I can drive, you know,' she said.

'No doubt you can.'

'Then why am I always the passenger?'

'In case you ever need to run, make a quick exit.'

He did drive well, she had to admit. He manoeuvred through the traffic with expert precision, anticipating the traffic lights and avoiding possible tailbacks.

'Why do you even care?' she said.

'Who said I did? I work for the Lewis family, and it's my job to keep you safe. Besides, I don't want to be caught in the crossfire.'

'Crossfire?'

'If someone threatens your life, it puts everyone around you in danger too.'

'Is there really a threat, after all these years?'

'There's no evidence to suggest it ever went away,' Mark said.

'Do you know who was behind it?' she asked, eyeing him with interest, the image of him as a muttonhead long gone.

'I have my theories, but no, I don't know for sure.'

'But you have an idea. Who?' she asked.

'Like I said, I don't know for sure.'

'But you weren't even part of this crew a decade ago.'

'Well, I am now, and like I said, it's my job to keep you safe and I take my job very seriously.'

'You are complicated. Wouldn't you care to share your theories with me?'

'No, not yet.'

'When then? This is my life we're talking about.'

'You didn't have to come back, you know, Danielle.'

'I did.'

'But why? I mean, you were safe in the UK. Why decide to come back here where it's dangerous?'

'I'm looking for answers.'

'And what if you don't like what you find? Or what you find isn't what you thought it would be?'

'What are you, the fucking Riddler? Just share what you know and make things easier on me.'

'You don't always find closure where you expect it to be,' he said.

'You know nothing about me.' Jesus, who was he to give her advice?

'I know enough. Do you really not remember me?'

Danielle looked at him properly. Now he mentioned it, there was something familiar about him that she hadn't seen before, but she couldn't put her finger on it. 'You weren't working for the Lewis family ten years ago.'

'But I was around.'

'*Around* had better not mean the Flynns.'

He turned to look at her, looking back just in time to avoid a car exiting the petrol station in Finglas. 'Do you think I am off my head?'

'No, but you wouldn't want to be crossing lines.'

'No danger of that. Currently, I work for Ged and you. And I make sure my focus is on my job. My advice to you is to keep your emotions out of your search for answers. It helps you see through the fog.'

'There is no fog.'

'Are you sure?' he said.

'Whatever. I think I preferred it when you didn't speak.'

'Fine. We can go back to that, so.'

She watched him veer left by the garage to join the M50. Crisscrossing the lanes, he stayed ahead of any traffic buildup.

'How serious is Ged's condition?' she asked at last.

'As serious as a major stroke can be.'

'Shit.'

'Yes. Decisions will have to be made.'

'What do you mean?'

'With the business.'

'Does that not pass automatically to Ann or Dean?' she asked.

'No. It passes to you,' Mark said.

'Me?'

'It's what Ged wanted.'

'What the fuck are you—'

'Isn't that the real reason why you came back?' Mark asked.

'No, no, not at all. I had no idea about that. Anyway, I told you why.'

'Taking over the running of the multimillion-euro Lewis empire seems a pretty good reason to me.'

'But why me?'

'Because Dean is destroying himself with drugs and tied to his mother's apron strings. He won't piss without her

233

approval. He acts the big knob when he's with the lads, but he's paranoid and unpredictable.'

'And Ann?'

'Ged has never trusted Ann. He has always doubted that Dean is even his.'

'Jesus. But there's no guarantee that either Ann or Dean will step aside—'

'They'll have to. All Ged's shares in his legitimate businesses are willed to you.'

'What? That's worth—'

'A hell of a lot of money.'

'Can he do that? Just leave out Ann and Dean?'

'He can do what he likes. He's the boss. They are his shares. They have always been intended for you, but about a year ago, he changed the executor.'

'To who?'

'Pat.'

'Wait.' *Their kiss.* 'Pat is privy to this information, but I'm not?'

'Not yet. Ged intended to discuss it with you. I doubt he anticipated getting a stroke.'

'I doubt he confided all this to you.'

'No. But I've been in the background when the discussions took place. You'd be surprised how much you learn if you shut the fuck up and listen.'

'Well, I'm all ears now.'

He grinned. 'I bet you are.'

'Fuck.'

'Exactly.'

'But it's a huge responsibility. I never asked for that.'

'I doubt you get much of a say in anything in this family.' Mark was now exiting the motorway and speeding along Brewery Road.

'Are we not heading back to the apartment, or going to get Ann and take her to Belfast?'

'That's already in hand. Pat has her.'

'Then where are we going?'

'Dean was arrested,' Mark said.

'Christ. What did he do?'

'Something about intimidation, dangerous driving. God knows.'

'Where?'

'Blackrock Garda station.'

Her stomach squeezed. 'You don't expect me to go in and get him, do you?'

'Why not?'

'I'm not rescuing that idiot.'

'As far as I know, he's being released.' The first drops of rain hit the windscreen. 'His phone is off, but if we wait across the way, we can pick him up.'

'If his phone is off, how do you know when he is being released?'

'The brief's been in, and anyway, they can only hold him for so long. We'll have to see what happens.'

'So we're not even sure if they're holding him, charging him, letting him out or what.'

'He doesn't know about his father yet.'

'If he even is his father,' Danielle muttered.

Mark was now approaching Blackrock Garda station, the rain pounding the car.

'Don't get too close.'

'Jesus, you're awful nervous,' Mark said. 'You'd think you were running from the law yourself.'

'Not me,' Danielle said.

Dean appeared at the top of the station steps and stopped to spark up a cigarette. Mark sounded the horn, but a taxi was right behind them. The wipers were now flying back and forth.

'I'll have to circle round.' As they did so, Ritchie's car sped past, Dean in the passenger seat.

'Well, that's that,' Mark said. 'He's out kind of quick, don't you think?'

'I suppose. He'd never have cooperated, would he?'

'Don't be heard saying that too loud.'

'They mustn't have had anything on him, then,' Danielle said.

'The solicitor said there was an accident. I think Dean nearly hit a child.'

'What an idiot.'

'We'll head for Clontarf,' Mark said, 'in case they're going there. We can meet them at the house and formulate a plan. I'll try ringing him again.' Mark pressed a button on the steering wheel. This time, Dean answered.

CHAPTER 40

The rain fell like arrows, ricocheting off the steps. Shivering
with cold, Dean stood outside the Garda station and peered
through the sheets of rain, looking for Ritchie. Eventually
he saw him, parked up on the corner of Temple Road. Dean
pulled up his collar, threw away his unlit cigarette and ran
for it.

'Pricks,' Dean said as he collapsed into the passenger seat.
He switched on his phone and dialled Brenno's number. No
answer. He rang Anto next. That went straight to voicemail.
He tried both numbers again. Still no luck. He shoved the
phone back in his pocket. At least Brenno had delivered the
cash. After Dean had run into him and Anto on the Old
Airport Road the previous Thursday, he had decided that, as
punishment for moving the equipment and money without
telling him, he'd make them wait a few days for payment.
Now, he was four hours late. Well, they'd have to understand
he got diverted — and getting arrested could be classed as
being *very* diverted. Their share of the money was safe at the
house in Clontarf. They'd just have to trust him and wait.

'What happened?' Ritchie asked.

'Some stupid bitch wasn't watching her kid.'

'What?'

Dean put on his seat belt. 'Just drive, Ritchie.'

'Why did they arrest you? Did someone make a complaint or something?'

'Someone did, according to what the cops told me.'

'You got charged, so?'

'Nope.'

'Why not?'

He shrugged. 'They let me out. Said they've to make further enquiries. That's all you need to know.'

'That so?'

'Yes, Ritchie, that's so. What the fuck is the third degree about? It's bad enough them scumbag cops interrogating me without you starting with the hassle.' Dean felt bad. Tar coated his tongue, and he was thirsty. His jaw ached.

'Stop for a bottle of Lucozade somewhere.'

'There should be a fresh one behind the seat.'

Dean swivelled around. There was a trayful. Thirsty enough to drink all twenty-four bottles, Dean picked one out and glugged it.

'I'm just checking, is all,' Ritchie said. 'I wanted to know that everything went okay. The guards can be right bastards when they want.'

'Why wouldn't it have gone okay?'

Ritchie shrugged. 'Dunno. They didn't try to get anything out of you?'

'They're always trying to get stuff out of us, or on us, you know that.'

'But nothing—'

'What are you trying to say? Come on, spit it out. Wait. You think I'm a rat? Because I've no bit of paper with me, no court date? Fuck you, Ritchie.'

Ritchie made a fast turn and drove towards Carysfort Avenue. 'No, Dean, I know you'd never—'

'You'd want to. Jesus Christ.' Dean put his feet up on the dashboard and stared out of the window. The sea looked rough, grey.

'I'll drop you to your ma. She's at the house in Clontarf.'

'You let her get home then, did you?'

'It's not like that, Dean,' Ritchie said.

'I don't know what anything is like, do I?'

'Look, just tell me what you got pulled in for.'

'Jesus. Will you let up with the questions?'

Ritchie waited.

'They said I was scaring some fella. The chicken shit. Then some stupid bitch wasn't watching where her child was, and I nearly hit it.'

'Who? The child?'

'Yeah. But I didn't. I managed to avoid them. I'm a quick thinker, I am.' Dean tapped his temple. 'Rapid reactions. Lucky, they were.'

'But they arrested you anyway?'

'Yeah, trumped-up bullshit. Pure intimidation.'

'Detectives?'

'No. But there was one when I got stopped. Some bitch called Teegan. I didn't recognize the face at first, but herself and the other fella with her came to see me in the hospital after the shooting. The drugs had me off my head; anyone could have been in to see me and I'd have had no idea. Anyway, I think we might do a little checking on them. Find out their story. She'd no ring or anything. Could be a dyke. Might live on her own. Who knows, but maybe a little spook or five might have her backing off. That other one, the detective sergeant, he's married, I know that much. I think there might be a kid or two there.'

'Intimidating officers.' Ritchie whistled. 'That's not a good road to go down, Dean. Not unless we need a diversion for something bigger.'

Dean stuck out his jaw. 'Think I couldn't do it?'

'It'd be better to target whoever made the complaint. Maybe that's what you meant. Is it?'

'You know what I meant. If I want to make their lives hell, I will.'

'You go down that road, you'll have the whole force down on top of you. They're the biggest gang in Ireland.'

'We'll see. When I decide what to do, I'll let you know.'

'At least run it by your da,' Ritchie said.

'You've found your respect for him again, have you?'

'I never lost it.'

Ritchie's phone vibrated. Dean saw Ann's name on the screen. Ritchie cut the call. It rang again, and again he cut it.

'Are you not going to talk to her? Afraid of me hearing something I shouldn't? Scumbag.'

'Drop it, Dean.'

'I'll drop it when I want to. Answer her. Don't keep her waiting. She might slap you about. Maybe you'd like a bit of that. Go on.'

'No. I don't want to talk on the phone while I'm driving. The cops'll give me points, or a fine, if I'm caught.'

'Bullshit.'

The East-Link Toll Bridge came into view. 'Have you got any change?' Ritchie came to a halt in the line of waiting cars.

'Do you not have one of them tags or something?'

'No. Too easy to get records from.' Ritchie felt around in his pockets, in the footwell, coming up with nothing but a dry balled-up piece of gum.

'Not a penny on me,' Dean said, patting himself down. 'Wait, there's a few bits here.' He put his hand in his track-suit pants. 'I told them to keep the coins for a tip and the wankers threw them back at me. Here. Two euros. You can have them.'

Ritchie paid and drove on, the traffic heavy now.

Dean's phone rang.

'Dean?'

'What's up, Mark?'

'Did you get a call from Ann or any of the others?'

'No. Why?'

'Your da is in hospital.'

'What? Where?'

'Belfast. He's been there a few days. Had no ID on him, which is why none of us was contacted until today.'

'How many days ago, exactly?'

'Five or six, I think they said. He's had a stroke.'

Dean swallowed. It felt like he'd eaten a tennis ball. He glanced over at Ritchie.

'Pat rang me after Ann got the call,' Mark continued. 'She couldn't get through to you, so she rang Danielle.'

'We're on our way to Clontarf. I'm with Ritchie.'

'Does Ritchie know about Ged?'

'If he does, he's not said.'

'Right, let's meet at your folks' house and cover what's needed while you and Ann travel north.'

Dean ended the call, shaking with rage.

Ritchie glanced at him. 'You okay?'

'When did you say Da sent you down from Belfast?'

'I don't think I did. But it was the day before you called. Why?'

'Well, he's in hospital. He's had a stroke. Five or six fucking days ago, apparently. Why the fuck did you not stay up there? In too much of a rush to get back, was it? My ma beg you to come back, did she?'

'What are you talking about, Dean? Wait, your da's in hospital?'

'You are nothing but a scumbag, Ritchie.'

'I had nothing to do with your da getting sick. What do you take me for?'

'A leery slime. Da up there alone, no one from his family or crew around him. You down here tapping my ma. You sick—'

The car lurched as Ritchie swerved right into Alfie Byrne Road. A passing van sounded its horn.

Ritchie reached into his jacket. Dean grabbed hold of his arm. The car veered across a yellow box junction, plunged into a mound of grass and struck a sign for Eastpoint Causeway. Ritchie punched Dean on the chin, sending him backward. Ritchie yanked at his gun, but it caught in the lining of his pocket. Dean lunged forward and took hold of his wrist, which was still caught in his pocket, pointing it up toward Ritchie's chin. Dean pressed the trigger. The bullet went through the roof, the sound of the blast like a hammer blow to the side of his head.

His eyes closed for a second or two. When they opened, Ritchie was mouthing words Dean couldn't hear. His ears ringing, Dean maintained his grip on Ritchie's wrist. They struggled, soundlessly, Ritchie twisting and turning, until the gun was pointing at Dean. With a final effort, his muscles screaming, Dean found the strength to bend the hand back.

Dean heard nothing but a faint *boom*. Particles of flesh landed on his face. He tasted metal. Half of Ritchie's face had been blown away.

Dean gagged. He needed to get out of the car. Shit, where was the gun? He was forced to reach down between Ritchie's feet to retrieve it, brushing against the mess that was Ritchie's face.

Outside the car, the ground wavered, then rose to meet him. The gun slipped from his hand and slithered across the road.

CHAPTER 41

The rain eased to a drizzle as Mark followed Ritchie's tail lights into Alfie Byrne Road. Ahead of them, a car at the roadside, its nose embedded in a signpost and beside it, a figure prone on the ground, rolling around in pain. Mark slammed on the brakes and leaped out of the car, followed by Danielle.

Mark took hold of Dean under his arms and dragged him into his car. He lay on the back seat, groaning, his hands at his ears. Danielle caught sight of the gun, lying a metre or so away, pulled the scarf from her bag and used it to pick up the weapon, which was covered in blood and something else that Danielle didn't want to identify.

They got back in the car, both of them breathing heavily.

Pat arrived, seemingly from out of the blue. He went to the boot of his car, took out a container and sprinkled its contents over the spot where Dean had been lying. The sound of sirens could be heard in the distance, growing louder. Pat legged it back to Mark's car, tossed the container into the boot and drove off in his own vehicle. Mark sped away after him.

Soon they were pulling up at the house on Castle Avenue. Mark pressed a button by the garage door, which slowly lifted to admit them. Pat's car was already inside. Mark parked beside Pat's car and switched off the engine, plunging them into darkness. A few moments later, a light came on and Pat appeared at a door leading into the house. He and Mark took Dean under the armpits, hauled him out, threw his arms over their shoulders and walked him towards the door.

Danielle remained in the car, looking down at the bundle by her feet. She felt as if she were trapped in some nightmare scenario: this gun, which had just killed a man, wrapped in the scarf of a woman whose body they'd found not long before. The handbag beside it contained another one with money and a memory card belonging to yet another victim.

Jesus Christ, how had things got so out of hand? How many crimes had she been complicit in up to now? She knew gang life could be harsh, but this was in a whole other league. There were stains on her T-shirt, blood on her fingers and still more blood on the seats. Traces of Ritchie's DNA were all over everything — they'd have to burn the car to get rid of them.

And what of her own quest? Her search for answers was fast becoming lost in the quagmire into which she sank, deeper and deeper, the longer she remained with this family. Why had she left the UK? Where was the plan Saoirse had come up with? There was evidence to be found somewhere, but where? Reason told her to bail out now, but if she did, she'd never be any the wiser. Mark had to give her more. Even those theories of his had to be based on something. She must persuade him to trust her. But how?

She tugged on the door handle but it refused to budge. She'd been locked in. She tried every door in the car, to no avail. She was sealed in a metal prison. She began to gasp for breath, afraid of suffocating. In ever increasing panic, she slammed her hand on the horn and left it there.

The door to the garage swung open. A masked gunman, followed by another, burst in. They approached the car, pointing their weapons in all directions, searching for something to aim at. To her horror, Danielle realized they had come for her.

CHAPTER 42

One of the men threw Danielle over his shoulder like a sack of potatoes and carried her into the house. He shouted something at her, but his voice was muffled by the mask and she couldn't make out the words. The man carried her inside, kicked a door open and plonked her on the closed seat of a toilet. He snapped his fingers in front of her face.

He pulled down his mask. 'Come on,' Pat said, 'you can't pike on me now we've come this far.' She saw Mark, hovering anxiously behind him. Pat began to tug at her clothing.

'What the—'

'Good. You're back to me. Now, out of those clothes, we have to get rid of them.'

'Jesus.'

'Unless you want to walk around covered in Ritchie Delaney's DNA,' Pat said.

'Fuck no.'

'Well, then, out of them, soon as you can,' Pat said.

'Christ, what was Dean thinking?' Danielle said.

'Who knows? He can't hear a thing. The gun went off right by his ear,' Mark said.

A high-pitched scream rose up the stairs. Someone howled.

'That's not Dean,' Mark said.

'No. Someone must have told Ann,' Pat said.

'I thought she knew about Ged,' Danielle said.

'Not Ged — Ritchie,' Pat said. 'Did you not know? He's been giving it to her for years, long before you left. How could you not have noticed?'

She remembered them together on the balcony, whispering. The looks that passed between them. She'd missed the signs.

'Rumour has it he is Dean's father, not Ged,' Pat said.

'Things have been happening so fast since I've been back that I don't know which way is up,' Danielle said.

'But you've returned to set everything straight, haven't you?'

Haven't you. It sounded like a challenge. 'What do you mean?' she said.

'Take charge. Run things as they should be run.'

'Ye . . . yes. That's right.'

'I didn't realize I'd locked you in — force of habit. Sorry.'

Sorry indeed. Meanwhile, she'd been thinking her end was near. 'The scene back there was pretty shocking.'

'Yes. It was.'

'I'll go down to Ann and Dean,' Mark said, and left.

'How come you got there so fast, Pat?'

'I was passing,' he said.

'Oh really?'

'Yes.'

'And what was the stuff you poured on the ground?'

'Something to break up the blood. It'll contaminate the DNA.'

'Traces of Dean will be all over that car. Besides, anyone could have seen him with Ritchie.'

'There's only so much we can do to sort it for him. He's reckless, thinks he's untouchable. And right now, it comes down to our own preservation. We need to get out of here,' Pat said.

'I've no clothes here.'

'Jesus. What's in that huge handbag of yours, then?'

Cheryl's stuff, a gun and her own wallet and phone. There was little room for much else, let alone a change of clothes.

Shit. Where is it? 'Did I leave it in the car?'

'No. I cleaned it up and left it downstairs,' Pat said.

'Did you look inside?'

'Why would you worry about that?'

'Oh, you know, a girl's handbag is sacrosanct.' Danielle tried to laugh. It didn't sound very convincing.

'If you say so.' He was on his knees wiping her shoes with a cloth.

'You still haven't said how you got to the scene so fast,' she said.

'Like I said, I was passing. Look, forget about that. The longer you stay here, the riskier it will be. And make sure you leave no trace of yourself behind. There should be clothes in the wardrobe. You'll find something to fit.'

'Are you taking Dean to the hospital?' she asked.

'I'm not sure if they'll be able to do much. He'd be better off trying to rest. He should be safe here.'

'So why can't I stay here, then?'

'Because you are needed elsewhere. Now, hop to it.'

Danielle bridled. 'Who the fuck do you think you're talking to?'

'Fine. Stay then. Listen to Dean roaring in pain.'

'All right, all right.'

Pat ran the water in the shower and left.

Danielle peeled off the rest of her clothes and stepped into the shower. The water swirling down the drain was tinged with pink. She scrubbed at herself until the water ran clear, but nothing could wash away what she had just seen. All she wanted was to get away, back to London. But she was in too deep now.

How many more times would she come close to being killed? Would Ritchie's death be avenged? There was a good chance his extended family would turn on them. They could well align themselves with the Flynn family and start a gang war. And she'd be stuck in the middle of it. Then there were all the legitimate businesses. She wasn't even sure which of them was legitimate. The Criminal Assets Bureau could come down on them and everything would be lost at the stroke of a pen. Her plan again, always her plan. Would Saoirse help? How could she, if it had all gone to shit?

The door opened. A hand appeared and shoved her handbag across the floor, along with a bundle of fresh clothes. She'd had more changes of outfit in the past few weeks than an episode of *Dynasty*. Her mind on Saoirse and the need to fill her in on what had been happening, she summoned the energy to get dressed.

Danielle rooted around in the pile of clothes and found a small-size hooded top and matching bottoms. Now, shoes. She was certainly not going to wear heels with a tracksuit; there was a limit. She searched again and found some trainers. They were about half a size too big, but needs must.

She went downstairs and joined Mark, Pat, Ann and Dean in the living room. Everyone except Dean was standing, ready to leave.

She was ushered into the back seat of a different car, parked at the front of the house. Ann struggled into the seat beside her. Her mascara had formed black smudges under her eyes and she kept blowing her nose. Pat helped Ann with her seat belt and got in behind the wheel.

'What about Dean?' Danielle asked.

'We've organized someone to pick him up and look after him,' Pat answered. 'He'll be fine.'

Ann continued to whimper. It would be a long journey to Belfast with that going on, Danielle thought.

'Mark?'

'He'll be along in a second.' Pat drove off.

Mark, carrying a bag, was waiting at the junction with Seafield Road. As they pulled away, Danielle turned to look at the vast, glistening sea. Two women in navy running tights jogged along the promenade, chatting. *Not a care in the world*, thought Danielle bitterly.

They passed the tall mast of Clontarf Garda station, reaching into the air. Two patrol cars were parked outside.

'I have to stop for diesel. The Applegreen is just up here. Get whatever supplies you need for the journey.'

While Pat filled the tank, Mark disappeared into the shop. Just to get a break from Ann's sniffling, Danielle got out too, and went into the shop for a bar of chocolate and a can of Lilt, neither of which she really wanted.

Mark, waiting with Pat in the queue for the checkout counter, glanced at her purchases. 'That all you want?'

Danielle returned to the car to find Ann folded forward, howling.

'Can I do anything for you, Ann? Get you anything?'

'He's dead . . .' Ann wailed.

'I know.'

She looked up at Danielle, her eyes red and brimming with tears. 'Not Ritchie. Ged. They just rang from the hospital. He died twenty minutes ago. It's all Dean's fault. We could have made it up there, if it wasn't for him. We could have said goodbye. Ohhh!'

'Oh shit.'

She met Pat and Mark as they were coming out of the shop.

'Ged is gone. He's dead. Ann just got the call.'

Danielle walked away to clear her own mind. When she looked back, Mark was pacing, his hands to his forehead. Pat was leaning against the bonnet, looking into space. Ann's phone was lying on the ground, its screen cracked. They were falling apart.

It looked like she was in charge now. There was nothing else for it. Time to step up and be the leader Ged had intended her to be.

249

CHAPTER 43

Bird stood staring at the seven-tonne Hitachi excavator, trac-tor and trailer parked up in the centre of one of his suppos-edly empty factories in Eastpoint Business Park. He turned to Brenno.

'What the fuck is this?'

'Your equipment. I said I'd get it back.'

'I don't fucking need it back. I'm claiming the insurance on it.'

'Grand, so. Sell it off and ship it to Poland or something, like you usually do. A win on the double.'

Bird took hold of Brenno by the throat and shoved him backwards. Brenno lost his footing and landed on his arse.

'What the fuck, Bird? I thought I was doing the right thing.'

'How?'

'By getting you back your property,' Brenno said.

'Jesus, Brenno. Weren't you listening? I told you three fucking weeks ago that this lot needed to be moved as soon as the owner was deprived of it. It's different this time, because the detectives were at my door last week asking about *these* pieces of machinery. That changes the situation. If you knew where it was, you should have told me sooner. I'd have got someone to pass the info to the cops and they'd have recovered it. They would think they're brilliant and I'd have got my machinery back — legally.'

'But you told them detectives to piss off, didn't you?' Brenno said.

'Something like that.' Bird paced, cracking his knuckles. He pictured his signature, the piece of paper the detective sergeant had tucked into his fucking file. He had to get it back, tell them he'd made a mistake. He didn't need to claim the insurance after all because he'd found the equipment. That would be reasonable, wouldn't it?

Why did Brenno have to find the fucking stuff? Now he'd have to grovel to the scumbags; it was the only way. First, he had to check if the paperwork had actually been sent off to the insurance company. Marion had said she'd deal with it. This was the one time he didn't want her to be efficient with the paperwork. Brenno had landed him in a big heap of shit. Maybe he meant to. Maybe Marion was in on it, too?

'I thought I was doing the right thing, Bird,' Brenno whined again, from the ground.

'The problem with you is you don't think. If the cops find it here after I've reported it stolen, I am fucked.'

'How could they find it?'

'I wonder, Brenno. You could be setting me up.'

'No way, Bird. Not me.'

'Brenno, cast your mind back three weeks ago, the day you failed to kill Dean Lewis. We were in my office, remember?'

'Yes, Bird, how could I forget?'

'Then you should remember what I said. How long did I give you to get the machinery back to me?'

'Um, forty-eight hours, Bird.'

'So, do you have difficulty reading? Like a calendar, maybe? You can add up, I suppose.'

'Yes, Bird.'

'Forty-eight hours is not three weeks, Brenno.' Bird raised his voice.

'I know, Bird, I know. I thought—'

'What did I say you should do if you couldn't get it back to me within those forty-eight hours?'

'Er, to leave it where it was, and you'd make an official claim.'

'Halle-fucking-lujah. So now, do you see how much of a fuck-up this is? Have them find my equipment in my warehouse the week after I've officially reported it stolen?' Bird was now shouting.

Brenno cowered. 'I didn't think it would matter that much, Bird. You could still get rid of it.'

'I'm talking to an empty vessel, aren't I? There's only one thing you understand.'

Slowly, Bird took off his suit jacket and laid it across the bonnet of the trailer. Carefully, he took out each cufflink and slipped it into the jacket pocket. He rolled up his shirtsleeves, one after the other, making sure the folds were tight. He turned his head to the right, then to the left. His neck clicked. He flexed his shoulders and stepped towards Brenno, who shuffled backwards on his elbows.

'Get up.'

Shaking, he did as he was told.

Bird landed a punch to the ribs that sent him spinning. He ended up flat on his face in a cloud of dust.

Bird had raised his fist to deliver a second blow when the sound of approaching sirens stopped him in his tracks. 'What the fuck have you done?'

'Nothing, Bird, I swear.' Brenno spat out pieces of grit. His lip was bleeding from the fall. 'Not a thing. I expect they're just passing. They'll be gone in a minute.'

They weren't. More sirens joined in the chorus. Bird turned and ran for his car. As he left, he pressed a button and the shutters slowly lowered, blotting out the sight of Brenno, on the ground in front of the machinery. A plan formed in his mind. He would deny all knowledge of its existence, blame the whole thing on Brenno. After all, he was inside with it.

He sat in the car, trying to gauge which direction the sirens were coming from, but, like the buzzing of a cloud of wasps, the noise seemed to circle round his head. Bird took a deep breath, put the car in gear and headed for Eastpoint Street. Keeping well under the speed limit, he drove past office blocks where anonymous figures sat bent over desks and stared at screens. Another world.

He crossed the bridge at Eastpoint Causeway and found himself heading straight for a cluster of flashing blue lights. 'Shit.' Then he saw a car planted into the sign.

Bird exhaled. Still in the clear.

He swung the car round, eager to get away. There was a screech of brakes, followed by a bang and a jolt. He glanced back. The front grill of the car that hit him was dented, but it didn't look serious. Then he noticed the blue light on the dashboard. Shit, it was an unmarked. The airbags had gone off, meaning the occupants wouldn't have been able to clock his car, so he jammed the gearstick into reverse. There was crunch of metal, and then he was free. He took off back the way he had come, thanking his stars that he'd taken Marion's car.

Bird floored the accelerator pedal and headed away from the scene, but one of the patrol cars had seen the collision and was now following him. He made a call to Sal.

'Where the fuck are you?'

'Heading for the factory, Bird.'

'Don't bother. Meet me beyond the container park, the road on to the M50, and be ready to go when you see me coming. I'll be on foot.'

'Will do.'

He ended the call. The car jerked forward. They had nudged him from behind. Scumbags. At the junction of Bond Road and Promenade Road, they nudged him again, this time driving him on to the concrete central island. Mounting the edge cost him the front bumper. He heard the loud crunch as he drove over it. If he put enough distance between them, he could abandon the car and leg it. He'd done it plenty of times as a teenager. He let out a whoop. He'd forgotten the adrenaline buzz of a chase. This was better than sex.

He veered right, put the car into reverse and yanked up the handbrake. The car spun. The patrol car sped past, just missing him. He mounted another concrete mound and bounced back on to the road beyond. The patrol car had just turned. He'd put enough distance between them to get away.

The whole car jolted sideways, tipped on to two wheels, then back down on to four. The impact seemed to rattle his bones and the airbags inflated. Glass rained down upon him and the car filled with smoke. When it cleared, he saw that the windscreen was shattered. An Audi SUV with damage to the side panel had hemmed him in. In navy suits, helmets — *Garda* emblazoned across their ballistics vests — they surrounded the car. He was fucked.

'Show us your hands.'

He wasn't even sure if he still had hands. He did a quick mental scan of his body. All the parts seemed to be where they were supposed to be. He was stiff but intact. Pieces of glass the size of teardrops were embedded in his bare arms.

He seemed to be having trouble breathing, however. He felt a weight on his chest as if someone was pressing hard on it. As if from a distance, he heard voices. Shouts. He managed to push open the door and collapsed on to the ground. Polished black boots came into his line of sight. Then nothing.

CHAPTER 44

Landing at Cork, Saoirse breezed through airport security. None of the Gardaí on duty recognized her. She took a bus to Dublin, ruminating on the little Danielle had told her. It was clear that the plan was falling apart and that Danielle was no closer to finding her answers.

She took the Luas to her apartment on Spencer Dock. She had been away from home a year now, and it was two since she'd received word that evidence relating to Gavin's murder still existed, and what it would take to hand it over intact. It took her the entire twelve months of her absence to formulate a workable plan. It relied heavily on the bond she shared with Danielle, and meant her accomplice had to return to her family. Throwing her lot in with them had been the only way they might draw out whoever was behind the shootings and obtain that vital evidence.

Apart from the sound of a door banging further down the corridor, the apartment was silent. Saoirse was used to living by herself since Gavin's murder, but now she found herself suddenly lonely.

She ventured along the corridor to the room she had kept locked since her husband's death. She hesitated outside, afraid of the pain that would surely overwhelm her, the hurt she had pushed to some small recess in her mind in order to get the job done.

Ignoring the warning voice in her head, she unlocked the door and was inside before she might find herself listening to it. The room smelled musty. She stood just inside and took stock. A foldaway bed by the window was open, barely covered by a thin grey mattress. A set of steps leaned against it. A chair stood at a small table beneath a large rectangular whiteboard. Traces of Blu-Tack were spattered across the wall as if someone had thrown it. A decade ago, that wall had been decorated with photos, lists of names, scribbled theories. All had been torn down in her frustration at the dead ends they represented. In the end, she had responded by fleeing to another country, putting thousands of miles between her and the events of that day. But the pull to return was always humming in the background, until it became too loud to ignore.

She opened the window, and then the wardrobe doors. Two suits. A navy fleece Garda jacket, trousers, some blue shirts. Rows of boxes, one cream, tied with a purple ribbon. She fetched the steps and took it down, reverently. Wiping away the film of dust with her sleeve, she set it down on the table and looked at it, tears forming in the back of her eyes. Printed in gold on the box were two little feet. She laid her hand on it and stood like that, wondering if she should open it.

She sighed, whispered 'Goodnight, baby,' and put the box carefully back on the shelf. The box and the room would stay closed, sealed up until it was finally all over.

Though she hadn't eaten since the previous day, she had no mind for food. A coffee would do her. She switched the kettle on.

She heard a noise behind her and tensed. It had to be him, coming to check on her. If he was here now, sooner than planned, something must have happened because he'd never risk blowing his cover. He was in too deep. She took a deep breath and gripped the counter.

'Hello again.'

Her breath caught, as if she'd just dived into icy water. The phone was on the table. Much too far. He'd have her flat on her back before she could even make a move.

'What are you doing here?' she said without turning.

'You obviously weren't checking for tails, were you?'

'No. I didn't think.' In the window, she could see his reflection. He stood with his back to the wall, arms crossed.

'What do you want, Jason?'

'Oh, I don't know. More guarantees.'

'Leave, unless you're here to hand over the proof.'

'Bird has been arrested,' he said.

'That's none of my concern.'

'I want you lot to lock him up and throw away the key,' he said.

'Why?'

'I want to get Dani back, and he's interfering.'

'How?' she said.

'Arsehole thinks he's better than me and should have everything for himself.'

'Including Danielle?'

'Yes.'

'I'm not interested in your family politics, Jason. You've broken into my apartment. I don't want you here. Go, before I have to arrest you myself.'

'You can't do that. Remember our deal? I have immunity.'

'No, if you remember, you were granted immunity for withholding evidence. That was the deal. Anything else you get up to is your concern.'

'I haven't held back any evidence. Dwayne has. I told you that.'

'Well, where is it?'

'Now that Bird is in custody, I can search his house and his offices properly.'

'But are we any closer to knowing who was behind Danielle's shooting and Gavin's murder?'

'I've been trying to get close to Dani, but she doesn't seem open to any kind of a reunion.'

'I couldn't guarantee you'd manage some grand reunion with Danielle. My part was to persuade her to come back here to Ireland to help draw out those responsible, while you looked for this evidence you overheard Dwyane saying existed. I did my part. So, I'll ask again, Jason. What are you doing in my apartment?'

'I just wanted you to know how easy it was to find you. And if I can, then so can others. You need to be more careful,' he said.

'Like what others? The ones who put out the hit on Danielle? Is it them who murdered Gavin?'

He stepped forward. 'Maybe.'

'You need to deliver on what you promised.'

'I will. I just need a little more time.'

'You'd better.'

'Or what?' He moved closer. 'You know, you need to be more choosy about who you trust.'

'That's rich, coming from you.'

The sound of a key turning in the front door echoed through the apartment. Jason reached into his jeans.

'Don't even think about it. Get the hell out of here now.'

She opened the patio door. 'The fire escape is to the left, although you probably know that. Now go, before you're seen.'

'I'll see you soon.'

'Not unless you have the information.'

'I will, and Danielle will be a Flynn and we'll be running Dublin.'

Jason had disappeared by the time the kitchen door swung open.

'Everything okay?' The Garda was in plain clothes.

'Yes. Christ. You look different.'

'Of course. I had to blend in, didn't I?'

'Any news?' she asked.

'Things are going a bit tits up.'

'Had to be, if you're here risking your cover. So, tell me how.' She shut the door to the patio, making sure it was locked. 'Go on.'

'I'm sorry to say the news is bad. It's Ged. He died in hospital in Belfast earlier today.'

'What?'

'Yes, a major stroke. Ritchie Delaney is dead too. Dean shot him.'

'What? Why?'

'No idea. It happened when Ritchie picked Dean up after he got himself arrested.'

'For what?'

'I'm not sure, intimidation or something. Next thing, Ritchie's brains were all over his car.'

'Did Dean get away?' she asked.

'Yes.'

'What is he saying?'

'Not a thing. He went deaf from the gunshot. All he's doing is moaning in pain.'

'Does anyone know about your connection to me?' she said.

'Give me some credit, will you?'

'Yeah. Sorry.'

'Oh, and Ann is in hospital.'

'For what?'

'She collapsed at the Applegreen in Clontarf after hearing the news about Ged.'

'Jesus Christ.' Saoirse began to pace. 'Right. Things need to be brought forward. Let Danielle know who you are and why you are there.'

'It's too soon. We haven't got the proof yet. It's on some memory card.'

'Yes. And where is that?'

'No one knows. Dwayne had it, apparently, but it's gone missing. I'd got one of the girls from the brothel onside. She was meant to find out about it. She contacted me to say she may have what I was looking for. She was meant to get it to me, but was murdered before she could hand it over. She must have stashed it, but I've no idea where — yet.'

'Shit. You relied on a prostitute?'

He smiled slightly. 'Says the person in league with major criminals.'

'Yeah, you're right. We do what we have to.'

'Maybe you are right I should let Danielle know who I am and why I'm here. Let's set up a meeting. Here?'

She glanced at the patio door. 'No, it would be safer somewhere else. Give me your number. I'll organize a place and message you.'

'Okay.'

After he had left, Saoirse sat at the window watching the sun disappear below the horizon. Her mind was racing. What a mess.

This needed fixing.

Fast.

CHAPTER 45

Bird had been put in one of the rooms off the custody suite. Cream walls, no windows. A poster advising the public about preventing burglaries. No camera. No desk. The seat wasn't bolted to the floor. Not an interview room. A uniformed guard stood outside the door. He asked for his solicitor, and someone made the call.

He had two cracked ribs. He was stiff and it hurt to breathe in, but it wasn't bad enough to keep him in hospital, so they discharged him, straight into custody.

Because of his injuries, they didn't handcuff him. He wouldn't have had the energy to run anyway, not after the chase. He wasn't fifteen anymore. What the hell had he been thinking? That he'd outrun them? Still, it had been a rush trying.

Dangerous driving, that's what they said he'd been arrested for. Ah, the good old Road Traffic Act. Always came in handy.

He'd been in there an hour when a woman carrying a briefcase walked in.

'Who are you?' he asked.

'Jo Hughes.'

'Why've you got a man's name?'

'It's short for Josephine. I prefer Jo.'

'Where's Geoff?'

'In the Special Criminal Court,' she said.

'So they send me you instead, huh? What are you — sixteen? Still in school?'

'I'm fully qualified, Mr Flynn.'

'You'd better be.'

After another thirty minutes, DS Dave Richards came into the room.

'Perfect timing, Miss Hughes. Your client's just about to be charged.'

'You can call me Jo.'

'She prefers that,' Bird added.

Reading from a sheet of paper, DS Richards proceeded to charge and then caution Bird. He asked if he had any reply to the charge. He glanced at the solicitor, who shook her head. Bird shook his. Richards noted that Bird had made no reply and gave him a copy of the charge sheet.

'That it?' Jo held his elbow to help him to his feet, but he shook it free. No point making him look like a helpless prick in front of the guards. He'd broken ribs before and, painful as it was, he knew it would be nothing compared to what he'd wake up with the following morning.

'If you fail to produce your driving licence and insurance certificate within ten days, we'll be looking at driving without either or both. The car's not in your name, so you'd better be covered,' Richards said.

'I am. I'm not letting you get me on a crappy charge like that.'

'Yet you drove like the clappers away from the scene of an accident. Did you honestly think you'd outrun us?' Richards said.

'No comment.'

'Expect more charges when the traffic accident file is complete. It will be someone higher than me investigating that.'

'Yeah, yeah.'

Richards's phone rang and he walked away to answer it. Bird and the solicitor headed for the exit.

He was through the door and into the evening air when he heard a familiar voice behind him.

'Just a minute, Bruce.'

He hated being called by his real name by anyone other than Marion. The way she said it was one of the few things he liked about her.

'What is it now — *Dave*?'

Richards placed his hand on Bird's arm. 'I'm arresting you under section eight, subsection three of the Criminal Justice (Theft and Fraud Offences) Act, 2001. You are not obliged to say anything unless you wish to do so . . .'

Bird glared at Jo. 'Can't you do something?'

She opened her mouth to speak, but Dave was still reading the caution. '. . . Anything you do say will be taken down in writing and may be given in evidence.'

'Why are you charging me again? I'm just on my way out. This is bullshit.'

'The guards driving the car you crashed into witnessed you driving away from a large storage shed. You weren't in too much of a hurry, but you left smartly enough to make us wonder what you were doing there. We were nearby, so we went to check it out. And guess what?'

Bird bit on his bottom lip.

'We heard a guy frantically calling for help and banging on the door from the inside. And who did it turn out to be? Only Brendan Ahearne, his lip all bloody. And guess what was in there with him?'

'It won't hold up, you know, whatever you saw. You need a warrant to search that place,' the solicitor said.

'We have one.'

Bird glared at her. She shook her head.

'I understand you'd submitted the claim for the stolen machinery to the insurance company, and had signed the declaration. Which we seized, by the way. The copies of the paperwork we found were very helpful. We seized them, too.'

'Nothing has my signature on it.'

'The paperwork does, and you also signed the statement I took from you at your house the other day, witnessed by me and my colleague. You've made a statement reporting goods stolen that were subsequently found on your property. We found metal parts in the digger bucket. I'll hazard a guess that they'll match parts of one of the ATM machines that were stolen. But let's not talk about this out on the steps. We'll do it in an interview room, under camera.'

Bird let Dave guide him back into the station. Someone would pay for this. Someone needed to be got to. It was time for Anto to step up and pay his debt. His chest throbbing, he turned to Jo. 'You are so fired.'

'Jesus, Bird, that's bad timing,' Richards said. 'You could really do with some legal advice now. Especially when the crowd from the National Bureau of Fraud Investigation have a word with you. I wish I could stay, but I have a murder to investigate.'

'Fuck you, Richards. I can buy and sell you three times over. On your shitty wages, you must be one meal away from a fucking famine. Don't tell me you do this for the money.'

'You think you can buy and sell me, do you? Keep going, Bird. Attempting to bribe an officer of the law is a chargeable offence.'

'Fuck you, Richards. You'll never prove I was there, or that I knew the equipment was there, either.'

As they came through to the main part of the station, the bitch cop Teegan handed Richards two see-through bags. Dave took them in his free hand.

'Oh, look. Does this look familiar?'

Shit. His wallet. And his engraved cufflinks.

'Maybe you could deny it, but I reckon you have — oh, I don't know — credit cards, bank cards, maybe even your driver's licence in here. It will save you having to produce that later anyway. One less thing for your to-do list. Oh, and look — *BF*. These wouldn't be your initials now, would they?'

'Bastard,' Bird muttered.

In her other hand, Teegan held a larger brown paper package, which she also handed to Richards.

'Yours too, I believe,' Richards said. 'It's a bit chilly, so, I'll get your suit jacket back to you as soon as I can. Matches those trousers really well.'

Bird called out to the retreating solicitor. 'You're rehired. You need to make some calls for me. Urgently.'

Richards looked him up and down. Bird wanted terribly to slam his fist into his face, but he could barely raise it.

'It's a pity,' Richards said.

'What is?'

'You might be right. I may never earn enough to afford a tailored suit on my wages, but your expensive taste in clothes will probably have you convicted.'

CHAPTER 46

Danielle ended the call and peeked into Ann's room. She had the nurse fussing over a piece of equipment, but seemed otherwise fine. Danielle peeled herself away, crept down the corridor and out of the ward. Linda had reassured Danielle that the baby was doing fine. 'Sleeping like an angel, she is.' There was no disguising the adoration in Linda's voice.

Mark and Pat had been gone for ages. Too long.

Danielle went out of the front door and lit up a cigarette.

'You can't smoke that here. You need to be off hospital grounds.'

The security guard didn't seem in the mood for a debate, so Danielle put it out against the wall and stuck it back in the box.

She rang Mark to find out where he was. She needed to get back to the apartment and check on the baby for herself. There was no answer, but the headlights of Pat's car appeared a few minutes later.

'How is she?'

'They admitted her for tests. She could be in a few days. She's alive, at least.'

'Yeah, I suppose.'

'Where's Mark?' she asked.

'He said he'd meet us back at the apartment at Clonliffe View.'

Her phone rang. It was Mark.

'Where are you?' Mark asked.

'With Pat, in his car,' Danielle said.

'Pick me up at the top of the road near the hospital.'

She took the phone from her ear. 'Did you hear that, Pat?'

He grunted. 'He could walk back from there.'

She was still on the phone when she saw him. 'There he is.'

Mark slid into the back seat. 'Is she doing all right?'

'As well as can be expected. Your husband and your lover both dead in the one day comes as a bit of a shock.'

Over his shoulder, Pat threw her a quick glance.

The rest of the drive to the apartment passed in a silence that even being packed into the lift failed to break. So much had happened in the course of that day it was hard to take it all in.

Danielle opened the door. 'I'm pouring us all a large drink or five.'

It took Danielle a moment to notice Linda and the arm around her neck, the gun pointed to her head. Behind her, cushions lay scattered on the floor. The place had been ripped apart.

Shit. The baby.

Pat reached into his jacket.

'Don't bother.' Anto pointed the gun at them and jerked it to the right. 'Over there, and don't open yer mouths unless I ask you something.'

Pat held his hands up. 'Anto, come on, what's this all about? I thought you and Dean were tight.'

'Fuck you, Pat. What do you know? Tight. Dean is a rat.'

'What are you talking about?' Pat asked.

Danielle took a step to the right, while Pat continued to talk.

'What about the raid on Bird's factory? All the equipment seized. Bird down at the cop shop,' Anto said.

'Bird?' Pat said.

'Yeah. I heard Dean got arrested and got let go again the same day. He must only have got out so quick because he ratted to the cops about Bird. He had to. One minute he's in custody, next thing he's back on the street with nothing, no charge sheet or anything, and now Bird is the one arrested. It doesn't sit right with me.'

'What station was Bird taken to?' Mark asked.

'Ballymun,' Anto said. 'Why?'

'Then Dean is no rat. He was taken to Blackrock Garda station, not Ballymun.'

'They're all the same,' Anto said.

'Not when they're on two opposite sides of the city. One's on the Northside, the other's on the Southside, nearly an hour apart. Makes no sense.'

'Well. Whatever. Dean owes me, and I want what Brenno gave him as insurance,' Anto said.

'And what's that then?' Pat said.

'A memory card, one of them micro SD cards. Brenno gave it to Cheryl, who was meant to pass it on to Dean.'

Pat looked at the others. 'No one knows what you're on about.'

Danielle tightened her hold on her bag. 'Where's the baby?'

'She's in the bedroom. She'll be all right so long as you all cooperate. Otherwise . . .' Anto pressed the gun into Linda's temple. She gave a small whimper. 'So I'd better get some answers.'

'What's on this card anyway?' Mark asked.

'Why do you want to know?' Anto asked.

'What if whoever killed Cheryl took it off her?' Mark suggested.

Anto withdrew the gun a centimetre or two.

Danielle took a step closer to him. 'Are you sure you know what you're doing, Anto? Shouting the odds about

Dean being a rat when you know he'd rather cut his own arm off than help the cops.'

Anto lowered the gun slightly, frowning. 'You think so, Danielle?'

'I'm sure of it. Now, lower the weapon, let Linda go and we can all put this down to a misunderstanding. You could be quite useful to us with your breaking and entering skills,' she said.

Pat went for his pocket again. Immediately, Anto swung the gun round and pointed it at him.

'No, Pat.' Danielle put out her hand. 'What I say here goes. I think Anto had a rush of blood to the head. Put that away and let's talk.'

'How do I know you won't just shoot me?' Anto said.

'I don't want to mess up my rug.'

Anto glanced at the floor, then back to Danielle. 'Bird has offered a reward for the card.'

'How much?' Danielle asked.

'He's talking a two-hundred-grand debt forgiveness.'

Jesus Christ. 'Then it must have incriminating evidence on it,' Danielle said. 'Wait. If Bird is in custody, how did he tell you to do this?'

'The brief rang me, some woman. Said she was at the station with him. Told me someone would call with instructions.'

'And you believe she was genuine?' Pat asked.

'Yes, because then Bosco Ryan called me,' Anto said.

'Bird sounds desperate to me,' Mark said.

Anto shrugged. 'I just did what Bosco told me to do.'

'We can't help you,' Danielle said.

Anto sighed, stuck the firearm into the pocket of his hoodie and slumped on to the couch.

Danielle rushed into the bedroom and rested her hand on the baby's back. She was warm and snuggled up, unaware of the drama taking place in the next room. When she returned, Anto was still on the couch. Mark was handing a glass of water to Linda. Pat was on the balcony. Danielle poured herself a glass of whiskey. 'What do you know about this card, Anto?'

'Straight up?'

'Is there any other way? Come on, spit it out.'

'I know nothing, other than Brenno wanted to give it to Dean to show him he could be trusted. He found it hidden in Dwayne's office, and now no one knows where it is,' Anto said. 'It's meant to have something on it to do with that cop's murder from years ago.'

Pat came in from the balcony. Danielle glanced at him, but couldn't read his expression.

She returned her attention to Anto.

'How do you know that?' Danielle asked.

'Between the brief and Bosco, getting info from Bird, it's what they more or less said.'

Danielle stopped pouring when she felt whiskey drip on to her shoes. *Why would Bird even mention evidence about a guard's death in the middle of a cop shop, and risk being overheard?*

'Does it show his murder? Are the Flynns involved?' Mark asked.

'Woah.' Anto raised his hands. 'I know nothing more than what I've said. Now you know the value of it.'

'It's only valuable to whoever has it,' Mark said.

Danielle had no laptop here and couldn't ask for one, not in front of Anto.

'How much did you say you were promised, Anto?' she asked.

'I told you, clearing a debt of two hundred grand. Brenno moved the machinery used in the ATM robbery and the haul. He gave the haul to Dean, who was meant to bring it to Brenno's the other day, so me and Brenno could get our share.'

'But he didn't,' Danielle said.

'He didn't. Look, just let me head off, would you?'

'Give me a moment to think,' she said and took a sip of whiskey. Anto was more useful onside than against them.

'Anything you want to say before you go?' Danielle nodded towards Linda.

He turned to Linda. 'Sorry, Linda. I was meant to meet Dean at Brenno's place and all I got was words on the street about arrests and searches. I just wasn't thinking. Sorry to you too, Danielle and lads. Look, I really wouldn't have done harm. Least of all to a baby. The brief said that Bird would do untold damage if I didn't get it back.'

'So you didn't actually speak to Bird?'

'No, just her, then Bosco. She said Bird all but threatened to kill me. I've seen what he's capable of.'

'You're safe if he's in custody, so,' Mark said.

Anto shrugged. 'There's always bail.'

Pat turned to Danielle, his face flushed and angry. 'You can't let him just get away with what he did.'

'I want no retaliation here,' Danielle said.

'Can I just leave in peace? I can be of use to ye.' Anto waved a hand around the wreckage in the room. 'I'll pay for any damage.'

'You can give us the card if you find it. We'll pay you more,' Mark said.

'Really?' Anto asked.

Danielle glared at him, hesitated for a beat and then faced Anto again. 'Yes, we will.'

'Fine by me,' Anto said, relief all over his face.

'Off you go.'

She watched his exit through the camera and then turned to Mark. 'When did you get the authority to offer rewards?'

'I just thought that if it contained something we could hold over the Flynns, we'd be better off having it than them,' Mark said.

'True.'

Meanwhile, Pat was pacing, shaking his head. 'You're really letting him get away with what he just did?'

'He's of more use to us like that. He owes us a favour,' Danielle said.

'We'll see.'

'It's my decision.' She went over to Linda. 'Are you okay?'

Linda croaked out a 'Yes'.

Danielle sat down beside her. 'I'm sorry you'd to deal with all that.'

Linda cleared her throat. 'I know what he's talking about. Cheryl got the card from Brenno. She told me she was meant to pass it on to some guy who could get it into the right hands. I don't know who murdered her or if the card was the reason, but I know someone who might — Aimee. Ask her.'

'Where is Aimee now?' Danielle asked.

'I haven't seen her for a few days, but she's due on tonight.'

'We need to find her. Mark, you check her flat. I'll go to Berkley Street. Let's hope she's not dead as well.'

CHAPTER 47

Aimee was at home in her flat, and she and Mark were now on their way to Berkley Street. Linda was convinced that Cheryl had hidden the memory card at work. Danielle pretended to search for it along with the others, while all the time the memory card was tucked securely into the lining of her bra. She was conscious of it pressing against her skin, itching to reveal its secret.

The door buzzed and Danielle looked up to see Aimee on the steps, wearing sunglasses but hopping from foot to foot, shivering in the cold. Mark stood beside her. Danielle released the door and called to Pat.

The moment Aimee stepped inside, Pat had her by the arms. Covering her mouth with his hand, he dragged her into one of the bedrooms. Danielle followed.

Pat slammed her against the wall with a thud, sending the sunglasses clattering to the floor. Someone had given Aimee two black eyes.

'Talk,' Danielle said.

Aimee shook her head. 'I'll be killed.'

'You will anyway if you don't tell us what you know.'

Aimee slid down the wall and sat hugging her knees. Danielle gripped her by the hair. 'Who killed Cheryl? You?'

'No.'

'Linda seems to think you had a hand in it.'

'No, not me,' Aimee whimpered.

'Who then? Come on. You must know something.'

Aimee looked up at Pat, and Danielle nodded towards the door.

When it had closed behind him, Danielle took a breath, telling herself to calm down. 'Did Dean kill Cheryl, Aimee?'

'No.'

'But she stole from him,' Danielle said.

'So you know about that then.' Aimee frowned.

Now she was getting somewhere. 'I do. But tell me what you know.'

Aimee sighed. 'Dean was so out of it he didn't realize she had taken the last few thousand from his cash box. I told her it was too risky to take the whole lot, but she did anyway. She even offered me some.'

'And did you take it?'

'Dean's money? You must be joking.'

Danielle sat on the edge of the bed. 'Okay, keep going.'

'He was so off his head he didn't even notice that Cheryl was in the bed with him. No way could he put out. He'd stopped paying her, but was still using her a lot. She was sick of it, especially because while she was with him, she wasn't earning here. She was down quite a bit of cash. She was a good earner because with her, nothing was off the table. So, after he passed out, Cheryl got his keys and tried every lock in the room. She found about ten grand in a cash box and figured he owed her about six, including interest.'

'Jesus — she must have missed out on a lot of clients for that amount. But didn't Hazel — when she was in charge — make sure she was paid from here, or tell Dean he couldn't book her unless he coughed up?'

'It had been going on a while. Hazel treated Cheryl badly. She held money back from her until, in desperation, Cheryl started ringing Hazel to persuade her to hand over her money. By then, the only thing Hazel was worried about was getting Ged to leave his wife. Nothing else mattered to her.'

Danielle shook her head. She hadn't realized Hazel mistreated her girls so badly. 'Would anyone have told Dean that Cheryl had stolen from him, and he killed her for it?'

'No. No way. I don't think anyone but me had any idea of what she'd done. Everyone who came to the house knew he kept cash there, but no one dared touch it. It was only a few of us who ever went there anyway, so he'd have narrowed it down pretty quickly. If there were parties on, he'd lock it away. I was with him about two weeks ago — he took me instead of Cheryl — and he didn't seem to have a care in the world.'

'I remember that.' *If Cheryl had been available that night, she might still be alive.*

'And I haven't heard from Dean since,' Aimee added.

'Then why was Cheryl killed?' Danielle demanded.

Aimee drew up her knees and buried her face in her arms. Danielle slid off the bed and sat on the floor, facing her. 'You can tell me, Aimee.' Danielle reached out and touched her on the arm. Aimee looked up and held Danielle's gaze.

'Because when Dean kept booking her and not paying up, she got no earnings at all. What money she did have was fast disappearing. She was also paying for some college course she was doing during the day. You don't argue with the son of the boss, and no one backed her. Hazel did nothing to help — she even made matters worse by holding money back from her. Hazel suspected that Cheryl wanted to leave, which she'd planned to do once she had enough money, and Hazel didn't want her to go. Cheryl started to give her number out to punters, though only to those willing to pay in advance. She earned more, but it meant she didn't have the protection of working out of here.'

'Oh, shit. Aimee, do you know who her last punter was?'

Aimee looked away.

'Please, Aimee.'

275

'It was Darren Holton. The guy who beat her up on your first day here. He contacted her privately, saying he wanted to apologize and make it up to her.'

Danielle's mind was in a spin. 'How do you know this?'

'She asked me to cover for her if anyone came looking. I was to say she was in too much pain to work. She told me it was Holton who had booked her. I tried to talk her out of it, but—'

'Are you absolutely sure he was her only booking?'

'Yes. He was always so rough with her that afterwards she was too bruised and sore to entertain anyone else that day.'

Danielle recalled the fine she issued Holton with. Five measly grand. Would he have done it if she'd stayed out of it? Oh, *fuck.*

'Holton is an auctioneer,' Aimee said. 'He deals with all the Lewis properties. He's a regular here. I try to avoid him. He's too rough for me.'

Now Danielle was glad she'd buried a golf club in his windscreen.

'He just dumped her body in the alley,' Danielle said, her voice breaking. She wanted to punch the wall in anger.

'I haven't slept since I heard. I keep seeing her busted face.' Aimee buried her face in her arms and wept.

'What else do you know? Have you heard anyone mention a memory card?'

'Yes,' Aimee whimpered.

'Really?'

'Brenno keeps asking Dean if Cheryl gave it to him, but he can't get a straight answer.'

'So that's why Anto came looking for it.'

Aimee's head shot up. 'Anto?'

'Yes. Why?' Danielle crouched down.

'He told Brenno that Bird is blaming him for some drugs bust mess-up. Says he's in debt to him for €200,000. Bird was arrested for fraud. He's called Anto's debt in. He wants him to do whatever it takes to get that memory card back.'

'How do you know that?' Danielle asked.

'I've been with Brenno for the past few days. He's good to us girls. He never tries anything on, he's like kind of a friend, you know?'

Danielle nodded.

'Bird beat him up, first for not finishing Dean off and then because he thought Brenno had ratted on him and got his gear taken by the cops. And then again when the cops questioned him about the equipment that Bird had reported stolen, but Brenno found. He thought he was doing the right thing by bringing it back, but Bird is meant to have signed some report or statement, which is where it got all fucked up.'

'Is Bird still in custody?'

'I'm not sure. I think he's due in court for running from the cops, so he must be, I guess. Something to do with dangerous driving. He's savage angry.'

'But how could he threaten Brenno if he's in custody? Surely the guards would have heard him.'

'As far as I know, the solicitor got Bosco Ryan to call. Anto was there, too. Anto was told to be on standby anyway. Bosco had gotten a call from a woman solicitor with messages from Bird.'

'Jesus Christ.' Danielle had heard Anto's account, and now Aimee's story appeared to back it up. 'And the lads discussed all this in front of you?'

'No, the walls in Brenno's place are thin. His mam's been at Bird's for the past week or so — she's moved in there, and he has the place to himself. Brenno usually leaves when Bird calls, 'cause he can hear them at it, and it makes him feel sick. Anto's been over a good bit all week. He's been very worried about the debt. They are very tight, them two.'

'What happened then?'

'Brenno told me to keep away from him for the moment. So I left. He was all stressed about Bird trying to pin everything on him. He reckons he'll get arrested next. Shitting it, he was.'

Danielle got Aimee a glass of whiskey, which she swallowed in a single gulp.

Linda rushed in and stood staring at Aimee, whose face was blotched and streaked with mascara.

Danielle stood in front of her. 'Is the baby okay?'

'She's fine. Sleeping.'

It had been a shame to disturb her, but they had needed to find Aimee, and Danielle wanted to keep the baby close. Linda was holding a brown envelope, which she thrust at Danielle.

Danielle stared at her name printed on it. 'A bike courier dropped it off,' Linda said.

'Is he gone?'

'He couldn't get out the door fast enough.'

'Is there anything else?'

Linda shook her head.

'I'll be up in a minute.'

Mark came in, bringing tissues and a towel for Aimee. 'Thought you might need these.' He indicated to the envelope. 'What's that?'

'I don't know yet. It was hand-delivered by a bike courier. Linda just gave it to me.'

'Well, open it then.'

She pressed the outside of the envelope. 'Feels like . . . like a credit card or something.'

'Not a memory card?' he said.

'No. Bigger than that.' Mark seemed as eager as Anto to get his hands on that card. Maybe he fancied a shot at getting a two-hundred-grand reward from Bird. So much for doing his job and protecting her.

She tore it open. Inside was a white card bearing the words *Green Acre Hotel*. With it was a tiny piece of paper. Scribbled on the back was *504. Just you*. She knew that handwriting well.

'I know where that is. Come on,' Mark said.

'But it says just me. Who knows what may happen if I don't follow the instructions.'

He shook his head. 'As if I'm letting you off alone.'

'I'm not asking your permission.'

'It could be a trap.'

'I am armed.'

Danielle pointed towards the hall. Mark exited ahead of her. As soon as the door closed behind them, she rounded on him. 'Don't ever think you can make decisions for me. I am looking for answers.' She held the hotel room card up and shook it. 'If this means I get them, then I am going. Alone. Like this note says. Now give me the keys. It's time I drove myself for a change.'

He bit his cheek. For a beat, she thought he would refuse to hand them over, but with a sigh, he held them out.

CHAPTER 48

Dean tried his best to comfort his ma, but he wasn't much good with weeping women. There wasn't much he could do except try to keep the business going. The most important thing was to get the message across that, despite the death of its head, the Lewis family still ruled. He'd do it with violence if that's what it took.

He left the hospital and climbed into his new van. He had a few calls to catch up on. His hearing was back in one ear, though the other was still fucked. The guards were busy trying to piece together what had led to Ritchie Delaney's death. So far, no one had mentioned it to Dean, so unless there was heat on him, it was business as usual and money to be collected.

Brenno and Anto had contacted him to ask for their share of the ATM hauls. He'd made them wait long enough, and now it was time to divvy it up. He didn't want to make enemies of them. Brenno's house was surrounded by blue flashing lights. Swarms of wankers in blue were scurrying in and out of the house carrying brown bags. A couple of them had their heads together, deep in discussion. What the fuck was going on? If Brenno had been arrested for something, he'd better not talk. He rang one of Brenno's numbers. To Dean's surprise, Brenno answered.

'What's going on at your place?'

'The cops are searching Mam's house. Something to do with Bird and fraud. They're looking for paperwork.'

'Did they arrest her?' Dean asked.

'No. She gave them the keys when they searched Bird's place, so as to show them she had nothing to hide, and she was cooperating with them.'

'Where are you?'

'Out and about near the city centre,' Brenno said.

'I'll ring you later, so we can meet up, and I'll give you what you're owed.'

'Right. Talk to you later, so.'

Dean ended the call.

He was almost at the junction with the M50. No point wasting the journey, there were collections to be done. He exited the motorway and drove through one of the many estates his family controlled and went for the easiest target — the Bradys. The lad might be grieving for his younger brother, but the debt of two grand remained and Dean wanted to collect. Besides, he was grieving too, for his da. It played havoc with his sensitivities. He couldn't be responsible for his actions in light of his sorrow. He'd better have what was owed, or there'd be hell to pay.

He parked the van. His wounds had almost healed. Doing his best not to limp, he strode towards the house.

A low buzzing sounded nearby. In the distance, a red dirt bike cut up the green doing wheelies and donuts. He smiled and shook his head indulgently. Soon, he'd have a few grand in his pocket, with Brady owing more in interest.

A car passed by at speed, nearly hitting him because it was on his deaf side. He turned and flipped him the middle finger. 'Fuck you!'

The driver did a handbrake turn at the hammerhead and drove towards him. He hopped on to the footpath. The driver didn't look at him. The red dirt bike had pulled in across the road. That had escaped his hearing, too. The bike rider raised his hand, as if to wave. But it wasn't a greeting. Dean darted left and right. Which way to go?

The decision was made for him. The bullet went straight into his chest. Dean tried to run. Indeed, in his head he was running — sprinting away as the gunman dismounted and laid the motorbike on the ground. The second shot pierced his stomach. A pool of red spread across the path, dripping slowly off the kerb. Dean lay slumped half on and half off the footpath, his face on the tarmac. The gunman strolled across and turned him over. Dean stared, empty-eyed, up into the sky. A group of crows took off from a nearby tree.

But he wasn't finished yet. One by one, the faces of every person he had killed rose into his mind. The shadow of the gunman, still in his motorcycle helmet, fell across him. He lifted the visor with the muzzle of the gun.

'This is for Jake,' Sean Brady said, and squeezed the trigger.

CHAPTER 49

Danielle drove towards Newlands Cross, conscious of the small card tucked inside her bra. The Green Acre was a small five-star hotel off the dual carriageway. The receptionist was busy on the phone, so Danielle headed straight for the lift.

The fifth floor consisted of four rooms, so 504 was at the end of the corridor. She was slightly relieved to see a camera in the far corner, and another closer to the room. A *Do Not Disturb* sign hung on the door handle. She raised her hand to knock, but dropped it. The writing on the card had been Saoirse's all right, but what if she'd been compromised? No point giving notice of her arrival, especially if it might lead to the death of either or both of them. She looked at the card in her hand. Gently, she slid it into the slot. A little light went green and the door released. She went in, leaving the door ajar in case she needed to get out fast.

Danielle reached into her bag, pulled out the gun and stepped forward on her toes. Her throat was dry. The swish of her leather trousers sounded loud in the silence. Her feet sinking into the plush carpet, she followed it past a large bathroom and into a bedroom with a lounge area beyond. A balcony leading off it appeared to be empty.

The door behind her opened. She was dressed in jeans and a blue-and-white striped T-shirt. She was smiling.

Danielle went limp with relief. Thank God. Saoirse would help her. Saoirse always had a plan.

CHAPTER 50

Saoirse picked up a small case and carried it over to a large writing desk in the corner of the lounge.

'No need for that. We're on the same side. Remember?' She pointed to the gun.

Danielle looked at it, she'd forgotten it was still in her hand. 'Oh. Sorry.'

'Did you come alone?'

'Yes.'

'Were you followed?'

'No.' Mark had seen the card with the name of the hotel, but she was pretty sure he hadn't followed her.

'So,' said Saoirse. 'Things have gone to shit.'

Danielle gave her a wry smile. 'You could say that.'

'I hope it won't interfere with our arrangement.'

'No, it won't. It's bad, though. There have been murders.'

Saoirse held up her palms. 'Don't tell me anything I can't unknow. Forget that for now, and let's talk about what you've gathered up to today. Have you got a suspect? And more to the point, any proof?'

'Yes, and yes.' Danielle reached into her bra and pulled out the memory card.

'How long have you had this?' Saoirse said, taking it from Danielle.

'I found it in Cheryl's bag. She was murdered too.'

'So I heard.'

'Oh? Where did you hear that?'

'He hasn't revealed himself to you yet?' Saoirse asked.

Danielle stared at her, confused. 'Who? No. What are you on about?'

'We've got someone on the inside.'

'Jesus Christ. Are you going to tell me who it is?'

'No need. He should be here any minute. Meanwhile, let's have a look at this.'

'I also found this.' Danielle took out the lighter she'd taken after the arson attack on the pub.

Saoirse turned it over in her hand. 'It's his. Where did you get it?'

'Ann had it. She said she took it from Bird.'

Saoirse held it to her chest for a moment, then laid it gently on to the desk. 'Right, let's get on with it.'

From the case, Saoirse pulled out a laptop. She plugged it in and inserted the card into an adaptor.

Before she could touch the keyboard, Danielle took Saoirse's hand. 'Before you go any further, let's take a moment and reflect on what we have done to get us this far. Whatever is on that card, whatever we see, there's no turning back. So far, we've been in control, but from now on, we'll have to go wherever it takes us. So let's just remember that we are together, doing this as a team.'

They stood hand in hand, just as they had in the maternity ward, united in their grief. After a few moments, Saoirse took a deep breath. 'Shall we?'

'I'm ready.'

'It's asking for a password,' Saoirse said.

Linda had shown Danielle a few computer hacks. She typed in her name, along with her date of birth. The screen cleared.

Saoirse turned to her. 'How did you know—'

An image appeared, blurry at first, then starkly clear. Danielle swallowed. Gavin Kelly had been tied to a chair, limp, slumped to one side. His face was cut and swollen. His own cuffs were around his wrists.

Saoirse pressed pause. The two women looked at each other.

'Are you sure you want to go on?' Danielle asked gently.

Tears had gathered in Saoirse's eyes, but she whispered a 'Yes'. She pressed play.

Now a woman's voice could be heard. The hoarse, rasping tones of a chain-smoker were unmistakeable. Ann Lewis.

'Finish him.'

A figure in a hood, mouth covered with a snood, stepped forward and aimed a pistol at the man in the chair.

A shot rang out, crackly in the sound recorder. The figure jumped at the impact and was still, his face now obscured by blood. Saoirse cried out.

The shooter, gun in hand, stood over the body and spat. 'That'll teach you to interfere, cop.' It was Dean.

Ann's voice was heard again in the background. 'Stupid fucker. He should have just let her get shot. But, oh no, he had to be the hero and fuck up all our plans.'

The screen went blank. For a long time, the two women sat staring at the empty screen.

'My own family,' Danielle said quietly.

'Who was doing the filming?' Saoirse added.

'It's not clear. We need to figure that out,' Danielle said, and gasped. She'd heard a noise behind her. 'Shit. I never closed the door properly when I came in.'

'Don't worry,' Saoirse said. 'I've been expecting him.'

CHAPTER 51

The two women turned to see Pat framed in the lounge doorway.

'What are you doing here?' Saoirse asked.

Danielle looked at her, puzzled. Hadn't Saoirse just said she was expecting him?

'My God. Look at you both, all cosy together.' He looked from Saoirse to Danielle. 'I never thought I'd see you side by side with the guards, Dani.'

'Stranger things have happened.'

Saoirse closed the laptop. 'You didn't answer my question. I asked you what you're doing here.'

'Protecting Danielle.'

'From what? Who?' Danielle said.

'You, of course. Ged's passing has changed everything. All the properties, all the businesses belong to Dani now. We can move forward.'

'Move forward to what?' Danielle said.

'To take command of the city. We have the power now.'

Danielle shook her head. 'Pat, enough people have died. We don't need any more blood on our hands, we need closure. I want no part in the family's criminal enterprises.'

'You said closure. Closure for what?' Pat looked from one to the other of them.

'We need answers to Gavin Kelly's murder, for one. The hit on me.'

'Well, good luck with that,' he scoffed.

'We already have most of the answers,' Saoirse said.

He took a step backwards. 'Go on.'

'We know who killed Gavin,' Danielle said. 'And who ordered the hit and possibly shot at me.'

'How?' Pat said.

'It's all on a memory card we just viewed,' Danielle said.

'Wait.' Saoirse stared at Pat. 'You said how, not who.'

Watching him closely, Danielle said, 'You had a strange look when Anto mentioned what was on the recording.'

'That's because he'd just broken in and the baby might have been in danger. I was worried,' Pat said.

'What are you talking about?' Saoirse asked. 'What baby?'

There was a moment of silence.

'Hazel's. She's Ged's baby. I, er, well, I have her. Linda is looking after her at the moment.'

'Jesus,' Saoirse said.

Danielle turned to Pat. 'Aren't you going to answer Saoirse? What did you mean by "how"? Well?'

Pat took another step back and pulled out a gun, aiming it at each of them in turn. 'Brenno had to be the smart arse, didn't he? He decided to get one over on the Flynn family by taking the memory card, not knowing what it contained.'

'You're risking everything for a pissy €200,000 reward?' Danielle asked.

'No. I'm making sure I don't go to prison for aiding the murder of a cop.'

'So it was you. You were the one recording it.' Danielle wanted to puke. She remembered their kiss, the warmth she'd felt. How she'd trusted this man, while all along he'd known who had shot at her, and who had murdered Saoirse's husband.

'Yes, it was me. And it was me who lured him to the factory with the promise of information on your shooting.'

'You animal.' Danielle started forward but he aimed the gun at her forehead. She stepped back. She hadn't come this far only to die in a hotel room at the hands of this bastard.

'You weren't even involved with the family a decade ago,' she said.

'I was around, all right. I was working for Dwayne when you headed off to London.'

'So, who are you working for now?' Danielle asked.

'Dwayne. My job is to keep close to the Lewis family and find out how they operate.'

'Was Dwayne involved in the murder?' Danielle said.

'No. I gave him the memory card to have something to hold over the Lewis family. It was like the nuclear button — never to be pressed unless there was no other choice.'

'And he never saw what was on it?' she asked.

'I never gave anyone the password. That was my insurance.'

'And Jason? Was he involved?'

'No. Neither he nor Bird.'

'Then why did Bird offer the debt forgiveness, the reward to Anto?'

'It wasn't Bird who did, it was the solicitor — my solicitor. She even duped Bosco into backing her up, so Anto would believe her.'

'Jesus.'

'Jason has always suspected that Ann or Dean was behind it in some way, but he could never prove it.'

'So you got close to me because you thought I knew something,' she said.

'When you arrived back, out of the blue, without telling anyone you were coming, I figured there had to be more to it. So, yes, I did.'

'Not that close, thankfully,' she said.

He smiled faintly. 'I was giving it time.'

'Jesus. Why didn't you just leave me alone?'

'Why the hell did you carry on with your wild goose chase? I never imagined you'd get your hands on that.' He jerked the gun towards the adaptor still sticking out from the side of the laptop. 'Now I can use it to get what I need from Ann and Dean.'

'No, Pat, no,' cried out Danielle.

He raised the gun, aiming it at Saoirse's forehead.

'Why shoot her?' Danielle said.

'Because she is one of them, a scumbag guard, just like her husband.'

'Pat, please.' Danielle took a step towards him, her eyes on the gun. 'You don't appear on the video, just Ann and Dean. Saoirse lost everything, like me. She is on my side.'

'She is on no one's side but her own. Did she tell you that Jason promised her information on the murder if she persuaded you to return?'

Danielle whipped around and stared at Saoirse. 'Is this true?'

Saoirse shook her head. 'Not the way he's telling it.'

'What way is that, so?'

'Jason was trying to find the proof, too.'

Pat made a movement with the gun. 'She's lying. The cops are never on your side. Think about it. She let you go back to that family, knowing you might have been killed.'

But Danielle had been well aware of the risk she was taking in returning.

'Like I told you, there was someone on the inside, protecting you,' Saoirse said. 'He was to be withdrawn after the drugs haul, but when he heard you were coming back, he stayed where he was. He was making sure you were safe, Danielle. You can trust me.'

Danielle hesitated. Saoirse had said she was expecting this person, so where was he? Then her eyes met Saoirse's. 'I believe her, Pat.'

'Fuck her, Danielle. Ask her why Jason was at her apartment earlier. That's right, I followed you. I saw who else was there too, the fucking rat.'

Pat began to pace the room, frowning. He seemed to be considering his next move.

Her eyes on him, Saoirse reached for Danielle's bag. Slowly, gently, she pulled out the Beretta.

Pat spotted her before she had a chance to raise it. He ran at her and punched her in the face. The gun flew from her hand. He snatched it up and stuck it in his jacket pocket. He pulled the adaptor from the laptop and yanked out the memory card. He tried to break it, but it wouldn't even bend.

He cast around him, then grabbed the kettle from the top of the dresser. He switched it on and waited for it to boil. Then he dropped in the card and replaced the lid.

'Try to prove anything now,' he sneered, as the lid began to rattle. 'You are both fucked.'

'Oh, I wouldn't say that now.' Mark appeared behind Pat and pressed a gun to the back of his head. 'Drop it.'

'Come on, Mark, don't be like this.'

'Drop it and get on your knees.'

'Christ, you sound just like a cop.'

Pat turned and swung his arm. An uppercut sent Mark hurtling backwards.

Saoirse leaped to her feet, grabbed Pat from behind. He threw her backwards against the tray, sending cups, saucers and teaspoons flying. Saoirse grabbed the kettle as she fell and swung it at him. The lid flew off, sending boiling water over his face. He howled. His gun dropped from his hand. Mark kicked it away and pointed his own gun at Pat.

Handing the gun to Saoirse, Mark turned Pat over, face down. Kneeling on his back, Mark pulled a set of cable ties from his pocket, bound his wrists together and pulled them tight. He retrieved the Beretta from Pat's pocket. Saoirse took it. He dragged Pat to the bathroom. Danielle heard the rush of water. She got to the bathroom as Mark was plunging Pat face first into a sink full of water.

'Christ, don't drown him.'

'I'm not.'

Panting slightly, Mark emerged from the bathroom. 'How are we all doing?'

'Great,' Danielle and Saoirse said together.

'Is that what I think it is?' He pointed to the wet SD card lying on the carpet.

'Yes,' Saoirse said, 'but what's on it is backed up on the laptop.'

'Is it clear? Good enough evidence?'

'Dean shot Gavin.' Saoirse's voice broke.

'Ann was involved, too,' Danielle added. 'Pat admitted to recording the whole thing. He gave it to Dwayne for safekeeping, and to have something to hold over the Lewis family.'

'That was a stupid move. Especially when Jason found out about it.'

'We were lucky you arrived when you did,' Danielle said. 'Thank you. And thank you for watching out for me.'

'You were doing a fine job on your own,' he said, and smiled. 'Anyway, I had a personal interest. I was one of the first on the scene when Gavin's body was found. My partner met him en route to the meeting with Pat, and said he sounded a bit vague about it. We know now that he didn't want to admit he was operating outside of his official capacity. But he did mention where he was going. That's how we found him — his body — so quickly.'

'Fuck.'

'The minute we had intel that proof was circulating about Gavin's killing, I stepped up. I built a relationship with Ritchie, with Ged. Soon they trusted me enough to run errands for them and I became privy to what they were up to. I had a sense this guy was playing both sides. A few times, I followed him to meetings with Dwayne. It was him ratted about the drugs, too. He set up some poor stooge to be killed for it. He fed bogus proof to Jason.'

Danielle looked down at Pat. 'You animal.'

'The money from the ATM was recovered in a search of Dean's place, along with pieces of the machine in Bird's warehouse. And Darren Holton has been arrested for murdering Cheryl.'

'Thanks, Mark,' Danielle said.

Saoirse nodded. 'This is a crime scene now. Would you care to caution this guy, Mark?'

'I'll leave you the honour of it, Saoirse.'

'There is a team on its way,' Mark added. 'You'd be better off staying and answering a few questions now, to clear matters up. But it might be a good idea if you put that Beretta away and didn't have it pointing at anyone.'

Saoirse grinned.

Mark's phone rang. When the call ended, he stood staring at the screen for some time, frowning. 'Dean's been shot. He was pronounced dead at the scene.'

Danielle and Saoirse looked at each other, wide-eyed. 'Do they know who shot him?' Danielle asked.

'They're asking at the house,' Mark said.

'What house?'

'Jake Brady's.'

CHAPTER 52

Ged's body lay in a Belfast morgue for a number of weeks awaiting collection. The necessary paperwork took time to complete, delaying the post-mortem. Danielle was the only member of the family left to organize its transportation to the Republic and its burial. She refused Saoirse's offer to accompany her or help with the arrangements.

On the day of his funeral, Danielle was just getting out of the car when she spotted Saoirse among the small crowd of mourners. They didn't acknowledge each other. Gavin could rest in peace, now that one of his killers had been caught and the other shot dead, so their connection had to be severed.

Linda emerged from the back seat, rocking the baby in her arms. She was nearly seven weeks old now, and getting cuter by the day. A DNA test confirmed that Ged was indeed the father. Hazel's family didn't step forward to claim her, and Danielle was in no hurry to encourage them.

With most of the Lewis family wiped out, Jason and Dwayne Flynn would inevitably fill the vacuum and take over the drugs trade. No doubt there would be opposition from somewhere, someone brave enough to step into the Lewis family's shoes and take them on. Who knew? Only one thing was certain, crime in the gangland world would continue.

Once the shares that Ged had left her were officially in Danielle's name, she planned to sell them and return to London. For now, she was enjoying having the baby to look after.

Danielle took her from Linda.

A navy-blue car pulled up behind Danielle's vehicle. Bird Flynn stepped out and regarded the mourners.

'What's he doing here?' Linda asked.

'He got bail,' Danielle said.

'I know that, but what's he doing *here*, at Ged's funeral?'

'Who knows why Bird Flynn does anything, Linda.'

'True.'

Smiling broadly, Bird made a beeline for Danielle. *Shit.* Surely he wasn't going to offer his condolences?

'You're still looking after the baby, then,' Bird said.

'Well, her mother certainly isn't going to claim her.'

'It suits you, Danielle.'

'What does?'

'Motherhood. Look at the two of you — you and that bundle of joy.'

Danielle didn't need his opinion on how like a mother she looked. She didn't want him near either her or the baby. He put his finger to the baby's cheek, and she couldn't help flinching.

'Adorable,' he said.

Bird glanced back at his car. Marion was just getting out of the passenger seat, wearing a floral hat more appropriate for a wedding than a funeral. Bird leaned forward and whispered into Danielle's ear. 'It could have been you and me in that car. It still can. You know where I am, when you realize that that's what you really want.'

Danielle shuddered.

'You still have her, then,' Marion said, tottering forward on her heels and straightening her skirt. She didn't seem able to meet Danielle's gaze.

Danielle sighed. 'Yes.'

'Would you not give her back to her family?'

Danielle said nothing.

'It's pathetic. You should give her to a proper family if her mother doesn't want her. You're a Lewis. You'll be condemning her to a life of violence. Look around you. Everyone is dead. There is no one left to back you up if someone wants to harm you. It's putting the child in danger.'

'Are you threatening me?' Handing the baby to Linda, Danielle stepped closer to Marion.

Marion jerked back. 'No, no, I'm just saying, if—'

'Shut up, Marion,' Bird said. 'Let's go to the graveside.'

Roughly, Bird grabbed Marion's arm and pulled her away.

'Ignore her, Danielle,' Linda said. 'She's nothing but a witch. I heard what Bird said to you. As if you'd ever want to be with him. He's toxic. She knows she'd lose him in a heartbeat if you showed an ounce of interest in him. That wasn't a threat, it was insecurity speaking.'

'I hope you're right, Linda.'

'Believe me, I am.'

But maybe Marion was right, the Lewis name was always going to be associated with violence. The baby needed protection, and as long as Danielle lived she was going to provide that for her. As soon as Ged was buried, she'd get herself and the baby back to the safety of the penthouse at Clonliffe View. Once there, she'd decide for herself what was best for both her and the baby.

'Here,' Linda said, and handed Danielle back the baby. 'Smell her gorgeous head, that'll ground you.'

Cuddling the baby close, Danielle made her way over to the graveside, making sure to leave as much space as possible between her and the poisonous couple. Linda stood at Danielle's shoulder.

A red car pulled up and a stocky, dark-haired man got out. Danielle recognized Ann's nephew from Adare, Martin McCarthy. Years ago, his picture had been all over the papers after the Criminal Assets Bureau raided his farm. Martin headed to the boot and unfolded a wheelchair, which he brought round to the passenger door. Ann, who was out on bail, struggled into it, gnarled hands on the handbag in her lap. Martin spread a rug across her knees and wheeled her to the graveside, close to where Marion and Bird were standing. Neither couple acknowledged the other. Ann glanced at Danielle, apparently unaware of Saoirse, who had edged closer to the four of them.

The priest began intoning the decade of the rosary to an answering hum of voices. Ann opened her handbag, sending tissues flying across the feet of the gathering of people. Marion's hat blew off and became trapped in the wheel of Ann's chair. As Marion stooped to retrieve it, Ann could be seen rooting around beneath the rug. Suddenly, she brought out a gun, which she pointed not at Marion, but at Danielle.

'I'm taking it all back!' Ann screamed.

Startled, Marion stood up, blocking Ann's line of sight, saw the weapon now pointing at her and caught hold of Ann's wrist. The gun went off, sending blood spraying over her and Ann. Saoirse raced across to them, followed closely by Mark.

Bird dropped to the ground, his hand at his throat, blood spewing between his fingers. Marion threw herself across him, pressing on the wound. The gun was still in Ann's hand. Saoirse prised it from her grip while Mark tried to stem the flow of blood.

By the time the ambulance arrived, Bird was dead.

THE END

THE JOFFE BOOKS STORY

We began in 2014 when Jasper agreed to publish his mum's much-rejected romance novel and it became a bestseller.

Since then we've grown into the largest independent publisher in the UK. We're extremely proud to publish some of the very best writers in the world, including Joy Ellis, Faith Martin, Caro Ramsay, Helen Forrester, Simon Brett and Robert Goddard. Everyone at Joffe Books loves reading and we never forget that it all begins with the magic of an author telling a story.

We are proud to publish talented first-time authors, as well as established writers whose books we love introducing to a new generation of readers.

We have been shortlisted for Independent Publisher of the Year at the British Book Awards three times, in 2020, 2021 and 2022, and for the Diversity and Inclusivity Award at the Independent Publishing Awards in 2022.

We built this company with your help, and we love to hear from you, so please email us about absolutely anything bookish at feedback@joffebooks.com

If you want to receive free books every Friday and hear about all our new releases, join our mailing list: www.joffebooks.com/contact

And when you tell your friends about us, just remember: it's pronounced Joffe as in coffee or toffee!

Printed by BoD™in Norderstedt, Germany